'A definite must read for crime thriller fans everywhere'
– *Newbooks Magazine*

'For lovers of crime fiction this is a brilliant, not-to-be-missed novel' – *Fiction Is Stranger Than Fact*

'An innovative and refreshing take on the psychological thriller' – *Books Plus Food*

'Russell's strength as a writer is her ability to portray believable characters' – *Crime Squad*

'A well-written, well-plotted crime novel with fantastic pace and lots of intrigue' – *Bookersatz*

'An encounter that will take readers into the darkest recesses of the human psyche' – *Crime Time*

'Well written and chock full of surprises, this hard-hitting, edge-of-the-seat instalment is yet another treat… Geraldine Steel looks set to become a household name. Highly recommended' – *Euro Crime*

'Good, old-fashioned, heart-hammering police thriller… a no-frills delivery of pure excitement' – *SAGA Magazine*

'*Cut Short* is not a comfortable read, but it is a compelling and important one. Highly recommended' – *Mystery Women*

'A gritty and totally addictive novel'
– *New York Journal of Books*

# ALSO BY LEIGH RUSSELL

**Geraldine Steel Mysteries**
*Cut Short*
*Road Closed*
*Dead End*
*Death Bed*
*Stop Dead*
*Fatal Act*
*Killer Plan*
*Murder Ring*
*Deadly Alibi*
*Class Murder*
*Death Rope*
*Rogue Killer*
*Deathly Affair*

**Ian Peterson Murder Investigations**
*Cold Sacrifice*
*Race to Death*
*Blood Axe*

**Lucy Hall Mysteries**
*Journey to Death*
*Girl in Danger*
*The Wrong Suspect*

*The Adulterer's Wife*
*Suspicion*

# LEIGH RUSSELL

# DEADLY REVENGE

A GERALDINE STEEL MYSTERY

**NO EXIT PRESS**

First published in 2020 by No Exit Press,
an imprint of Oldcastle Books Ltd,
Harpenden, UK
noexit.co.uk

ISBN
978-0-85730-305-9 (print)
978-0-85730-306-6 (epub)

2 4 6 8 10 9 7 5 3 1

Typeset in 11.25pt Times New Roman
by Avocet Typeset, Bideford, Devon, EX39 2BP
Printed and bound in Great Britain by Clays Ltd, Elcograf S.p.A.

For more information about Crime Fiction go to @crimetimeuk

*To Michael, Jo, Phillipa, Phil, Rian, and Kezia*
*With my love*

# DEADLY REVENGE

## Glossary of acronyms

DCI   – Detective Chief Inspector (senior officer on case)
DI     – Detective Inspector
DS    – Detective Sergeant
SOCO – scene of crime officer (collects forensic evidence at scene)
PM    – Post Mortem or Autopsy (examination of dead body to establish cause of death)
CCTV – Closed Circuit Television (security cameras)
VIIDO – Visual Images, Identification and Detections Office
MIT   – Murder Investigation Team

# Prologue

'A lot of men would have given up on you a long time ago, the way you carry on,' he told her. 'You don't appreciate how lucky you are.'

'Lucky?' she retorted before she could stop herself.

She bit her tongue and lowered her gaze, but it was too late.

'It's all just one big game to you, isn't it?' he replied, his voice rising as his anger escalated. 'You like to see how far you can go before I snap. What about my feelings? You don't care about me, do you? Do you? Answer me, you stupid bitch.'

She shook her head, struggling to control her trembling. He had that effect on her. However hard she tried to hide her fear, he could see it in the craven drooping of her head, and the way her legs shook.

'Take your clothes off,' he commanded, stepping back to watch her as she stripped.

He sat on the bed and waited until she was naked. She could feel his eyes crawling over her skin, from the top of her head to her bony feet, lingering on the small mounds of her breasts and the darkness between her thighs. She clutched her shoulders, hiding her breasts behind her crossed forearms.

'Drop your arms,' he snarled.

'I'm cold,' she whimpered.

'Did you hear me?' he demanded. 'I want to see the whole of your body, not just your scrawny arms.'

Shaking violently now, she let her arms fall to her sides. He pounced like a panther then, teeth bared in a grin as the soft

11

flesh of her belly gave way beneath his weight, and she cried out in pain.

'Don't you ever do that again,' he hissed, his breath hot against her hear.

'What did I do?' she whimpered. 'What did I do?'

She closed her eyes and tried to imagine she was somewhere else, somewhere far away.

When he had finished, he strode away leaving her sprawled on the bed. She waited until the door closed behind him before bursting into tears. For now, all she could do was suffer. He had drawn all the strength out of her, and now even the sound of his breathing in bed beside her at night was enough to shatter her will. But one day she would summon the strength to resist him. She made that promise to herself. Only when she was out at the shops, or walking along the street, did her terror abate. She never felt safe inside the house.

# 1

GERALDINE WASN'T CURRENTLY INVOLVED in a murder investigation, where her position as a detective sergeant working in serious crime often placed her. There was still plenty for her to do, like questioning a young delinquent who had threatened an elderly man with a knife. Geraldine adopted a friendly tone. The boy was less likely to talk freely if he felt intimidated. He looked several years younger than his nineteen years, was articulate, and seemed intelligent enough to know what he was doing. After questioning him for some time, Geraldine finally worked out that his victim had berated the youngster for spraying graffiti.

'He was bang out of order calling the cops on me. I got every right to express myself.'

'By threatening a stranger with a knife? How is that expressing yourself?'

'I know my rights,' the youngster insisted.

Geraldine dropped her relaxed approach and spoke severely. 'Everyone has the right to walk along the street without being attacked.'

'But he wasn't just walking along the street. He was interfering with my right to express myself.'

'Your right to express yourself doesn't stretch to vandalising property and threatening to stab someone, and your victim wasn't trying to suppress your right to free speech,' Geraldine said. 'He was protecting his property from your graffiti.'

'There's nothing wrong with free speech,' the youth

13

persisted. 'I should be able to say whatever I want to anyone I like.'

'You know perfectly well that you're missing the point,' Geraldine said.

'But how else am I going to get them to listen?' the youth burst out angrily.

'Who?'

He shrugged. 'I dunno. The government, the council, everyone in power. They don't do anything to help us.' He leaned forward. 'My mother and her boyfriend threw me out on the street the day I turned sixteen and left me to fend for myself. I'd be dead now if a homeless shelter hadn't taken me in and given me somewhere to stay. And now the council want to cut their funding.' He was nearly in tears. 'The council are the ones who should be arrested, not victims of their cutbacks like me.'

That evening, over supper, Geraldine discussed her day with her boyfriend and senior officer, Ian.

'Are you defending what he did?' Ian asked.

'Of course not. But no one should find themselves homeless in a civilised society.'

'Granted he didn't have much of a start in life, but he's hardly helping himself, is he? Sooner or later he's going to end up in the nick, no matter how much help is thrown at him. Some people are too damaged to become functional adults.'

'So we just wash our hands of them and lock them up?' Geraldine replied angrily.

Ian shrugged. 'Of course that's not what anyone would want. All I'm saying is that there's nothing we can do. We're not social workers, Geraldine, and our job is to keep our streets safe so people can walk around without fear of being attacked. This boy threatened an old man with a knife. Members of the public should be able to feel safe anywhere, not just in their own homes.'

Geraldine sighed. Ian was right when he said there was nothing the police could do about the young man's situation but pass him on to overstretched social services. It was a pity the council were cutting their funding for homeless shelters.

'This is ridiculous,' Ian grumbled later that evening, returning from the bathroom, a bottle of aftershave in his hand.

Geraldine looked at him, hiding her dismay behind a smile.

'What is?'

'This.' He gesticulated, waving the bottle in front of his face.

'What's wrong with it? Haven't you always used it?'

'There's nothing wrong with my aftershave. That's not what I'm talking about. I'm complaining about living in two places at once. I can never remember where anything is. Now this bottle's empty and I've not got any more here.'

Geraldine smiled. 'I'm sure you can manage for today.'

'For today?' he repeated quizzically. 'What about tomorrow? Or are you throwing me out?'

Geraldine frowned. She had been in love with her colleague, Ian, for years without disclosing her feelings. Now that Ian and his wife were finally getting divorced, and he had revealed that he reciprocated Geraldine's feelings, he had begun spending the night at her flat. There was nothing stopping him from moving in with her, other than her reluctance to share her private space. She had not lived with anyone else since her early twenties, and was not sure how she would cope with having him there all the time.

'You know that's not what I meant,' she replied. 'I couldn't throw you out.'

Ian tossed his empty bottle on to the bed and raised his

hands, his fists clenched in an exaggerated boxing pose.

'I'd like to see you try.' He glared at her from beneath his lowered brows.

Geraldine laughed and he grunted in response.

'What does that inarticulate noise mean?' she demanded.

'It means: "Do I really have to go through the motions of telling you how wonderful this all is, and how you are the most beautiful woman in the world, and I'm the luckiest man in the world to be here with you," and so on and so on. I went through all that bullshit with my wife and look where that got me. You know how I feel about you, and if you don't then you're not the brilliant, intelligent, sensitive woman I'm in love with, and this is all a mistake.'

He leaned over and kissed her on the nose and she laughed.

'I'll settle for that,' she said.

'What? A peck on the nose?'

'For you saying you're in love with me.'

They smiled at one another, a comfortable, affectionate smile.

'All I'm saying is that living like this in two places is driving me nuts,' he said. 'Apart from anything else, the parking is terrible.'

It was true; he was rarely able to park close by. Geraldine had a reserved space in the underground car park beneath the block of flats where she lived, but Ian had to cruise around looking for a space on the street, and it wasn't always easy to find one. She felt guilty about refusing to drive him to the police station where they both worked, he as a detective inspector, she as a detective sergeant, but she wasn't ready to announce their relationship to their colleagues. Not yet. She was still wondering whether it was unfair of her to insist they keep their relationship a secret when she left for work the next morning. But at least Ian had his own flat to go to. Her thoughts strayed to the young man who had been thrown out by his mother, and was now losing his place in a homeless shelter thanks to council cutbacks.

# 2

SHE RECOILED, SHOCKED INTO silence.

'Well?' he demanded, taking a step towards her, his fists clenched but not yet raised. 'Well?'

On his lips the innocuous word sounded charged with malevolent power, forcing her to edge away until she felt the wall pressing against her back.

'Well? Have you lost your tongue, you stupid bitch?'

'I'm – I'm sorry,' she stammered. 'I didn't mean...'

'You didn't mean, you didn't mean,' he sneered.

His fists rose and she winced, waiting for him to hit her. Instead, he spat in her face with such violence she felt the impact of the saliva as it struck her cheek, warm for an instant, then cooling as it dribbled down her face towards her jaw bone. She didn't dare move.

'Well?' he repeated. 'How long are you going to stand there staring at me like an idiot?'

She shook her head. Her tears mingled with his saliva as her trembling fingers reached up to wipe her cheek.

'I won't do it again, I promise. I didn't think it would matter... I thought you wouldn't mind – I should have asked you – I'm sorry, I'm sorry.' Once she began, she couldn't stop babbling. 'I won't see her again without asking you first, I promise. It won't happen again. I should have asked you first...'

'You're not to speak to that witch again. Not for any reason. I won't have it, do you hear me? I won't have it.'

His voice rose as he lowered his fists and she breathed more easily. She tried to explain that she felt sorry for his mother, but he interrupted her.

'I won't have you listening to her lies, spreading her poison about me, behind my back. If she's all on her own, she's no one to blame but herself. I won't have you drawn into her toxic games. You're my wife. My wife! She drove my first wife away with her filthy lies. She's not going to do the same to you.'

'She never breathed a word against you – I wouldn't have let her –it's not like that...'

'I've said all there is to say on the subject. If she calls here again, hang up. I won't have you talking to her. Not a word. As soon as you hear her voice, hang up. Do you understand?'

'Yes, yes, I understand. I understand. I was wrong. I'm sorry.'

They both knew that she would never have capitulated so readily if he hadn't threatened her with his fists. He glared at her and she lowered her eyes, terrified of infuriating him even more while he was in such a temper. He must have moved silently because a moment later she heard the door close and looking up saw that she was alone in the room. Her legs buckled beneath her and she slumped to the floor, sobbing quietly.

With hindsight it was easy to see that she should have recognised the signs earlier, but the abuse had begun very gradually. Of course it had. Unless the victim was crazy, or a masochist, that must be how it always started, because no normal person would deliberately court pain. It had begun with the odd pinch, an occasional slap on the arm, nothing serious. He had been too circumspect to let himself go until he was confident of her collusion. She still found it hard to believe how easily she had allowed him to deceive her, but to begin with he had been relentlessly charming. He still could be, although the mask slipped more often the longer they were together. It maddened her to remember that she had been over the moon when he had asked her to marry him. For a while everything had seemed perfect – until the first time he had hit her.

After that, her life had been a sickening rollercoaster of pain and emotional torment. She had learned to recognise the threats: the heightened colour in his face, his sweaty forehead and flared nostrils, and the wild glare in his eyes, but sometimes she noticed these warnings too late to escape his punches. After a violent outburst he would treat her so kindly, it made her yearn for him. She wondered if it was his way of showing he felt contrite, because he never apologised for hurting her. To do so would have been an admission of his guilt. The really stupid part of it was that she had seen that kind of domination before; she, of all people, should have known better. For a while she had refused to acknowledge what was happening. Only when her mother had commented on her bruised wrist had she been forced to admit the truth to herself.

Even then she had done her best to shrug off her realisation. 'Jason doesn't know his own strength.' Her words had sounded hollow to her own ears while she thought, 'Oh my God, is it really possible that I've married a violent man?'

Her mother had given her a curious look and Jessica had let out a braying laugh, so loud it sounded forced. It had taken her another year to recognise that she was not only miserable, she was actually at risk, but by then it was too late for her to walk away. She was trapped.

'That's my baby you're carrying,' he said to her, 'yours and mine. There's no way you're taking him away from me.'

Jason made it quite clear what he would do to her if she tried to leave him. On the few occasions she attempted to remonstrate with him, he lost his temper, although he never once hit her while she was pregnant with Daisy. In a way that made her feel worse than before, knowing that he could control his violent outbursts when he chose. In any case, it made no difference by then, because physical violence was only one of the methods he used to intimidate and control her. He had subtle ways to break her will, and she had learned to become complicit in tolerating his abuse.

What made the situation more difficult was that she had to conceal her injuries. In one of his fits of rage, he had clouted her so hard on the side of her head that the hearing in one of her ears was impaired. She dared not go to the doctor about it for fear they would discover the cause of her partial deafness. Of course she could have claimed she had fallen over, but somehow lying like that seemed complicated. And whatever happened, she couldn't risk Jason finding out she had spoken about her injuries to a third party.

'If you tell anyone,' he had whispered in her undamaged ear, 'I'll make sure you never see Daisy again.'

With every small concession to his will, she surrendered a little more of her freedom, and lost another shred of her self-respect, until she no longer had the power to resist his bullying. Looking back, she could hardly believe how readily she had come to tolerate his domination, yet the truth was it had all come about so slowly she had scarcely noticed it happening. And now it was too late to leave him and start again. Life, with all its potential and its opportunities, had slipped from her grasp while she had been looking elsewhere. And still she could not leave him. Where would she go? Brought up by an overbearing father, she had never learned to fend for herself. The last thing she wanted to do was go crawling back to her parents. They had warned her that her marriage wouldn't end well.

'There'll be tears before bedtime, you mark my words,' her father had told her.

He had been too blinkered to realise that his opposition to her marriage only made her more determined to be Jason's wife. In any case, she hadn't wanted to stay and witness her parents' tormented relationship any more than they wanted her there to see it. And then the baby had come along, and that changed everything. Although Jessica's love for her baby was overwhelming, Daisy wasn't exactly company. Jessica talked to her, but Daisy only cried and gurgled. Watching her lying in her cot, curling and spreading her tiny fingers in the air, Jessica wondered how she was going to protect her daughter from Jason. Since the birth he had become unapproachable, and she had learned it was best to avoid trying to start a conversation with him. Any communication other than his animal grunting in bed ended in an argument, and the likelihood of violence. Jessica's only other adult human contact, apart from her parents, was with the health visitor, who encouraged Jessica to visit the local children's centre.

Although she said she would definitely go along, Jessica rarely went out, existing in a state of exhaustion in a strange silent world punctuated only by the baby's cries and brief exchanges with a cashier when she went to the supermarket. She could have been living on the moon with only a small dumb alien for company. But as long as Jason didn't hit her, she was content to keep her head lowered and carry on. One day the baby would be old enough to talk, and they would become friends. Considering the future, Jessica resolved to make sure Jason never lifted his hand against their daughter.

'I'll kill him before I let him touch you,' she whispered to the gurgling baby as she stroked the downy hair on her head. 'I promise you, I'll kill him.'

# 3

THE MOOD IN THE room was volatile. Feeling threatened by the angry muttering, Anne watched her husband glare around at the assembled crowd. Balding and well built, his customary air of confidence had been torpedoed by the level of hostility he faced. Every time he wiped his sweaty forehead with the back of his sleeve she winced, knowing he had been taken by surprise on seeing how many people had turned up for the council consultation meeting. The closure of a small library hardly warranted much fuss, yet the local community had turned out in force.

A tall man who had grumbled loudly all through David's speech called out again. 'Why can't you be honest with us? The council could keep this library open if they wanted to. You're just choosing to close it because you don't give a toss about the needs of disadvantaged people.'

A small group of people standing with him mumbled their agreement.

'This is just a cost-cutting exercise, isn't it?' the tall man went on in an unpleasantly nasal voice.

David raised a plump white hand for silence. 'Unfortunately, you've hit the nail on the head, sir,' he replied with a shrug of his broad shoulders. 'Like everyone else, we're having to cut costs.'

While David was speaking, the tall man leaned down to speak to a ginger-haired man beside him.

'How much did it cost to produce this glossy questionnaire?'

the ginger-haired man shouted out, sounding excited.

The tall man flapped the brochure above his head and raised his voice. 'Every question in this extravagantly produced leaflet is pushing us to provide evidence that the library is underused. There's no space for comments, just a load of tick boxes which are all geared in one direction. Look at the last one: how would you feel if this branch library closed? And now look at the options we're given: pleased, indifferent, or disappointed.' He turned back to the councillor. 'Why isn't there an option to express outrage, which is what most of us are feeling right now? "Disappointed" doesn't come anywhere near describing it. Disappointed?' He let out a snort of derision. 'We're bloody livid!'

'You all know that libraries up and down the length and breadth of the country are facing closure,' David replied, wiping his brow on his shirt cuff. 'Some people feel strongly enough about the closures to keep the facilities open as community libraries, run by volunteers, and there's nothing to stop you from taking over this library and running it yourselves.'

'While all the trained and experienced librarians who curate the stock are put out to grass,' one of the librarians commented sourly.

'And there won't be any funding for purchasing new books,' another librarian added. 'Community libraries survive on volunteers to run them and books donated by readers.'

Anne listened with growing disquiet as local residents heckled her husband. Ranging from children to the elderly, all appeared passionate about keeping their library open.

'I'm afraid these are the times we live in,' David said, looking around with a bland smile. 'I assure you I share your dismay and deeply regret that this is necessary.'

'Oh, it's "necessary", is it? And you "share our dismay"? How very decent of you,' the tall man retorted with a sneer.

Anne shuddered. These people were fuming about the

threatened closure of their local library, and even she had to admit that David was behaving like a smarmy bureaucrat. His protestations of sympathy fooled no one.

'Stop avoiding the issue!' his tall antagonist countered. 'You're the people who are making this happen. You can pretend you're helpless to prevent it, but we all know you're the leader of the council. You have the power to keep this library open if you want to, along with all the other libraries in the borough. You have the funds; you're just not releasing them.'

'There are other priorities –' David began.

'Like your council dinners and your glossy brochures,' the tall man replied, brandishing the questionnaire in the air again.

As a murmur of support for the complainant rumbled around the room, a small boy raised his hand.

'If the library closes, what will happen to all the books?' he asked, peering earnestly at David.

'And where will Miss take us to get our library books?' another pupil demanded shrilly. 'We can't get library books if there isn't a library.'

'We come here once a month, in term time,' their teacher explained. 'It's a very important outing for the children. And a lot of our parents bring the children here for the story-time sessions in the summer.'

'Who's going to organise that if we have no librarians?' someone else asked.

David nodded and forced a smile. 'It's admirable that you want to encourage children to visit the library. No one would want you to stop doing that, and you have the full support of the council in what you are doing. There are other libraries that would welcome your visits.'

'Not within walking distance of the school,' the teacher replied testily.

'You won't be the only school in York that doesn't enjoy the luxury of having a public library near enough to walk to,' David pointed out.

'Which is surely a reason for opening *more* branch libraries,' the tall man called out, with a note of triumph in his voice. 'It's hardly an argument for closing the ones we have.'

A lot of people began shouting their agreement, and the librarian who was chairing the meeting stepped forward.

'We can't all talk at once,' she said, 'or Mr Armstrong won't be able to answer any of our questions.'

'He's not answering them when he *can* hear them,' the tall man pointed out. 'All he's done is blame "the times", and tell us this isn't the only library that's closing. He knows perfectly well he has no reason to close this library, none at all. It's a shabby policy from an incompetent council, and we need to stop them before they do any more damage to our community.'

The listening audience cheered this statement. A few people stamped their feet. Anne had been nervously watching the tall man who was so strident in his attacks on her husband. She recognised him from other such meetings. With a long, thin nose and sunken cheeks, his eyes burned with a zeal that made him look positively evil, like a villain in a James Bond film.

'I'm not here to listen to political haranguing,' David announced. 'But in any case, I'm afraid that's all I've got time for. Thank you all for coming along today and making your views known. If you'd like to hand your completed questionnaires to the librarian before you leave, she'll make sure they are delivered to the council offices and I assure you that all of your views will be taken into account when we reach a decision about the future of this library, along with all the other branch libraries currently under threat of closure. Rest assured, we pay close attention to the wishes of each and every one of you, but you must appreciate that the libraries can't all remain open.'

'No, we don't appreciate that,' the tall man shouted out angrily. 'And no one here accepts your lies. This whole meeting has been a sham. You didn't come here to listen to us; you're just ticking the box so you can say the local community has been "consulted". This wasn't a consultation. It was a meeting to announce your decision.'

David picked up his coat and swept out of the room without deigning to respond, while the librarian trotted anxiously at his side, talking breathlessly. Anne hurried after them, buttoning up her coat as she walked.

'And we really hope you will reconsider,' she overheard the librarian saying as David left the building. 'You've seen for yourself how strongly the local community feels about the proposed closure.'

Anne caught up with her husband in the car park. As they reached David's black BMW, the tall man who had been so obstreperous at the meeting charged up to them, a couple of middle-aged women and his younger ginger-haired companion at his heels.

'This isn't over!' he yelled at David, shaking his fist in the air. 'If you think we're going to take all your cutbacks lying down, you couldn't be more wrong. You'll see! You're going to be sorry you ever tried to close this library! You think you're going to get away with it, but you're going to see how wrong you are. Someone's going to call a halt to your interventions before it's too late. You just wait and see. One way or another you're going to be stopped before you do any more damage.'

He turned to his followers, still protesting loudly about what David and his Tory council were doing to the area.

Urging Anne to hurry, David climbed into the car. 'I've heard enough of this nonsense,' he muttered as he turned the key in the ignition.

'They're just passionate about the library,' she replied nervously.

David scowled. 'Repeat your defence of those scurrilous troublemakers when we get home and you'll be the one who's sorry.'

Anne shrank back against her seat and lowered her head, making herself as small as possible. She knew from experience that her husband was not a man to tolerate opposition.

'I'm sorry,' she mumbled. 'I didn't mean to question your decision. I know you must have very good reasons for what you're doing. You always do. Those people just don't understand the extent of your responsibilities. They're only thinking about their own local interests, and you have the whole area to look after.'

Even as she spoke she despised herself for caving in, but she had no strong feelings about the proposed closure of a branch library and was anxious to placate her husband.

'I'm sure you know best,' she went on. 'It's only one library. There are plenty of others. And like you said, they can run it themselves if they're so concerned to keep their library open. There are enough of them who seem interested in keeping it going.'

'Oh, shut up,' he snapped. 'I'm sick and tired of talking about bloody libraries.'

# 4

ON HER WAY TO the shops one morning Jessica spotted a sign pinned on a notice board outside a local church:

Parent and baby drop-in session with toys and tea in a welcoming, safe environment. Come in and chat to other parents every Tuesday 11am-1pm.

Although not a churchgoer, she went in, driven by loneliness and drawn by the promise of 'safety'. A group of young women were seated together, seemingly all talking at once, their shrill chatter amplified by the dusty wooden floor and painted walls. Used to sitting at home with no one but a baby for company, Jessica was overwhelmed by the noise. She hesitated on the threshold, and was about to turn and leave when she noticed a thin blonde girl sitting apart from the rest of the women. Taking a deep breath, Jessica went and sat next to her, and the other girl looked up. Her greasy hair was dyed blonde, the roots dark against her pallid skin. She looked scraggy and she had a spotty face, her pimples poorly masked by cheap concealer that was too dark for her pale complexion. As she gazed at Jessica, her blue eyes softened in a smile. They both had young babies.

'I wondered if Lily was too young for something like this,' the other girl said, nodding towards her baby so that untidy wisps of hair flapped around her face. 'It's my first time here.' She looked down at her bony fingers fidgeting in her lap.

'Mine too. I'm not sure it's my kind of thing.'

They were both silent for a moment and then the blonde girl looked up again.

'My name's Ella.'

She seemed anxious to be friendly, and Jessica had the impression that she too was unused to adult company.

'I'm Jessica. And I know what you mean. It seems a bit cliquey, doesn't it? It's like they're all ignoring us.'

'I know. The sign said "welcome", but you're the only person here who seems to have noticed me. Until you turned up, I was just sitting here wondering how soon I could leave.'

Jessica glanced round at the group of chatting mothers who still all appeared to be talking at once. It didn't look as though any of them would have noticed, let alone cared, if Ella stood up and scuttled out of the room. Jessica turned back to smile at her nervous companion.

'Not exactly friendly, are they?'

Neither of them admitted they had gone there because they were lonely, but they recognised that unspoken need in one another. After a few minutes, her new acquaintance smiled at something Jessica said, and she felt her mood lift. No one had smiled freely at her like that in a very long time. Jason never smiled at all, and her mother's expression was always tinged with anxiety. Even the health visitor was only doing her job, focusing on Daisy with brisk efficiency, paying scant attention to Jessica herself. She made only the most perfunctory enquiries about her, readily accepting Jessica's assertions that she was fine without any question.

In the course of a stilted conversation, Jessica discovered that Ella was only nineteen, five years younger than her, and Lily was just a week older than Daisy.

'I might come back next week if you're going to be here,' Ella said after they had sat in silence for a while, and Jessica felt an unexpected surge of happiness. She could not recall the last time anyone had expressed anything like pleasure in her company. She mentioned her husband, and Ella said she lived alone.

'Apart from Lily, that is,' she added with a shy smile.

'What about her father?'

Ella shrugged. 'Oh, he pissed off as soon as Lily was born. He wasn't interested in her, or me.'

'But he must still support you?'

Ella shook her head. 'No chance. You've no idea what an evil bastard he was. I'm better off without him, even though I'm skint. It's not easy trying to care for a baby with no money.'

Jessica gazed at Ella's baby, noticing for the first time how puny and lethargic she looked compared to Daisy.

'That's wrong,' she said. 'You ought to chase him for child support, for Lily's sake. He has a duty to pay maintenance. He can't just walk away from his responsibilities.'

Despite her indignation, Jessica felt a twinge of envy on hearing about Ella's untrammelled status.

'You don't understand,' Ella muttered. 'He's not my husband. We weren't married.'

'That's beside the point,' Jessica said. 'He's still Lily's father. She's his child too, and he has a duty to pay towards her upkeep. You shouldn't let him get away with it. The law is on your side. Go and see him and insist he helps you.'

'I might try and chase him if I knew where he was, but he'd be more likely to kill me than part with any money,' Ella replied, with an angry snort. 'And anyway, it's none of your business.'

Reluctant to antagonise her new friend, Jessica let the matter drop. Ella was right in saying it was not her business and even though she knew her advice was sound, Ella was clearly unwilling to follow it. Jessica smiled sadly. They had more in common than Ella realised, despite the difference in their circumstances. Jason was an evil bastard too. She fervently wished there was a way she could get rid of him. If she could have been certain he would never find her, she wouldn't have hesitated to pack a bag, walk out and not look back. She would have gone anywhere to keep Daisy safe. But she was terrified of making the situation worse if she tried to run away. And in any case, with no money of her own and no friends, there was nowhere for her to go to be free of him. She did not want to end up penniless on the street, starving, with a baby as spindly as Lily.

She left the parent and baby drop-in session early, despite Ella's request that she stay, and hurried home. Jason was at work, but occasionally he appeared in the middle of the day, purportedly to join her for lunch. She knew he was checking up on her. Before going home, she dashed into the corner shop and bought a few pieces of fruit and a bottle of milk, and filled another bag with nappies, although she had plenty. If Jason had come home, she had her excuse lined up for having gone out. He was not there, and he did not return until the evening, and she spent the afternoon comparing her own situation with that of the woman she had met for the first time that morning, the woman who was poor but free. Given the chance, she would swap places with Ella, whatever hardship she might have to endure as a result. At least she would be free of fear.

# 5

GERALDINE FROWNED ENQUIRINGLY AT the constable. 'And how is that *my* job, all of a sudden? I do have a workload of my own to get through.'

As a detective sergeant it was true there was always plenty for Geraldine to do, but nothing on her desk was currently urgent.

'Please, Sarge,' the constable wheedled, pressing his palms together in mock supplication. There was an edge of desperation behind the comical gesture. 'I'm convinced that nothing short of your magic touch will be able to get any sense out of her, if there is any sense to be had.'

'Oh, all right, I'll speak to her.' With a sigh, Geraldine stood up. 'It's not like I'm that busy right now, to be honest.'

She knew the constable had approached her for help not only because she was an experienced detective sergeant, but because she had a reputation for dealing effectively with hysterical women. It was not a reputation she relished.

'I don't know why he assumes I'll be able to persuade her to talk,' she muttered to Ariadne, the sergeant who sat opposite her.

'It's because you're always so calm,' Ariadne replied. 'You make other people feel calm.'

'Huh! I don't know about that.'

'Look how calm I am now that I know you're going to deal with this, and I don't have to worry about it,' Ariadne grinned.

'Wish me luck.'

Geraldine thought about Ariadne's comment as she made her way to the interview room. Ariadne had spoken lightly, yet there was an element of truth in what she said. Geraldine had always regarded most of the people she met as moody and emotional. On reflection, she wondered whether she should look at things from a different perspective, and consider that she herself might be unusually phlegmatic. Certainly she had never regarded herself as especially placid by nature, yet she supposed she must be. It had taken a chance remark by a colleague to reveal that aspect of her own character to her. She had always assumed it was her training as a detective that had helped her to remain outwardly composed regardless of circumstances, but she now realised that it was in her nature to control her emotions. At forty years of age, it seemed she still didn't know herself very well.

'She's distraught, Sarge,' a female constable murmured as Geraldine entered the small interview room. 'We can't get any sense out of her.'

'OK, leave her to me,' Geraldine replied quietly. 'Perhaps you could bring us some tea?'

The woman they were discussing was sobbing loudly. Thick shoulder-length blonde hair hung down like a veil, concealing one side of her face completely, and the other side was mostly hidden by a large white handkerchief. Geraldine spoke softly to her, and after a moment the woman blew her nose rather loudly, lowered the handkerchief and pushed her hair back off her flushed face. Her lips trembled as she gazed at Geraldine with frightened eyes, her make-up smudged and moist. Despite her strained expression, Geraldine could see she was beautiful, with large blue eyes, a small straight nose, slightly turned up at the end, and high cheekbones. If her looks hadn't been marred by crying, she would have been exquisite.

'I'm sorry,' the blonde woman stammered, 'it's just that

–' she hiccuped, and then said in a rush, 'my baby's gone'. Emitting the final word in a low wail, she hid her face in her handkerchief again and sobbed.

Geraldine felt a stab of fear, but she kept her countenance steady as she responded, careful to divest her voice of any emotion.

'You need to stop crying so you can help us to find him,' she said briskly. 'Please, pull yourself together. We can't help you if you don't give us any information.'

Her suspicion that sympathy would only prompt the woman to cry more seemed justified when, with a few loud sniffs, the woman put away her handkerchief and looked up.

'I'm sorry,' she said.

'Right, now, how old is the missing infant?'

'She's six months,' the woman stammered.

'And where did you last see her?'

'I put her in her cot yesterday at about seven, as usual, and when I went in to her this morning, she was gone.'

Geraldine nodded. She had expected to hear that the baby had been asleep in her pram in the park, or at the shops, that the mother had turned away for only a few seconds, and in that short space of time a stranger had run off with the baby. Someone who had stolen the baby away from her home ought to be easier to trace. She relaxed slightly, while the mother hid her face in her handkerchief once more and wept.

'Now, you need to tell me exactly what happened,' Geraldine said firmly. 'Let's start with your name.'

'Jessica Colman.'

The constable brought in a cup of tea and Jessica sipped it gratefully.

'I'm sorry if it isn't very hot,' Geraldine apologised with a slight smile, maintaining her attempt to normalise the conversation, despite the circumstances that had brought Jessica to the police station. 'Now, tell me everything that happened, and please be as detailed as you can.'

Jessica explained how she had woken up late that morning. 'Usually Daisy wakes me really early. She's a good sleeper but she's only six months old.' A tear slid down her cheek, but she retained enough self-control to continue cogently. 'This morning I didn't wake up till half past nine and she wasn't crying, which was odd, but at the time I was pleased because it meant she was still asleep and not calling out to be fed. But when I went in to check on her, she wasn't there.'

Jessica dropped her head in her hands and began to cry again. Through her sobs, Geraldine made out a few words: 'disappeared' and 'so little'.

'So she wasn't in her cot?' Geraldine repeated.

'No. It was empty.'

Gradually Geraldine learned that Daisy was Jessica's first baby. Her husband, Jason, was the baby's father and the only other person living in the house.

'My mother has a spare key,' Jessica said in answer to a question about who else had access to the house.

'And have you spoken to your husband and your mother?'

'No. I came straight here. Jason's away. He's on a stag do this weekend.'

'A stag do? Where is he? Can you call him?'

'I don't know where he is.'

'Where does he work?'

Jessica mentioned the name of an estate agent in York. Geraldine sent the constable to contact his office to see if anyone there knew where he was, but all they could tell the police was that he had booked that Friday and Saturday off work and was due back early in the week. Meanwhile, Geraldine continued to question Jessica.

'All I know is that he went away with a group of friends. I think they might have gone to Amsterdam but I'm not sure. He did tell me,' she added quickly, as though realising her ignorance of her husband's whereabouts might strike Geraldine as strange. 'It's just that, I don't know, I'm in such a state, I don't know what's going on. My father's David Armstrong, leader of the local council,' she added, as though she thought that might be important.

Geraldine had heard of David Armstrong, a controversial councillor who was forcing through unpopular cutbacks in local services. He had been the subject of several virulent attacks in the local press for closing libraries and threatening the survival of a local school.

'A lot of people hate him,' Jessica said, her eyes wide with fear. 'You don't think...' She broke off, unable to complete her sentence.

'I doubt if the disappearance of your baby has anything to do with your father's activities. Most people probably don't know about your connection with him. The likelihood is that your husband has taken the baby and left her with someone. Does he have family living nearby?'

'No. He doesn't see his mother or his brother and his father's dead.'

Geraldine spoke gently. 'Jessica, I suggest you go home and wait there while we speak to your husband and your mother. You're sure no one else had a key to your house?'

Jessica nodded. 'I'm sure,' she whispered. 'No one.'

'Well, you can go home now and leave this to us, and don't worry. It's unlikely anything has happened to your baby if only your husband and your mother could have had access to her. I expect we'll find her very soon. This is probably all a misunderstanding.'

Geraldine spoke reassuringly, but Jessica's account troubled her. The obvious explanation for the baby's disappearance was that her father or grandmother had taken her out, and had not wanted to wake her sleeping mother. But if that was the case, they would surely have had the sense to leave a note, or at least have called Jessica by now. They must have realised she would worry. And Jessica not contacting her husband also struck her as slightly odd. Jason must have a mobile phone with him, even if Jessica wasn't sure where he was, which in itself seemed strange, given they had a six-month-old baby. It was almost as though Jessica was keen to involve the police before approaching her family.

'She's probably annoyed with her husband or her mother for taking the baby out of the house without asking her permission, or at least informing her,' Ian suggested, when Geraldine arrived home that evening and told him about the interview.

'To be fair, there's no way anyone should have removed the baby from the house like that without letting her mother know,' she agreed. 'It's a cruel thing to do. But what I don't understand is why she didn't at least try to contact her family before coming to report the baby missing.'

Ian frowned. 'If you ask me, the mother's deliberately creating a fuss to make them feel guilty.'

'That's harsh,' Geraldine replied. 'But in any case, let's hope you're right and she's panicking unnecessarily, and her baby will be found with the father or grandmother.'

'And now, let's forget about work and focus on what you're going to make for my dinner tonight,' Ian said, grinning.

'I hadn't thought about it.'

'Well, why don't you leave it to me?'

'If you're sure?'

'I just need to pop out for a few things and then I'll make you an unforgettable curry.'

'Is it a threat or a promise?'

Geraldine sat on the sofa in her living room, and not long afterwards the front door closed and she heard Ian humming to himself in the kitchen. He brought her in a large glass of red wine.

'All these years I've known you, and I had no idea you could make a curry,' she said.

He smiled at her. 'Bev was never happy to spend time in the kitchen unless we had guests,' he said. 'I don't know why really, because when she did cook, when we had her friends or family over, she did a good job of it. But she never wanted to bother when it was just the two of us. So it was a case of necessity, really. If I wasn't going to starve, and we weren't going to cripple ourselves financially by eating out every night, which is what she would have preferred, one of us had to learn to cook, and she made it clear it wasn't going to be her.'

'Poor you.'

He shrugged. 'On the contrary, I discovered I enjoy cooking.'

'It's a good way to relax and take your mind off things,' she agreed.

'Yes. And if it works, you get a decent meal out of it, which doesn't happen with meditation. So she did me a favour, really.'

'She certainly did *me* a favour,' Geraldine grinned. 'I don't know exactly what you're concocting in there, but it smells wonderful.'

Ian went back to the kitchen where she could hear him chopping and frying and, she suspected, experimenting. She loved Ian and he was happy and, for one evening at least, nothing else seemed to matter.

# 6

ANNE AND DAVID ARMSTRONG lived in a large detached house on the outskirts of the city, towards Driffield. Anne came to the door. Slim and middle-aged, she was expensively dressed in a cashmere sweater and pearls, and her short, fair hair was neatly cut. She looked faintly puzzled as Geraldine introduced herself, and smiled politely without inviting her into the house.

'I take it this is about my husband? Did he ask you to call here? I know he's had some problems recently with political extremists. It's an unpleasant fuss over nothing, and it's high time you put a stop to it.'

Quietly Geraldine explained that her visit had nothing to do with David. 'But I am here in my professional capacity. Is there somewhere we can talk?'

'What's this about?'

'Your daughter came to see us.'

'My daughter?' Anne echoed faintly, her air of slightly righteous outrage fading. 'Has something happened to her? Is she all right?'

'Your daughter is fine, but she's very upset. Is there somewhere more comfortable we can talk?'

'I'm sure this must be a mistake,' Anne said. 'Jessica would have come to me if there was anything wrong.'

Still remonstrating, she led Geraldine into a small study at the back of the house.

'Do you know where your son-in-law is?' Geraldine

asked as soon as they were sitting down.

Anne scowled. 'I might have known he would be at the bottom of this. What's he gone and done? If he's got himself in hot water, I'm afraid he's going to have to face the consequences himself. My husband and I are not going to shoulder the responsibility for any trouble he's got himself mixed up in.'

'Jessica told us he's away this weekend at a stag party, possibly in Amsterdam.'

She hesitated before adding that Jason had lied to his wife. A quick passport check had indicated that he had not left the country, and his car had been discovered abandoned not far outside the city. Wherever he had gone, he had not wanted to be followed.

'So what you're telling me is that he was off enjoying himself with his friends for the weekend, and he didn't want Jessica to know where he was because he didn't want to be interrupted at his stag party. I'm sorry to say this, Sergeant, but what you're telling me doesn't surprise me. Our son-in-law is a selfish man.'

Anne gave a dismissive grunt, as if to say that no decent man would be off gallivanting with his friends, leaving his wife at home with a baby. Geraldine inclined her head. It was certainly possible that Jason had lied to his wife about where he was going, but equally, Jessica might have lied to mislead the police for some reason that was not yet clear.

'The problem is, he's left home and your granddaughter's missing,' she said quietly.

'I'm sorry, what did you say?' Anne shook her head, looking baffled. 'I don't understand. What do you mean, Daisy's missing?' The reality of the words seemed to hit her for the first time as she uttered them aloud. 'I have to go and be with Jessica... We have to find my granddaughter. Have you spoken to Jason? Where has he taken her? But I don't understand. Why didn't he say anything? Have you spoken to him? Please…'

Her distress seemed genuine.

Geraldine leaned forward. 'Please, Anne, take a deep breath. And another. I need you to think clearly. My colleague is tracing your son-in-law right now, and he will most likely clear this up. But we do need to talk to you.'

'I need to be with Jessica. You're telling me he's taken Daisy without telling her where he's gone. He must have planned it. He can't just take her away from her mother like that, without a word. There must be a law against it. Surely that's kidnap?'

'Can you tell me exactly what your movements were yesterday, please? I'd like you to think very carefully about what happened after you woke up. Did you see your daughter and her baby?'

Anne frowned. 'No.' She broke off and stared at Geraldine in bewilderment. 'How can this have happened? My granddaughter can't have just disappeared. Find her.' She drew in a deep breath. 'There must be some mistake,' she muttered. 'This can't be happening. Jessica's not…' She broke off, flustered.

'Not what? What were you going to say about your daughter?'

'What about my daughter?'

'You started to say something about her,' Geraldine prompted her gently. 'What were you going to say?'

Anne sighed again. 'You've met her, haven't you? She has a beautiful soul, and she's a wonderful mother, but she's not… she's not the most level-headed of people at the best of times. I thought she'd begun to settle down lately. For the past six months, since Daisy was born, my daughter's been emotional. Very emotional. Very difficult. She's always been highly strung and obstinate. I suppose we spoiled her. She's so beautiful, and yet she went and married that man. Where's the sense in that? My husband introduced her to so many nice young men –'

She gazed at Geraldine, seemingly pleading for reassurance.

'I don't think it's uncommon for new mothers to be emotional,' Geraldine replied. 'Her hormones will have been –'

'No, no,' Anne interrupted her, and Geraldine let her talk. 'I'm not talking about normal emotional changes in a new mother. I mean, she's always been excitable. Even before she was pregnant, she was volatile. She used to burst into tears for no reason, any time anyone challenged her. The slightest thing seemed to set her off, sometimes nothing at all. She's always been –' she broke off and heaved a sigh. 'She's always been irrational. We hoped, my husband and I, that she might change once she was married, although we never thought that boy was right for her. She was such a lovely child – I mean, she still is lovely, she's a really lovely person, but look, I don't want to make this sound worse than it really is, but she's a very emotional person. She becomes hysterical at the smallest provocation. She's fragile, you see. We did our best, bringing her up, making sure she had the best of everything. And we never asked her to do anything that pushed her too far out of her comfort zone. She couldn't cope, you see. We were always very careful with her. She can't take any pressure. Some people are just like that. It wasn't anyone's fault. She wasn't able to stay in a job because no one she worked for ever understood her. She can't be corrected, you see. She just crumbles under any criticism. Jason knows what she's like. How could he do this to her?'

She dropped her head in her hands and burst into tears. 'Find her, please find her,' she mumbled. 'Oh God, what is he doing to her? She's so vulnerable. This will drive her crazy. My daughter has never been a strong woman. She needs to be cared for and handled gently, not tormented.'

Geraldine was only slightly reassured that Anne did not appear worried that Jason might mistreat the baby. Anne's concern was all for Jessica.

'Of course, she was frightened,' Eileen replied, when Geraldine reported her impression at a briefing on her return to the police station. 'Her granddaughter's disappeared. They must all be going out of their minds with worry. But from what you said, she was more concerned about her daughter than her missing granddaughter.'

'That was certainly the impression I got.'

'There are plenty of women who are scared of upsetting their precious children, especially teenage girls,' a constable chipped in, and several of his male colleagues voiced their heartfelt agreement.

'Jessica sounds like a very spoiled young woman,' one of them commented tartly.

'And you *were* speaking to her mother, Sarge. She's hardly going to be an impartial judge of Jessica's character.'

'Let's focus on what's important here,' Eileen snapped. 'A baby has disappeared from her home. Missing Persons Unit are co-ordinating the search. The likelihood is that the father has taken the baby, but this investigation must be treated as urgent so we're going to do whatever we can to assist the search. We can start by continuing to make every attempt to trace the father. Now, you all have plenty to do so let's get back to work. Finding Jason Colman is a priority. As far as we can tell, Daisy's grandfather has nothing to do with the infant's disappearance, but please bear in mind that he is the leader of the local council, which means that he is not only a very unpopular figure, he's an influential one too.'

They all understood the implications of Daisy's family connections. The local press were already pernicious enough in their attacks on the police. They did not want the local council to whip up any more hostility towards them.

'But,' Eileen concluded, 'as far as we are concerned, this has nothing to do with the councillor.'

'I certainly can't imagine Jessica's parents would have anything to do with this,' Geraldine said. 'They seem to have idolised their daughter.'

The mood at the police station was troubled over the disappearance of the baby and the team set about their allotted tasks with a will. Feeling apprehensive, Geraldine went to question Jessica's parents further. Anne opened the door again. She had clearly been crying. Her eyes were bloodshot and swollen, her cheeks blotchy, and her hair dishevelled.

'My daughter's suffering dreadfully,' she said. 'Something has to be done. My husband's spoken to one of your senior colleagues.'

Geraldine had read the report of the meeting, and knew there was no need for her to speak to David in person. Nevertheless, she decided to see him. She had been criticised in the past for insisting on doing everything herself, and told that she ought to place more trust in the other members of her team. On this occasion, she deliberately ignored any risk that she might be criticised for disregarding her colleague's report. The priority was to find the missing infant and return her to her mother as swiftly as possible. Every other consideration was insignificant by contrast. And, however unlikely, the chance that David Armstrong could somehow be implicated in his granddaughter's disappearance could not be dismissed out of hand. He seemed to have garnered a few enemies in the course of his political career, and it was possible he was the target of a cruel attack on his family.

'I just wanted to tie up a few loose ends,' Geraldine said.

'Oh, I'm sure he won't mind,' Anne replied. 'Anything you can do to help find Daisy as quickly as you can…' She gave a lame smile. 'To be frank, we're pleased at any interest the police show in finding her. The more you can do, the sooner our little girl will be returned to us.' She broke off with a sob. 'Where do you think she is?' She reached out and put her hand on Geraldine's arm, a ruby and diamond ring sparkling on her finger. 'She will be all right, won't she?'

'We're doing everything we can to return Daisy to her mother as quickly as possible,' Geraldine replied.

This time Anne led Geraldine across a spacious hall into a large square kitchen that overlooked landscaped gardens at the back of the house. They sat down at a scrubbed wooden table where a stout middle-aged man gave a peremptory nod, as though giving Geraldine permission to speak.

'How has your daughter taken to motherhood?' Geraldine asked.

David's florid face reddened more and his eyes hardened at the implied query over Jessica's suitability for parenthood.

'It's only natural for a woman's hormones to be all over the place for a few months,' Anne replied before her husband had a chance to speak. 'It wasn't an easy birth, but Jessica's over the moon at being a mother. She's been devoted to the baby right from day one. We all are. She always wanted a daughter, didn't she, David?'

Her husband grunted assent.

'And the father?'

'Jessica insists he's been supportive,' Anne replied tersely, dropping her gaze and staring at the table.

David's grunt this time was less enthusiastic than before.

'Was Jason happy about having a daughter?' Geraldine persisted.

Anne's reply was cagey. 'Yes, I suppose so. He didn't really say much, not to us anyway. He's back at work, so we don't see much of him. Not that we ever did,' she added almost under her breath.

'Thank goodness,' David interjected. 'That man was a waste of space. I could see that from the first moment I set eyes on him. A freeloader if ever I saw one.'

'Didn't you get on well with him?'

'Yes, of course we all got on. Why wouldn't we?' David demanded.

He glared at Geraldine as though she had made an improper suggestion although, given his previous remarks, his claim that he was on good terms with their son-in-law did not exactly ring true.

'And your daughter gave up her job when she had the baby?'

'Yes. She told us she was planning to go back, but she never really settled in the world of work,' Anne replied.

'There was no need,' David interrupted. 'We have always been able to provide for her and she's never wanted for anything. There was no call for her to work. We help them out.' He muttered something about his son-in-law being nothing more than an estate agent. 'And now she has Daisy...'

Hearing her granddaughter's name, Anne broke down in tears.

'Where is she?' she cried out. 'Find her for us. Oh please, just find her.'

'For goodness sake, stop snivelling. How is that helping?' her husband snapped. 'Pull yourself together. And as for Jessica, her talk about going back to work was all nonsense. She never managed to hold down a job for longer than a few weeks, even after I'd pulled strings to get her a really nice position. She said she couldn't cope with the pressure. It was better for all of us when she stopped that charade and admitted that working wasn't for her. Stop blubbering, Anne. You're not making this any easier for the rest of us.'

The rest of us being himself, Geraldine thought. Aloud she asked, 'When did you last see Daisy?'

Anne blew her nose and raised her head, making a visible effort to control her sobbing.

'Jessica brought her here on Thursday, around teatime.'

'With Jason?'

'No, he was working.'

'And when did you last go round to Jessica's house?'

'Oh, I can't remember. A few weeks ago, maybe more. She brings the baby to see us every week. Daisy knows us,' she added with a tearful smile. 'She –'

Geraldine interrupted her. 'You have a key to Jessica's house?'

'Yes. And she has our key as well, in case we lock ourselves out. She drives by occasionally when we're away, just to keep an eye on the place, and we do the same for her. We've always done that, ever since she married that man and moved out.'

With further assurances that the police were doing everything in their power to find the baby, Geraldine left. Nothing about Anne's responses had struck her as strange. Clearly she wasn't close to her son-in-law, but that wasn't unusual. David also, although gruff and almost rude in his responses, was behaving as might be expected from a man deeply upset by his granddaughter's disappearance. The visit had thrown up no new lines of enquiry, although it had established that the Armstrongs were not fond of their son-in-law. There was nothing more Geraldine could do to help so she went home, feeling frustrated. They could only wait for the results of the search for the father, who must surely be the key to the mystery. It could not be a coincidence that the baby had disappeared just when her father went away. The fact that no one had been able to contact him, or establish his whereabouts, was telling, as was the fact that his mobile phone had somehow been disabled and was impossible to trace.

Most of the team subscribed to the theory that Jason hadn't gone to a stag party at all, but had deserted his overly emotional wife, taking their baby with him.

'There's probably another woman involved,' Eileen muttered darkly. 'There usually is.'

'Or a man,' someone added.

# 7

GERALDINE WAS INTERRUPTED IN her work by her phone ringing. She didn't recognise the number.

'It's me, Jessica,' the voice babbled. 'I need to see you right away.'

'Would you like to come to the police station –' Geraldine began, but Jessica interrupted her.

'No, no, this can't wait. You have to come here. You left me your card and said I could call you at any time. Please. You need to come here and see this for yourself.'

Anne had described her daughter as highly strung and emotional, and had mentioned that Jessica had been particularly vulnerable after the birth of her baby. All the same, Geraldine took the call seriously and drove straight to Jessica's house. She wished that Jessica had not flatly rejected the appointment of a family liaison officer to support her through this difficult time. She seemed to suspect the officer would not only be tasked with helping her, but would also be reporting back on her conduct.

Jessica opened the door at once, as though she had been standing right beside it, waiting for the bell to ring. Her blonde hair was scraped back in a pony tail, looking greasy and uncombed, and she was wearing no make-up. Although her cheeks were pale and her blue eyes bloodshot, the elegant bone structure of her gaunt face was perfectly proportioned.

'You called me,' Geraldine reminded her gently, when Jessica stood staring at her like a rabbit caught in headlights.

'Yes, yes, I know. I did. I did. Come in, please, come in. You have to find her before it's too late.'

Geraldine went inside and closed the front door. Jessica appeared to be raving, but it was understandable that a woman prone to hysteria might become temporarily unhinged by the shock of her baby going missing.

'Jessica,' Geraldine began, 'we're doing everything we can to find Daisy. I think it might help you to see your doctor and ask him to prescribe something to help you cope while you're waiting. It must seem interminable, but we will find her –' she hesitated to add, 'if that's possible.'

Jessica shook her head vehemently. 'No, no, you don't understand. This is different. There's something I have to show you.'

Grabbing Geraldine by the arm, she dragged her towards the stairs. For a second Geraldine resisted, wondering what Jessica wanted with her. She regretted not having summoned backup, even though there was nothing as yet to indicate she might require help.

'Come on, you have to see this,' Jessica insisted, her eyes blazing with despair.

Geraldine nodded and followed her up the stairs into a nursery. The walls were covered in pale pink paper where pink rabbits cavorted, amidst a sprinkling of tiny pink flowers. Matching curtains hung at the window. A white cot stood in the centre of the room beneath a brightly coloured mobile. For an instant, Geraldine felt a fleeting hope that she might see a small baby sleeping peacefully in the cot, and discover that the disappearance had only ever existed in Jessica's febrile imagination.

Jessica pointed at the cot and gestured frantically to Geraldine to look inside it. With a frown, Geraldine stepped forward to peer at a few red dots right at the edge of the pale pink sheet. She bent down to examine the sheet more closely.

She had not been mistaken. The red marks were there, and they looked as though they might be bloodstains.

'I was just changing the sheet – I came in here to make sure it was all tidy for her –' Jessica stammered.

'Please, don't touch anything in here,' Geraldine said, taking Jessica by the elbow and ushering her firmly out of the room. 'Go downstairs and wait for me outside. I need to make a call.'

Eileen had said there was no evidence of a crime having been committed. With a sickening feeling, Geraldine hoped she had not just seen something to prove Eileen wrong. Gently Geraldine told Jessica that while the house was being treated as a crime scene, she would have to leave.

'Can you stay with your mother?'

Jessica looked stunned. 'But – I don't understand. What do you mean? I've just made a pot of tea.'

Carefully Geraldine explained that the marks on Daisy's sheet would have to be forensically examined. In the unlikely event that they turned out to be bloodstains, then the whole house would be searched for fingerprints and the DNA of any intruder.

'We have to act fast,' Geraldine said. 'If a stranger did somehow gain access to your house and take the baby, then the quicker we trace his or her identity, the sooner Daisy will be returned home. Now, I need you to come with me to the police station.'

'The police station? Why? You just said I could go to my mother's.'

'Yes, but first we need you to give us as many details as you can of anyone who has been in or around your house since Daisy was born. Anyone at all.'

Jessica nodded. She was trembling and pale, and she scarcely seemed to understand what was happening.

'Is it blood?' she whispered. 'Is it...'

'It may well turn out that the marks on Daisy's sheet are not blood at all,' Geraldine added, in as reassuring a tone as she could muster. 'Someone might have been eating, and dropped a few drops of food or drink on the sheet. But we have to be sure.'

'Yes,' Jessica repeated dully, as though the words held no meaning, 'we have to be sure.'

Bursting into tears, she allowed Geraldine to guide her into a police car that had just drawn up. Geraldine watched thoughtfully as Jessica was driven away. As if the disappearance of a baby wasn't dreadful enough, the investigation had just taken an alarming turn. With a sigh, she watched as the search team arrived. Pulling on plastic overshoes and a white protective suit, she went back in the house, keen to learn what they could discover.

'It looks like a chaotic household,' a scene of crime officer told her. 'Apart from the nursery, which is beautifully kept, the whole place is a mess. Clothes, toiletries, toys, nappies, food, everywhere.'

Geraldine left shortly after. Nothing more could be determined until the search was concluded, and results of forensic tests on the bloodstains had been received. Walking slowly to her own car, she wondered whether they should have discovered the blood spots earlier. It was going to be a long day and there was still no sign of Jason. Jessica had told them he had gone to a stag do, yet none of his friends they had been able to trace knew anything about it. A marriage where the husband lied to his wife about his whereabouts for the weekend, and then ditched his phone, did not sound normal. Either Jason had wanted to mislead his wife, or the beautiful fragile Jessica was deliberately lying to the police. Whatever the truth might be, the motive for concealing it could only be malevolent.

# 8

'I FEEL REALLY SORRY for her,' Ariadne said. 'I can't think of anything worse than a baby going missing like that, whatever the circumstances.'

Geraldine nodded in agreement. 'Yes, not knowing what's happened must be torture for Jessica. We have to find Daisy soon.'

'The mother seems a tad bonkers,' said the female constable who had first spoken to Jessica. 'Hysterical doesn't even come close.'

'You'd be hysterical if you were going through what's happening to her,' Geraldine replied. 'Show some compassion, for God's sake! We don't yet know what's happened to her baby.'

A young constable called Naomi interrupted her. 'We know the baby's been stolen. Whatever happens, this can't end well.' She shook her head glumly.

Geraldine disagreed. 'Hopefully she'll be found very soon and it will turn out all right in the end. But what must be making it even worse for the family is that they have to be questioning whether they can trust each other.'

'You're right. We have no idea who's responsible,' Ariadne said.

'It could only have been one of the family, because no one else had access to the house,' Naomi pointed out.

'As far as we know,' Geraldine replied.

'It's feasible someone could have broken in,' Naomi said,

'but it seems pretty obvious the father's run off with the baby.'

'It may be obvious but that doesn't mean it's necessarily true,' Geraldine replied.

'The obvious explanation often is the right one,' Ariadne pointed out.

'But surely the father can't have taken the baby away, knowing how vulnerable Jessica is?' Geraldine said. 'She's already mentally fragile. This could tip her over the edge.'

'Maybe that's why he did it,' Naomi replied.

'If the marks on the sheet turn out to be bloodstains from the baby, that would suggest one of the parents injured her and they're trying to avoid discovery,' Ariadne said, tentatively.

'Anything's possible,' Geraldine replied heavily. 'It may not have been deliberate. The baby could have been accidentally killed, and the parents panicked and conspired together to cover it up, to protect one or both of them.'

Silence greeted this suggestion. Several officers shook their heads as though they were refusing to consider such a horrible suggestion, even though the idea must have occurred to all of them. No one could deny it was possible, and since the discovery of suspected blood spots in the cot, it was beginning to seem a likely explanation.

'Let's wait and see what the scene of crime officers come up with before jumping to any conclusions,' Eileen said. 'They're going to be looking for evidence of anyone else having entered the nursery.'

'And it might turn out not to be blood at all,' Geraldine added.

After running over the case so far, and reiterating what needed to be done, Eileen dismissed the assembled team to their various tasks. Geraldine went back to Jessica's parents' house and Anne let her in. If her eyes had not been bloodshot and puffy, she would have given no indication that there was anything amiss. Glancing around, Geraldine noticed a pushchair folded in a corner of the hallway, and she caught a glimpse of a highchair in the dining room as they passed the open door.

'Can I offer you some tea, Detective Sergeant?' Anne asked.

Geraldine declined the offer, and Anne led her into an elegant living room, where Jessica was weeping hysterically. Once they were all seated, Geraldine explained what the police needed to know. It took a while, but at last she was able to gather a list of people who had visited Jessica's house since Daisy was born. Jessica was an only child and she had few friends, so the list was short. To begin with, Jessica's parents had been frequent visitors to the house during the first three months of Daisy's life, after which Jessica had taken to going to visit them.

'It was good for her to go out,' Anne explained, as though Jessica was incapable of going anywhere other than her parents' house.

Jason's parents lived further north, in Harrogate, but they had been to see the baby when she was born. According to Jessica, they had not been back since, but she and Jason had taken Daisy to see them several times, on family birthdays and over the Christmas period. Jason had a brother who lived in Sheffield and he had met Daisy at his parents' house but had never visited Jessica and Jason. Apart from that, Jessica had taken her baby in to her former workplace to show her off to her colleagues, none of whom had been to her house.

'She's not exactly friends with any of them,' Anne explained, once again answering Geraldine's questions as though Jessica was unable to speak for herself. 'My daughter's been very tired since the birth, and is often up at nights with such a young baby. She has little energy for socialising.'

Geraldine told them that all of the relations they had

mentioned had been visited by local police officers and no one had any idea where the baby was. Only Jason had yet to be questioned.

'When is he due home?' Geraldine asked.

'He's supposed to be back tonight or tomorrow,' Jessica replied. 'He said he was going away for the weekend.'

The accusation hung in the air unspoken, that he had gone away for two or three days, leaving his unstable wife and six-month-old baby alone at home. Jessica was crying so much she could barely string two words together, but even so Geraldine had the impression that Anne was used to speaking for her daughter. Back in her car, Geraldine studied the list Jessica had given her. Since Daisy's birth, the most frequent visitor to the house had been Jessica's health visitor. Geraldine went to talk to her next, in the expectation that she would be an expert and independent observer of Jessica and her baby.

It was the weekend, and Geraldine found Mary Spinner at home. Mary was in her fifties, thin and single, with no children of own. With a kindly gentle manner, she resembled a middle-aged aunt rather than a health visitor. As soon as she understood who was calling, and why, she invited Geraldine in.

'This is a shocking business,' she said, gazing at Geraldine with a mournful expression. 'Shocking. Do you have any idea what has happened to poor Baby?'

She referred to Daisy as though Baby was her name, a habit she had perhaps acquired through having too many babies' names to commit to memory. While she was speaking, she ushered Geraldine into a small front room, neatly furnished with chintz armchairs and a low wooden table.

'We're building a picture of the family, and the circumstances of the baby's disappearance,' Geraldine replied, saying nothing about the stains on Daisy's sheet.

The officers associated with the case were under instructions to say nothing about what had been found inside the cot. The sheet and mattress had been sent away for forensic examination, and until they heard otherwise, they were all hoping the marks had been made by wine or food of some kind. It was the kind of detail that would be of interest to the media, and Eileen judged it best to keep the case out of the public eye until they had some idea what they were dealing with. So far the baby had been missing for at least twenty-eight hours.

'Baby was healthy,' the health visitor assured Geraldine, as though that was the most important information. 'She was gaining weight nicely, and sat up unaided at three months. Mother weaned her from the breast at four months which is perhaps a little earlier than we recommend these days, but longer than many mothers manage. I hesitate to say it's probably just as well, given what's happened,' she added solemnly. 'Baby was sleeping well, not unduly bothered by her teeth, and really everything was progressing nicely.'

Geraldine recalled Anne saying Jessica had not been getting much sleep.

'Was Daisy sleeping through the night?' she asked.

Mary nodded. 'According to Mother, little Daisy was a good sleeper. She had the occasional bad night, of course, when her teeth bothered her or she had a cold, but that's only to be expected.'

'But generally she slept well?'

'Well, of course I wasn't there to see,' the health visitor replied sharply, as though she felt her assertion was being questioned. 'But Mother reported she slept well as a rule. In fact, she assured me Daisy was no trouble at all.' She smiled as though the baby's satisfactory progress was a testament to the efficacy of her own supervision.

'Did you notice anything unusual in the household? Any cause for concern?'

'No, as I said, Baby was healthy.'

'I meant,' Geraldine went on, choosing her words with care, 'did you notice anything about the behaviour of the parents that might possibly have given you any cause for concern? Anything at all? Were there any signs that Jessica was suffering from post natal depression, for example?'

The health visitor's greying eyebrows rose. 'No, certainly not,' she replied.

She sounded slightly indignant at the question as though she were somehow responsible for Daisy's parents. Perhaps she was concerned that she might be accused of negligence if something was amiss that she had failed to notice.

'We need to know everything we can about the family to help us find the missing infant as quickly as possible,' Geraldine explained.

She wondered if Jessica had been entirely honest with the health visitor. Although she held back from saying so, Mary was clearly sharper than Geraldine had suspected, and seemed to pick up on what she was thinking.

'Jessica was perfectly comfortable with me,' she said frostily, 'and I've no doubt she would have confided any worries she had to me. If I had been alarmed in any way, I would have acted on my concerns at once.'

'Yes, I don't doubt that,' Geraldine reassured her. 'Now, is there anything else you can think of?'

Seeming to take Geraldine's questioning as an attack on her professional competence, the health visitor merely sniffed.

'Mary,' Geraldine said gently, 'you are clearly a very shrewd observer, and very perceptive when it comes to the parents of very young children.' Hoping she was not overdoing the flattery, she was pleased to see Mary's expression soften visibly.

'What do you think happened to Daisy?'

Mary assumed that Jason had taken the baby, and once

Geraldine gained her trust, she was vociferous in her censure of a father who would take such a young infant away from home without the mother's permission. Geraldine thanked her, and hoped she was right, but Mary had not really offered any deep insights into what had happened.

Meanwhile, Ian had organised a team which was going from door to door questioning neighbours.

'As far as we have been able to gather so far,' he reported, 'no one but the immediate family went to the house, and Jason was out at work all day and Jessica was rarely seen.'

Geraldine nodded. Anne had said something similar to her. Apart from the fact that the health visitor seemed to think the baby was sleeping through the night, all accounts of the family appeared to agree.

'Do you believe Jessica was lying to the health visitor?' Eileen asked.

'I don't know. We know Jessica is volatile and there does seem to be an element of duplicity in her dealings with the health visitor, but I think it's understandable an insecure new mother might want to convince anyone in authority that there was no call for them to intervene.'

'She's a new mother,' a female constable pointed out. 'I'd say that's par for the course.'

Eileen nodded. 'There's nothing to suggest Jessica is unreliable. Unless she was confused, which is possible, we have to conclude Jason lied to her about going to a stag do.' She sighed. 'We need to find that young man, and quickly. And when we do, hopefully we'll find the missing baby.'

# 9

THE REPORT FROM THE forensic laboratory arrived later that day.

'That was fast, for a Sunday,' Naomi commented.

'They work quickly when they want to,' Eileen replied.

She didn't add what all experienced officers knew. In a murder investigation, days of the week meant nothing. Nothing mattered but information gathering to discover leads that resulted in an arrest. Eileen summoned the team to a briefing and glared around the room so aggressively that Geraldine gathered straight away the news was bad. She held her breath, praying that the baby's body had not been discovered. Having worked on numerous cases investigating the brutal murders of adults, she had considered herself more or less impervious to shock in a murder case, but the prospect of the victim being a six-month-old baby, whether killed accidentally or otherwise, horrified her.

'The stains found on the cot sheet were human blood,' Eileen announced angrily, as though she was personally affronted by the results. 'Forensics have confirmed the blood was from Jessica's child.'

For a few seconds no one spoke.

'But no body has been found,' Ariadne said. 'She might still be alive.'

'And the blood spots were tiny, as though the baby had been pricked with a pin, not...' Naomi's voice tailed off. 'She wasn't stabbed or anything,' she muttered.

'You mentioned the missing baby was identified as Jessica's

61

child,' Geraldine said, with a slight frown, picking up on Eileen's statement. 'What about Jason? We have a sample of his DNA from the house, don't we?'

Ian nodded. DNA samples had been taken from Jessica directly and from Jason's toothbrush.

'Yes, and it appears that Jason is not the father,' Eileen replied, with a fierce nod at Geraldine. 'Jessica never mentioned this to us.'

She gazed around the room, as the team absorbed this new information. No one said anything for a minute, but they must all have been thinking it was curious that neither Jessica nor her parents had told the police Jason was not the baby's biological father. In all probability David and Anne were not aware of the truth, although if they were it might perhaps explain why they were so hostile in their comments about him.

'So who was the father?' Ariadne asked.

'The father's DNA isn't on our database, so unless he comes forward, or Jessica shares that information with us, we have no way of knowing,' Eileen told them.

'He might not even be aware that he has a baby,' Geraldine said. 'Jessica might have had a casual affair and lost touch with Daisy's biological father before she told him, or even before she discovered she was pregnant.'

'I wonder if Jason knows the baby's not his,' Ian muttered.

The expression in his blue eyes was troubled, and his square jaw jutted out more than usual as he clenched his teeth. Geraldine guessed he was thinking about his own wife, and the father of his wife's baby. But Bev had left Ian and gone to live with the father of her child. She hadn't stayed with her husband and tried to pass the child off as his. Jessica might not have been so honest with Jason.

'We don't yet know if Jessica is aware that the baby is not Jason's,' Ariadne pointed out.

They urgently needed to find out what had passed between

Jessica and Jason before their daughter's disappearance. Reluctantly, Geraldine set off on her next task, to question Jessica about the father of her missing baby. It was likely to be a tricky interview, but the baby's life might depend on what Geraldine managed to find out, and time could be running out for Daisy.

Jessica's father, David, came to the door and frowned imperiously at Geraldine. She returned his gaze levelly. Noting his heightened colour and aggressive stance, she thought he might be prone to losing his temper, but she was aware that appearances could be misleading. It was possible he was a mild-mannered man who happened to be particularly irritated by her arrival. This impression seemed to be borne out by his first words.

'If you're from the local press, we don't want to talk to you,' he growled.

His expression altered when Geraldine held up her identity card, and he relaxed his hold on the front door while his expression became eager, almost pleading.

'Yes, of course,' he mumbled. 'I should have recognised you straight away. I do apologise, Sergeant. I'm somewhat preoccupied, as you can well imagine. Have you brought us news of Daisy?'

He glared ferociously, but there was no mistaking the desperation in his voice.

'Not yet, but we're making progress.'

That was partly true. They had identified bloodstains in Daisy's cot, incidentally establishing that Jason was not her father, but none of that had helped them discover the baby's whereabouts.

'I would like to speak to your daughter again.'

'Jessica's been upset enough over all this,' David replied firmly. 'The only words she wants to hear from you are that Daisy's been found, safe and well.'

'That's what we all want, and we're doing everything we can to find her. Now I need to speak to Jessica.'

David did not stir from his position blocking the doorway. 'My daughter is too upset to answer any more of your questions right now. I sent your police liaison officer packing and now you can return to the police station as well. Go and do your job and find my granddaughter.'

As he began to close the door, his wife appeared in the hallway behind him.

'Who is it, David?'

Her face grew taut on seeing Geraldine on the doorstep and her eyes glowed with longing.

'Is it–? Have you found her? Is she–?' she stammered, starting forward.

'I'm afraid we haven't found Daisy yet, Mrs Armstrong. We're following several leads. I'm sorry to disturb you, but I do need to ask Jessica a few more questions.'

'I told you to leave my daughter alone,' David said. 'This constant badgering isn't helping her –'

'Let the sergeant come in,' Anne interrupted him, giving her husband what appeared to be a warning frown. 'We must help the police in any way we can. Let her do her job.'

'If they were doing their job properly, Daisy would be back with us by now,' he replied.

'I'd like to speak to your daughter,' Geraldine repeated.

'You can speak to me,' David said. 'Daisy's my granddaughter.'

'I have a few questions to put to Jessica. It won't take long.'

'I'm not leaving her alone with you,' he replied firmly.

Geraldine stared at him. 'Are you concerned about what she might say? Is there something you would like her to keep quiet about?'

David flushed with irritation. 'I don't know what that's

supposed to imply, but I resent your tone, Sergeant, and if you can't keep a civil tongue in your –'

'I need to speak to your daughter,' Geraldine interrupted him impatiently. 'We can do this at the police station, if necessary, but it would be easier and quicker to talk here and now, and we don't want to waste time. I'm sure Jessica would feel more comfortable talking to me here, in familiar surroundings. We are all keen to find your granddaughter as quickly as we can and reunite her with her mother. So shall we stop wasting time in pointless argument?'

David sniffed, and seemed about to retort. Thinking better of it, he withdrew and stomped away along the hall, grumbling irascibly. Anne took Geraldine into the living room where Jessica was staring fixedly at a game show on the television.

'I'd like to ask you a few questions,' Geraldine said.

David followed Anne and Geraldine into the room. 'Don't let her hector you, Jessica,' he barked.

Jessica seemed calmer than she had been on the previous occasions when Geraldine had seen her. As she sat down, Geraldine asked Anne and David to leave her and Jessica alone.

'I'm staying right here,' David retorted.

'You might as well do what she wants, or she'll never go away,' Jessica said. 'Go on, please.'

Anne shooed her protesting husband out of the room.

'Jessica,' Geraldine began as soon as the Armstrongs had gone, 'how long have you and Jason been married?'

'Just over three years.'

Geraldine stared directly at Jessica, studying her reaction, as she posed her next question. 'And who is Daisy's father?'

Jessica gave a credible appearance of being surprised. 'What do you mean? I don't understand the question. Jason is, of course.'

'I need you to tell me the identity of Daisy's biological

father.' Geraldine leaned forward. 'It's possible he abducted her. That kind of reaction isn't unprecedented in situations like yours.'

'What are you talking about? What situations? I don't know what you mean. Jason's her father –'

'Jessica, we know that's not true. DNA found in Daisy's cot establishes that you are her mother, and someone other than Jason is her father. The longer you continue lying about it, the less chance there is that we will find her. Your husband needn't necessarily find out the truth, unless that turns out to be unavoidable, but the priority now is to find your daughter and return her safely to you. So, let's go through this again. Who is Daisy's father?'

Jessica shook her head. 'I don't know,' she whispered, looking terrified. 'I had no idea… I always thought Jason was her father… I'm telling you the truth.'

Geraldine was inclined to believe her. 'Very well, but there must have been another man in your life around fifteen months ago, because there's no question that Jason isn't Daisy's father.'

Jessica had gone pale and she was trembling. 'I don't know,' she mumbled. 'I don't know.'

'Think very carefully. Who were you having an affair with?'

'No, no, it was nothing like that. Please, you mustn't say anything like that. We have to pretend it never happened. If you say anything, I'll deny it. No, no. It's not true. It's not true.'

'Jessica,' Geraldine said, very gently, 'the DNA confirms it. So I'll ask you again, who were you having an affair with?'

'No, no, it wasn't like that. It wasn't an affair. You can't say it was an affair.'

'What wasn't an affair?'

'There was this one, but it was just the once, one time, that's

all. It was just a fling, a stupid one-night stand. I went out...
Oh God, this is all so horrible.'

'Who was he?'

Jessica shook her head helplessly. 'I don't know. I don't
know. I was drunk. I've no idea who he was. It was just a
ghastly mistake that should never have happened. I didn't
even know his name. We barely spoke before we... outside
a pub... I don't know why I did it. Jason had gone away for
the weekend with his friends.' She shuddered. 'I thought she
was Jason's. Oh God, this is awful.' She looked at Geraldine.
'Don't tell Jason. Please, please, don't tell him. I never meant
him to find out that I had... it didn't mean anything. There's
no reason why Jason should ever know. Please. And please
don't say anything to my parents.'

'Does Daisy's biological father know about her?'

'How could he? I told you, I don't even know who he is. If
I passed him in the street I wouldn't recognise him. I was too
drunk to know what I was doing. It was a long time ago. And
I had no idea at the time... How could I have told him? I never
told anyone. No one knows. No one. Jason mustn't ever find
out. He would –' She broke off suddenly, her eyes widening in
shock. 'He'd be so upset,' she concluded lamely.

'It was fifteen months ago,' Geraldine said. 'And Jason
knows nothing about this fling you had?'

Jessica shook her head, seemingly too overwhelmed with
fear to utter a word. 'Please don't tell him,' she pleaded, when
she recovered sufficiently to speak. 'It would destroy our
marriage. I know my husband, and he's not the type of man to
forgive something like that. Please don't tell him.'

'I think it's something you should probably tell him
yourself.'

'How can I tell him now, after all this time? I can't tell him.
And if you try to tell him, I'll deny it. No, you can't tell him.
Please. It would destroy us.'

'Well, it's up to you whether you ever tell your husband or not, and, in any case, maybe it should wait until Daisy has been found. But she might want to know about her father when she's older. For now, can you tell me anything about the man you had sex with? Anything at all?'

Jessica shook her head, making her blonde hair swing around her face. 'I can't tell you what I don't know.'

Geraldine drove away thoughtfully. There seemed to be a motive for Jason to have resented Daisy, if he had discovered the truth about her parentage. But if Jessica had genuinely believed Jason was Daisy's father, she couldn't have said or done anything to make him doubt that, and Geraldine was fairly convinced Jessica had been telling the truth when she insisted she had always believed Jason was Daisy's biological father. On the other hand, with Daisy gone, Jason would never need to learn the truth about Jessica's deception. If Jessica had disposed of the baby, then she had not counted on the police discovering those drops of blood in the cot. Yet it was Jessica herself who had drawn Geraldine's attention to the blood, and it stretched credulity to suppose that Jessica would have done that if she had killed Daisy herself to cover up the fact that Jason was not her biological father. On the contrary, she would have disposed of the sheet and replaced it straight away. Somehow the case seemed to be growing more complicated with every passing day.

# 10

'WHAT DID THAT POLICEWOMAN want?' David demanded. 'Tell me everything she said. I want to know exactly what they're doing to find Daisy.'

'I don't have to tell you anything,' Jessica replied, scowling.

'Jessica, don't speak to your father like that. He's trying to help,' Anne said.

'This is all the fault of that bloody good-for-nothing,' David fumed. 'I told you he was a waste of space. You should have listened to me before you went running off to marry him. I told you all along, he's not right for you.'

Jessica returned her father's glare with what she hoped was an equally ferocious scowl of her own.

'If you say another word against Jason, I'll leave this house and go and find a hotel to stay in, on my own, and you'll never see me again. How dare you insult my husband like that, when he's not even here to defend himself. You wouldn't dare say that to his face.'

Her fists clenched in an involuntary response to David's belligerent outburst.

'I'll say what I damn well please about my own son-in-law in my own house,' he snapped.

'Not in front of me, you won't.'

'Whose fault is it that all this has happened?' David asked, too angry to think about what he was saying.

His voice dropped to a reasonable tone, but the expression in his eyes remained as furious as before. 'I can't begin to

69

understand why you agreed to marry that man. Don't kid yourself we are ever going to be pleased if you insist on staying with him.'

'Here we go again. You never wanted me to marry him. You and my mother, you never approved of him, did you? But be honest, for once, this isn't about me and my happiness, is it? You don't think he's good enough to be your son-in-law.'

Anne stood up, flustered and trembling.

'Stop shouting, please, both of you. They must be able to hear you halfway down the road. David, what's got into you? Keep your voice down, for goodness' sake. Do you want the whole street to know we're fighting here?'

She stared at her husband and her daughter, aghast. David was on his feet, red in the face and sweaty, looking like he might have a stroke at any moment, while Jessica stood facing him, her fists clenched at her sides as though she was preparing to launch a physical assault on her father. Watching them, Anne let out an involuntary whimper. David spun round and frowned at her.

'What's the matter with you now?' he demanded, turning the full force of his temper on her.

'Stop it, both of you!' she cried out. 'Listen, I know we're all feeling frazzled, but how is this going to help the situation if you two fall out? Don't you think Jessica needs all the support we can give her right now? We all do,' she added plaintively, staring at David.

Jessica whirled round and dashed out of the room, and they heard her footsteps pounding up the stairs.

Anne turned to her husband. 'Arguing like this isn't helping. David, Jessica's upstairs crying. I'm going to speak to her.'

'I'll go –' David began but Anne interrupted him.

'You've already upset her enough for one day. You stay here and I'll go.'

With that she scurried out of the room, leaving David

muttering darkly under his breath that he wasn't the one who had upset his daughter.

'One day you'll go too far,' Anne called out over her shoulder as she left the room.

'I don't know what you're talking about,' he replied.

After about an hour, Anne returned. 'I'll put the kettle on and make us all a nice cup of tea,' she said.

'That's your answer to everything, isn't it? A cup of tea. Is a cup of tea going to help us find Daisy?' David replied.

She shook her head miserably, and slunk away to the kitchen to put the kettle on. Returning through the hall with a tray, she noticed a letter had been dropped through the letter box. Having put the tray down in the living room, she went back to the hall to collect it.

'What's this?' David asked as she held it out to him.

'It must have been delivered by hand,' she replied, sitting down and pouring out the tea.

David swore suddenly.

'What is it now?' she asked, glancing up anxiously.

There always seemed to be some drama unfolding in her husband's life, and she was sick of it. Having taken early retirement from his firm of solicitors, David had become increasingly crabby sitting around at home. She had advised him not to retire before he was ready, but he had been adamant that he was not going to carry on working now that his office had been invaded by arrogant young know-it-alls. When he had first entered local politics she had been pleased that he would be kept occupied away from the house, leaving her to pick up her life as it had been before her husband was at home all day during the week. On Mondays she resumed her painting class, on Wednesdays she returned to Pilates, and once Daisy was born she helped look after her every Friday. She had welcomed David's election to the local council where she thought he would be kept happily occupied. But he seemed to be constantly falling out with one council member or another, and his temper had not improved. When he became leader of the council, if anything he had become even more curmudgeonly. But at least he was kept busy.

'You don't understand the pressure I'm under to resist these changes,' he would tell her. 'You have no idea how difficult they're making it for me to just get on with the job. It's becoming impossible.'

But when Anne suggested, hesitantly, that he might resign from his position, he dismissed the notion with an impatient shake of his head.

'And how do you suppose they would manage without me?'

Anne could have replied that the council would manage perfectly well without her husband just as they had managed before his election, but she wisely refrained from making any such comment. Not only would it have incensed him further, but she dreaded the prospect of his quitting and being at home all the time.

Instead, she had said, 'All that responsibility must be hard. They are an ungrateful bunch.'

'Louts,' he replied. 'Ignorant louts, the lot of them.'

'Surely you have a lot of support among them,' she said. 'You were elected, after all.'

David scowled and told her she didn't understand. 'You never do.'

He stared at the letter he had taken out of the envelope, and Anne noticed that his normally ruddy cheeks had turned pale.

'What is it?' she asked, putting down her mug of tea. 'Is something wrong? Are you feeling a bit ropey? Can I get you anything?'

Without answering her questions, he held out the letter, and Anne was surprised to see the sheet of paper was trembling in his hand. Afraid the council might have voted to remove him from his office, she took the letter. As she did so, an even more terrible thought struck her.

'Is it about Daisy?' she whispered.

Although she and David were not wealthy people, their circumstances were certainly comfortable. She had a small pension from the years she had spent teaching part-time while Jessica was at school, and David received a decent pension from his law firm which seemed to have been very happy to pay him to retire. She wondered if it was possible that someone was demanding a ransom for her granddaughter's safe return. Or they might be attempting to blackmail David for reasons that were still obscure to her. Taking a deep breath, she read the letter. It was typed on an A4 sheet of paper, addressed to David Armstrong, Leader of the Council, so there could be no mistaking its intended recipient. There were just three words on the paper, printed in a very large font size so that each word took up a whole line on the paper. The message itself was short and stark: YOU WILL DIE.

Anne raised her eyes from the message.

'This is a nasty prank,' David said.

Snatching the piece of paper from her, he crumpled it in his huge fist but she remonstrated before he could destroy it completely.

'No! Wait. We should keep it.'

'Keep it? Why?'

'Because we ought to show it to the police. David, don't dismiss this so lightly. That's a death threat. Remember the crazy man who was shouting at you at a meeting in a library the other day? What did he say to you in the car park?'

David shook his head. 'I can't remember. I wasn't really listening.'

'Well, I was. He shouted that it wasn't over, and he said you won't get away with what you're doing. He said someone was going to stop you.'

'Idle threats from an impotent heckler.'

'Maybe, but what if it was more than that? What if he really is out to stop you? I mean, really stop you. David, we have to go to the police before anything else happens.'

David scoffed at her fears, telling her with false lightheartedness that of course he was going to die. Didn't everyone, sooner or later? Reluctant to let the matter drop, she determined to convince him to report the hate mail to the police.

'I'm a politician,' he told her airily. 'This sort of thing happens all the time.'

His face had resumed its normal florid glow.

'All right, but if there's one more threat against you, we're going straight to the police.'

When David didn't respond, she replaced the crumpled sheet of paper in its envelope and put it safely away in a drawer in the kitchen.

# 11

GERALDINE WAS WORRIED. IT was rare for her personal life to distract her from her work, but she could not ignore the fact that something had gone wrong between her and Ian. Having been friends for many years and, as it turned out, both been secretly in love with each other for a long time, she had been confident they would prove compatible when they finally embarked on a relationship. For the past month they had lived together in harmonious companionship which she had believed was a deep and genuine love. She had almost been ready to invite him to move in with her, and disclose their relationship to all their colleagues. Now it seemed that their honeymoon period had been no more than a short-lived fantasy. Ian had abruptly stopped visiting her at home, and was virtually ignoring her at work. If she had not known him well, she might have suspected he was annoyed with her for hesitating to agree to his moving in with her. But their friendship was too well established for such games. If he was angry with her, he would have discussed his feelings, not avoided her in order to get back at her. She knew he would not abandon her lightly. Something was amiss.

On Saturday afternoon he had rushed away from the police station, muttering to Geraldine that he had to attend to some business and might be gone all night. She did not hear from him again that day. They had arranged to go out for Sunday lunch, so the following day she arrived at the pub, hoping to find him in better spirits. He wasn't there. She waited for nearly an hour but he neither joined her nor answered her calls. She had been stood up by the man who had recently started spending the night at her apartment, but she knew Ian too well to believe he would ever willingly let her down. Undecided whether to be angry or apprehensive, she studied the menu, and ate on her own. She should have been used to her own company but, after just a few weeks living with Ian, the thought of returning to her independent lifestyle made her nervous. She hadn't expected to lose Ian. Not yet, and not so suddenly. Not ever, if she was honest. She had not understood how lonely she was, until she had stopped being lonely. Now the prospect of living without Ian troubled her, like a physical ache.

Ian didn't contact her on Sunday afternoon, nor did he come to her flat that evening. She waited up until late, and was growing really worried by the time he finally returned her call.

'Ian, it's nearly midnight. Where are you? What's happened?'

'I can't explain right now. I only called because I don't want you to worry. Everything's fine.'

'How can you say everything's fine when you've gone off without a word, leaving me to –'

'I'll explain as soon as I can.'

'Ian, what's going on?'

'It's complicated.'

'Ian, talk to me. I need to know you're all right.'

'It's fine. I'm fine. Don't worry.'

Before she could reply, he rang off. Clearly everything was far from fine, but she still had no idea what had happened. Helpless and miserable, she resisted the temptation to phone him back to demand an explanation. Instead, she went to bed and spent a restless night worrying about what might have happened to prompt this unexpected breakdown in their relationship, so serious that he wouldn't even talk to her, when she had been confident that everything was going well between them. She could hardly believe she had been so wrong about him. She could not help recalling how she had felt there was something odd about Jason concealing his movements from Jessica. Geraldine had interpreted that as a sign of an unhealthy relationship. The suspicion that Ian was behaving in exactly the same way filled her with apprehension.

On Monday morning she arrived at work early hoping to speak to Ian on his own, but he wasn't in his office. Eileen called a briefing and there was no opportunity to speak to him before the team gathered. When she saw him in the incident room, she was dismayed by how tired he looked. His face seemed more lined than she remembered it, and his eyes were slightly bloodshot. Once or twice she caught him looking at her without seeming to register who she was. His shirt collar was askew, and he was unshaven. Normally he was very careful with his appearance, and she suspected he had been drinking. With a horrible pang, it occurred to her that she might somehow be the cause of his wretchedness. Finally she managed to catch his eye, and a faint smile of recognition flickered across his face, as though he had only just noticed her and was relieved to see her.

Ariadne had been in charge of a team of constables looking for Jason. Her report was frustrating. Having booked the time off work, Jason had simply disappeared. It could be no coincidence that he had gone missing at the same time as the baby had vanished. The mood at the police station was generally slightly less sombre than it had been, as it seemed the baby must be with her father. But there remained the issue of the bloodstains in the cot, and not everyone was confident the baby was still alive.

Geraldine had no chance to speak to Ian before the briefing began but, as they were leaving the room, she caught up with him and asked to speak to him.

'Yes, I need to speak to you,' he replied, without meeting her eye.

'Ian, what is it? What's wrong?' she demanded in a low voice, aware that they might be overheard in the corridor.

'Not here,' he muttered. 'We can't talk here.'

'Let's go to your office then.'

He shook his head. 'No, we can't talk now. It's too complicated. It'll take too long.'

'Ian, what is it? What have I done to upset you?'

'You?' He turned to face her at last, looking surprised. 'You haven't done anything. Nothing at all. Please, don't think this is anything to do with you.'

'Of course it's to do with me if you're refusing to see me,' she hissed furiously. 'Tell me what's wrong.'

'Can't you guess?'

'I have absolutely no idea what's going on,' she replied. 'And I'm not playing stupid guessing games. It's time for you to be honest with me. This isn't doing either of us any good. Please, just tell me what the problem is. I'm a grown woman. I can take it.'

Ian sighed. 'OK,' he said, 'I'll come to the flat this evening and we can talk there.'

He turned and strode away. With difficulty Geraldine quelled an impulse to run after him like a love-struck teenager. She was desperate to grab hold of him and force him to explain himself; only his devastated expression held her back. If he was making her unhappy, there was no doubt he was feeling at least as miserable as she was. In addition to pity, pride kept her from following him. She guessed that the problem had something to do with his divorce but, whatever had gone wrong in his life, she had a right to know. The more she thought about the situation, the more furious she became with him for refusing her the chance to show him that he could rely on her support whatever happened. He was being unfair to her in every way possible, but there was nothing she could do about it. She could not force him to share the truth with her, and she was definitely not about to make a scene at work. She would have to let him speak to her in his own time. Meanwhile, she went back to her desk, fearing the worst.

With a sigh, she tried to settle down to her morning's work, but the memory of Ian's pale, tired face haunted her. Wherever she looked, his weary eyes seemed to stare at her, alternately taunting her and pleading with her. At last she could bear it no longer and went to his office to confront him. He wasn't there. She tried his phone but he declined to answer her call. She had no choice but to wait as patiently as she could until he came to see her that evening. She refused to consider the possibility that he might not turn up after he had said he would. But she was beginning to wonder if she had been a fool to believe that she had ever really known him at all.

# 12

ONCE AGAIN SHE WAS woken in the night by the sound of a baby crying. With a groan, Ella flung off her duvet and clambered out of bed. The walls of her apartment were thin, and she was often disturbed by noises from other people living in the building. If it wasn't babies crying, it was children shrieking or adults quarrelling. When they weren't shouting at each other, she would hear her next-door neighbours' television blaring so loudly it could have been in the room with her. The people living in the flat above her never seemed to wear slippers or trainers indoors, and she was convinced they stamped their hard heels on the floor deliberately, to ensure the sound reached her through the ceiling. But more often than not, the noise came from a teething and miserable baby in her own flat.

'There, there,' she soothed the fretful baby, picking her up and rocking her gently in her arms. 'It's all right, I'm here. Don't cry, little one, don't cry.' In the same soft tone of voice she added, 'Just shut the fuck up will you? You're doing my head in. Just shut the fuck up, for fuck's sake.'

The baby finally settled into a fitful sleep, but usually Ella barely had time to drift into a light doze before the crying started up again. The hours passed in a haze, until her whole life seemed to revolve around feeding, soothing, and nappy changing. Late that morning she was finally managing to doze when the doorbell rang. She tried to ignore it, but the caller was insistent. Swearing at the neighbour who was no doubt coming to harangue her about keeping her baby quiet at night, Ella dragged herself off the sofa where she had been resting, and shuffled towards the door.

'What do you want?' she called out crossly. 'I'm trying to get some sleep in here. Is it a crime to want to sleep? I hardly shut my eyes once last night. Is it my fault the baby cries from time to time?'

'Ella, it's me, Jessica. Let me in.'

'Oh, shit. Hang on.'

Fumbling to tie the cord of her dressing gown, Ella hurried to open the door. She forced herself to smile at her unwelcome visitor and put on a convincing show, pretending she was pleased to see her. For a few months they had been no more than casual acquaintances, but since her baby had gone missing, Jessica had been coming round to Ella's lodgings more and more often. Jessica was so grateful to Ella for allowing her to hold the baby that she offered to pay her to help her out. She said she was doing it as a friend, but Ella knew she was only parting with so much money so that she could come and see the baby. Not for the first time, Ella cursed her own poverty that forced her to accommodate Jessica's wishes.

'Jessica, come in, make yourself comfortable. I'll put the kettle on.'

'No, please, don't fuss. There's no need. I don't want anything. I just want to hold her,' Jessica said.

For once, Lily was sleeping peacefully on a blanket on the floor.

'How is she?' Jessica asked.

'She's all right, but I wish she'd sleep better at night.' On the point of launching into a rant about being kept awake all night, Ella glanced up and caught sight of Jessica's expression. Stopping herself in time, she said, 'She's fine, really. I'm not complaining. I know how lucky I am to have her. I'm just tired and that makes me irritable. But I couldn't be happier, really I couldn't. In fact, I'm very happy with things as they are. So, how have you been? It must be so difficult for you.'

Jessica picked the baby up very gently, and held on to her as though she was never going to let go. Lily stirred in her arms and settled back to sleep as Jessica rocked her from side to side.

'It's awful,' she admitted, with tears streaming down her cheeks.

The baby woke up and began to whimper.

'Give her here,' Ella said, 'she must be hungry. If I don't feed her soon, she'll start yelling.'

'I can do it,' Jessica said eagerly. 'Let me feed her.'

'OK. I'll go and get her bottle.' At the door, Ella turned back. 'It'll be all right, you know. You just have to be patient and carry on believing that everything will work out. Babies don't disappear forever.'

Jessica nodded. 'I don't know what I would have done without you,' she said. 'No one else understands.'

Ella grinned. 'That's what friends are for. I'll go and get that bottle now.'

In the kitchen, Ella glanced around and quickly shut the door. Hurriedly grabbing a couple of empty beer bottles, she chucked them in the bin. Having shoved an empty cereal box on top of them she turned round. Spotting another empty bottle by the sink, she pushed it out of sight underneath the cereal box. Grabbing a full ash tray, she tipped the contents into the bin as well, thanking her lucky stars she hadn't left it in the living room for Jessica to see. The kitchen stank of stale cigarettes. The tiny window was painted shut so she flapped a grubby tea towel, and wafted the reeking air around without lessening the smell. Having concealed her drinking and smoking as far as she could, she warmed the baby's milk and took the bottle through to Jessica who was still sitting where Ella had left her, cradling the baby in her arms.

'Here you are,' Ella said, holding out the bottle.

'Don't make any noise,' Jessica replied in a whisper. 'She's gone to sleep.'

That was hardly surprising. The baby lying so peacefully in Jessica's arms must be exhausted after keeping Ella awake virtually all night, crying and whimpering, but Ella thought better of complaining. At least she still had a baby to wake her up at night, unlike Jessica. So she didn't answer honestly, nor did she comment on how it must be wonderful for Jessica to be able to have a proper night's sleep. Somehow that didn't seem very tactful under the current circumstances, and Ella couldn't afford to upset her visitor.

'How are you coping?' she asked quietly. 'Are you all right?'

Jessica shook her head and a tear slid slowly down her cheek. 'It's been really awful,' she admitted. 'Sometimes I wish I'd never had her.'

'Don't say that,' Ella replied. 'You'll have her back with you soon. You just have to be patient. It'll all come right in the end. You have to believe that.'

Jessica seemed to want to stay there forever, staring at the baby lying in her lap, her face concealed by a veil of blonde hair. Ella sat watching in silence, too tired to ask her visitor when she might be thinking of leaving. At last Jessica stirred and handed the sleeping baby to Ella who took her to her cot in the bedroom without waking her.

'You know it's not a problem, you coming here like this,' Ella said hesitantly.

Instead of offering her money, Jessica smiled and thanked her. She stood up to go.

'I wouldn't ask, wouldn't even mention it,' Ella said, 'only I'm a bit short this week.'

'Short?' Jessica echoed, looking faintly puzzled.

Ella took the plunge. Jessica would be leaving soon, and there was no knowing when she might be back.

'Money,' Ella muttered. 'I hate to ask but I'm skint.'

There was a slight hiatus. Ella held her breath. Jessica had pots of money and so far she had been almost unbelievably generous. Of course, she thought she was helping Ella out with supplies of milk and nappies – endless nappies – all for the baby, but that was only partly true. Jessica's contribution meant Ella could afford more than her usual meagre fare, and Ella had begun to dread the day when her friend's generosity ran out. This could be the moment when she shook her head and refused to part with another penny, and Ella was down to her last packet of cigarettes. But Jessica reached for her bag and took a fistful of notes from her purse. Ella tried not to gawp as Jessica counted out five twenty-quid notes and handed them over.

'Is that enough?' she asked.

When Ella hesitated, Jessica added another note. Somehow Ella resented her more than ever. She was loaded, without having done anything to deserve her good fortune. It wasn't Jessica she hated so much as life that was so unfair. What had Jessica done to deserve all that? She had been born to a rich father, that was all. But Ella still had something Jessica didn't have. Ella had her baby. Her face twisted in a smile as she pocketed the cash. Jessica rose to her feet, dabbed gingerly below her eyes so as not to smudge her make-up and took her leave, promising to return the next day.

As soon as the front door closed behind Jessica, Ella burst into tears of relief. She was not used to having visitors in her flat, and Jessica's presence made her nervous. Ella did feel sorry for her friend, but she wished she wouldn't come round so often. Sniffling to herself, she went to the kitchen for a drink and a smoke. With a lit cigarette in the corner of her lips, she screwed up her eyes against the thread of smoke rising into the stale air of the kitchen, and carefully hid the cash in a jar of tea leaves. Fortified with beer and nicotine, she checked all the doors were locked, before flopping down on the sofa. No sooner had she begun to doze than she was woken by the sound of a baby crying.

# 13

'WHAT IS IT?' ANNE asked. 'What's happened?'

He knew she was thinking about the baby. That was all she had been thinking about for days. He glared at her for a moment, too wound up to say a word.

'It's unspeakable,' he spluttered at last. 'They could have caused a serious accident. Jesus, someone could have been killed.'

'David, what are you talking about?'

He sat down, feeling shaken, his anger giving way to what he could only assume to be some kind of delayed shock.

'I'll put the kettle on and then you're going to tell me what's happened,' Anne fussed.

He shook his head. 'No, no, not tea. Pour me a whisky.'

'Are you sure?'

'Are you deaf? I said pour me a whisky.'

Anne hurried to fetch his drink and he took a gulp before speaking. Holding the tumbler in the air, he gazed at the amber liquid through the glass.

'What's happened?' Anne prompted him.

'I'm telling you, they could have killed someone.'

'Who?'

'That loud-mouthed hooligan who follows me around heckling me whenever I speak in public. You know who I mean?'

'Yes.' Remembering the man who had threatened her husband in the library car park, Anne nodded. 'Yes, I know who you mean. So what did he get up to this time?'

'That imbecile and his bloody henchmen! I was driving through the car park and they must have followed me. Before I knew what was happening, he threw eggs at my car!'

'What?' Finally Anne was startled out of her preoccupation with Jessica and Daisy and listening to him. 'You mean while you were driving?'

'Yes, the car was moving. I could have been killed. I could have killed someone else.' He shook his head in disgust and finished his whisky. 'If I wasn't a steady driver, there would have been a collision!'

He held out his empty glass and waggled it at her. Without remonstrating, she refilled it with a generous second slug.

'David, you have to tell the police. That man must be stopped. The police will speak to him, give him a warning, and he'll back off. This has gone too far.'

David nodded. 'Yes, they can see the evidence for themselves. If I call them before I get the car washed they'll see the mess that idiot's made of my car.'

'And you can show them that letter,' Anne reminded him.

David sniffed and threw his shoulders back, feeling revitalised. 'Good thinking. Have you still got it?'

For answer, Anne stood up and left the room, returning a few minutes later with the letter. David made a call to the police station and barely ten minutes later a constable arrived. She listened intently to David's account of recent events.

'Have you been drinking, sir?' she asked when David finished speaking.

He sniffed, muttering about the ineptitude of a police force that sent a junior officer to hear his report.

'Had you been drinking before the incident took place?' she repeated patiently.

'Listen, Constable, I had a drink when I got home, yes. You can see that for yourself,' he added, indicating the empty tumbler on the coffee table. 'But I hadn't been drinking before I got home, and certainly not while I was driving, if that's what you're trying to imply.'

Anne looked tense, worried by the hostile turn the conversation appeared to be taking.

'Officer,' she said, 'my husband arrived home very shaken by what happened to him while he was in the car, so he had a whisky. But he hadn't been drinking before he got home. You can see from the letter we showed you that my husband is being targeted by some maniac. He needs your protection.'

'This is a politically motivated campaign to frighten me into resigning from the council,' David stormed. 'But I can tell you right now, anyone deluded enough to think they can bully me into stepping down couldn't be more wrong. Now, this has gone far enough. I want the police to warn this imbecile to keep away from me. If necessary, I'll apply for an injunction to stop his shenanigans, but hopefully a stern word from one of your senior officers will put an end to this tomfoolery without the need for any action from me. Surely even a junior officer like you must appreciate that I'm a very busy man. I don't have time for this kind of foolishness. Please tell your chief constable that I expect this to be sorted out without any further shillyshallying.'

The constable nodded. 'This letter you received was sent anonymously, but we'll have it checked for prints.'

She picked the letter up carefully by one corner and dropped it into an evidence bag.

'Shouldn't you be wearing gloves?' Anne asked.

'Be quiet,' David snapped at her. 'The woman knows what she's doing. They're going to have the letter forensically examined by – by a forensic team.'

'And you're certain you could identify the man who threw eggs at your car, sir?'

David nodded. 'Oh yes, I saw him clearly. He darted out

from between two parked cars as I was driving past so I got a clear view of him, and that's when he chucked a handful of eggs at me. I can't have been doing more than five miles an hour because I was in the car park, probably three miles an hour at most. He made no attempt to hide and I'd have no hesitation in identifying him.'

'Did you manage to get a picture of him while you were both in the car park?'

'Don't be stupid. I was driving. A few of the eggs hit my windscreen and it took all my concentration not to swerve into another vehicle. Fortunately there were no other cars driving around the car park or there would almost certainly have been a collision. As it was, I barely managed to avoid hitting any parked cars. It really was a dangerous attack, and potentially lethal.'

'You didn't take a photograph of the incident at the time?'

'No, of course not. I didn't stop. I thought I should get away from there. Listen, Officer, I'm not the one who should be gathering evidence, that's your job. Now, I want this man locked up before he causes a serious accident.'

The police officer put her notebook away. 'There should be CCTV in the car park to confirm your account, and your description of your attacker.'

'Is that really necessary?' Anne asked. 'Surely you can take my husband's word for what happened. He's a councillor.'

'The leader of the council,' David added loudly.

The constable appeared to be on the point of responding but she said nothing, and merely lowered her head. David could almost hear her thinking that being a politician was no guarantee of honesty. Meanwhile he was growing increasingly tetchy.

'So,' he barked, 'what exactly are you going to do about this? I want to be kept fully informed of your actions.'

'Of course, sir,' the officer replied. 'I assure you we take complaints like this very seriously, and we will do everything in our power to assist in resolving this conflict.'

'Conflict? What conflict? I made it perfectly clear that this was an unprovoked attack. Now, what are you, personally, going to do about it, right now?' he insisted.

'Leave it with me, sir,' the constable replied evenly. 'I'll make a report and make sure you are kept informed.'

With that, she turned to leave.

'Is that it?' Anne blurted out. 'Someone's threatening to kill my husband and you're going to write a report about it?'

'That man nearly killed me today,' David said, his face now bright red. 'As for resolving the conflict, don't you understand, this was a completely one-sided attack on an innocent victim? I'd take care how you represent it in your report, Officer. Members of the public are entitled to drive around the streets unmolested. It's your job to protect the public from violent hooligans.'

'What would you like us to do?' the policewoman asked quietly. 'I assure you, sir, we'll do our utmost to track down whoever did this. It shouldn't be difficult, given your very detailed description of him. And once you have identified him, we'll have words with him and make sure he leaves you alone in future.'

'That man sent me a death threat and then tried to cause an accident which could easily have been fatal. I want him charged with attempted murder and, in the meantime, you need to give me police protection. I won't settle for anything less.'

'You do know my husband's the leader of the council?' Anne said.

'We will speak to your attacker as soon as we have evidence that indicates who was involved.'

'What if something happens to me before you've had

a chance to establish his identity? He's a lunatic. What if I'm attacked again before you speak to him?'

'Are you planning on going out tonight, sir?'

David shook his head. 'Only to the car wash,' he replied.

'I suggest you leave that until the morning, sir, as you've been drinking,' the constable said.

'I can't leave that shit all over my car overnight,' David replied. 'The sooner it's washed off, the better. It's probably already drying on the paintwork. I only left it this long so you could see for yourself what happened.'

After the policewoman left, David snatched up his car keys.

'Don't you think you ought to wait until tomorrow?' Anne asked anxiously. 'You heard what the police officer said.'

About to respond, David drew in a deep breath, feeling a horrible lightheaded sensation, which he put down to stress. It was all the fault of that maniac who was hounding him. David would never have admitted as much to anyone else, but he was frightened by the threats he had received. Of course he knew that his enemy's aggression was nothing more sinister than a lot of hot air, but it was unnerving all the same. In a way he was almost pleased about the letter he had received. It was extremely unpleasant, but at least now the police would have to do something about it. He imagined the chief constable speaking sternly to the tall ungainly campaigner, the imbecile who thought he could do whatever he liked with impunity. Well, he was about to learn that there were laws protecting the rights of responsible citizens, and sending hate mail was a serious crime, especially when it threatened the life of an important public figure. The wooziness faded and he glared at Anne.

'I'll get my car cleaned when I damn well like. Can you believe it? They sent a constable to take my statement. A woman at that, and barely out of school. I've a good mind to call and speak to the chief constable about it.'

Still grumbling, he stomped out of the house. Glancing through the window, Anne saw that it was nearly dusk. The street lamps were lit.

# 14

'WE NEED TO TALK,' Ian said gruffly to Geraldine as he caught up with her in the police station car park.

The sky was overcast and the air felt damp with a hint of rain. It wasn't even drizzling, but she suspected it wouldn't be long before there was a cloud burst.

'Yes, we certainly do,' she agreed, thrusting her cold hands in her pockets as she turned to face him. 'It's about time you told me what's going on, Ian. You can't just breeze in and out of my life and expect me to –'

'Let's not talk here,' he interrupted her quickly, glancing around to check no one could hear them.

Geraldine nodded. They were alone but one of their colleagues could walk past at any moment and, like Ian, she was reluctant to expose their private affairs to their colleagues. It was difficult enough dealing with Ian's unexpected coldness, and her own bitter disappointment, without the additional barb of questions from her colleagues, some of whom already seemed curious about her relationship with Ian. Geraldine's friend, Ariadne, had started to become quite intrusive in her concern.

'I just hope you know what you're doing,' she had said. 'Believe me, there's nothing worse than being stuck working with an ex, especially if you didn't part by mutual agreement.'

'You sound as though you're speaking from bitter experience?' Geraldine replied, doing her best to hide her irritation.

'Not exactly. Not me, at any rate. I had a girlfriend in my last station who kept running after this complete tosser. She was convinced she would wear him down in the end, and get him to divorce his wife and marry her, when all he wanted was to get his leg over. Everyone but her could see he was just fooling around. It didn't end well. She must have been the only one who didn't see it coming when he went back to his wife.'

'I'll be careful to make sensible decisions,' Geraldine said, hiding her irritation.

She didn't point out that where emotions were concerned, decisions were frequently neither sensible nor voluntary.

'Let's go to my flat,' she now said to Ian. 'We can talk there. I don't want to give you a hard time about what happened between us, but I do have a right to know what's going on,' she added.

She hated herself for sounding apologetic, when Ian was the one who was behaving badly, but he looked so dejected she couldn't give voice to her rage.

He nodded. 'I'll see you there.'

With that he turned and strode off to his car, leaving Geraldine standing alone in the car park. She half expected not to see him again that day, but he was waiting on her doorstep when she arrived home.

'Come on in and I'll put the kettle on,' she said. 'Or would you prefer something stronger?'

'Stronger than one of your cups of tea?' he smiled. 'I'll have whatever you're having.'

Now they were alone together in her flat he seemed relaxed in her company again, displaying none of the tension he had shown earlier. Uncertain how long he intended to stay, she decided not to spend time brewing tea, and cracked open a bottle of red wine. After pouring two generous glasses, she sat down opposite Ian who was sprawled out on the sofa.

'Now talk,' she said.

'It's not straightforward,' he replied, sitting up and taking a sip of wine.

'I don't understand. What have I done?'

'It's not you,' he replied, his eyebrows raised in surprise. 'This has nothing to do with you. With us. My feelings for you haven't changed. You must know that. It's important to me that you understand how much I respect you, and how deeply I care about you.'

Geraldine held her breath as Ian sat gazing gloomily into his glass, swishing the deep red wine around.

'I sense a "but" is coming,' she said at last, unnerved by his use of the word 'respect'. She wanted so much more than that. 'What?'

'You said you respect me and care about me. Thank you very much,' she said frostily. 'So, what comes next?'

She paused, waiting for a response, but he just sat staring at her as though he was seeing a ghost. Despite her dismay, Geraldine felt sorry for him.

'Ian, if you're struggling to end this relationship we've started, please, just say whatever it is you need to say. There's no point in procrastinating, that's only going to make it harder for both of us. If you want to revert to how we were before we got together, just say so. Don't worry about upsetting me. My feelings are my problem, not yours. We've been friends for a long time and we both agreed that neither of us wanted to spoil that. As long as we can still be friends, whatever happens I'll cope with it. So please, speak to me.' She paused but he didn't reply. 'Tell me you're all right, please, because you're starting to really worry me. What's wrong? You know I'll always be here for you if you want my help.'

Instead of answering, Ian placed his wine glass carefully on the table and dropped his head in his hands, covering his face. She waited, feeling helpless.

'Please, Ian,' she said at last, speaking very gently, 'just tell me what you want to say. It's all right. Everything's going to be all right. Whatever it is, you don't need to worry about me. We can work this out.'

'But we *can't* work it out,' he burst out in an anguished tone, dropping his hands and staring wildly at her. 'Geraldine, all I want is to be with you. These last few months have been... I never thought life could be so wonderful. You have to believe me. I've never been happier in my life.'

'Nor have I. So what's going on? You know I'll be here for you –'

'No,' he interrupted roughly. 'Please, stop it. I know you're being kind but it's not helping.'

'You have to tell me. What's wrong? Are you ill?'

'No, I'm not ill. I wish it was as simple as that.'

'Don't say that! Now, just tell me what's going on.'

'Bev came to see me,' he replied.

Geraldine felt as though she had been kicked in the stomach, hearing the name on Ian's lips. She had been doing her best to believe that his strange behaviour had nothing to do with his ex-wife.

'So?' she said. 'What does she have to do with us? Do you want to give your marriage another shot? Is that it?' she asked, no longer attempting to hide the bitterness in her voice. 'Do you still love her? Because if you do then please let's stop this farce and we –'

'No,' he interrupted her again. 'I don't love her. And I honestly don't know that I ever really did, not in the way that I love you. It was a youthful infatuation that went on for too long, and in the meantime we grew apart as we grew up. It's different with you.'

'What's the problem then? If she refuses to go along with a divorce, we can live with that, can't we, until –'

Ian interrupted her brusquely. 'She says the baby's mine.'

For the first time, Geraldine was shocked. 'What?'

'She's left the man she's been living with, the man she told me was the father of her child, and now she swears blind the baby's mine. He's three months old!' The expression in his eyes softened, despite the set line of his jaw. 'So it seems I'm a father. She wants to come home with the baby and be a family. A family with me and her and the baby. Geraldine, I still feel the same way about you, but you must see this changes everything.'

Geraldine nodded. Ian had been offered something she might never be able to give him: a son. A wild thought crossed her mind that she could lie and tell him she was expecting a baby herself. She could even try and fall pregnant. But she knew it was too late. Even if she could conceive straight away, Bev's baby was already born and he wasn't going to disappear.

'What do you want me to do?' she whispered. 'What do you want to do?'

Ian shook his head. 'I don't know,' he admitted. 'I just don't know. I never thought about having a child. It was never even a consideration. But now he's here and I'm a father, and it's all so overwhelming.'

Geraldine frowned. 'Before you get carried away, in your own interest as well as my own, I have to ask you the obvious question. Are you positive the baby's yours? Ian, I'm not saying he's not, but either your wife lied to you before, when she told you the child was someone else's, or else she's lying to you now trying to pass someone else's baby off as yours. Whichever is true, she's behaved badly, to put it mildly. You must see that. Given how untrustworthy she is, you ought to at least insist on a paternity test. That's not to say you shouldn't take care of the baby regardless of whether you're his father or not. Bev is still your wife, until the divorce is final, and whatever happens, the baby deserves to have parents who will take care of him. But in any case, you have a right to know if he's yours or not, and so does his biological father if he's not yours. That's all I'm saying. And if he is yours, whatever happens between you and his mother, he has a right to be a part of your life.'

They both knew that more lay behind her words than she would ever admit. She had learned as an adult that she had been adopted at birth, and her quest to find her birth mother had been a long and painful process.

'Don't hate me for saying it, Ian,' she begged. 'Being a parent gives your child a lifelong claim on you. I'm thinking of the baby as well as you. He has a right to know who his parents are. Every child needs to be offered the chance to know their parents, when it's possible. And if this baby is yours, Bev is making that chance possible. You don't have the right to take that chance away from your child.'

She thought of Daisy who would never know her father, and felt an overwhelming sadness.

'You know I want to be with you,' Ian interrupted her thoughts with a twisted smile, 'but this changes everything. It's all so complicated. I wish she'd never come back into my life! But you're right, I need to find out the facts and then –' He gave Geraldine a troubled look. 'I don't know where we go from here. I just don't know.'

'You have to find out the truth about the baby's paternity before you can make any decisions about what to do. That way there'll be no more surprises to deal with.' Geraldine stood up. 'I think you'd better go now.'

It sickened her to think that, for the three months she had been with Ian, he might unwittingly have had a child. Ian hesitated for a second then rose to his feet in one lithe movement and left without looking back. As she closed the door of the flat behind him, Geraldine burst into tears. Alone once more, she poured herself a second glass of wine and collapsed on the sofa, sobbing quietly. After just a few short months, her only chance of happiness had been snatched away and she had no resources left to comfort herself. She had assured Ian that everything would be all right, but that was a lie, at least where she was concerned. For the rest of her life, nothing would ever be all right again.

# 15

TURNING ON THE IGNITION, David could hardly see anything through the film of slime on his windscreen as he drove round the bend in the drive, out of sight of the house. It was going to take a few minutes for the glass to clear, so while he waited he fished out his phone to check his emails. However furiously he worked his wipers, the mess continued to smear back and forth across the glass without seeming to clear. An automatic car wash was unlikely to remove all the traces of slime and fragments of shell left by the eggs that had been thrown, but he had no other choice until the next day as the hand valeting service at the garage would be closed by the time he reached the garage. The car wash machine was better than nothing, although he might be better off to wait until the morning when it could have a more thorough hand wash, but if he left the car as it was overnight, the viscous muck might dry and be more difficult to remove. He was still undecided what to do, and couldn't help feeling the situation had become more challenging than it ought to be for an intelligent man accustomed to dealing with problems.

It was tempting to go home and forget about the mess on the car until the morning. He was feeling nauseous and a little giddy with every breath he took, which was understandable after the fright he had suffered. At the same time, he was impatient to get the muck cleaned off his windscreen. In addition, if he went to the car wash he could stop off at the police station on his way home to register his dissatisfaction with the treatment his complaint had received. He would do himself a favour if he lodged a complaint without delay. Fiddling with the windscreen wash, he changed his mind again, mainly because he had just felt another wave of nausea and his stomach hurt. Thinking he might actually be sick, he opened his window, hoping that a blast of fresh air would revive him. Looking out, he blinked furiously. His windscreen still had a film of sludge on it, making the street look hazy, but outside a fog had descended quickly and what he could see through the open window was equally blurry.

He kept his wipers going at full speed, but the fog in front of the car did not clear. By now he was more concerned about his drowsiness, which he was struggling to overcome. Delayed shock at the attack on his car had finally caught up with him. At the time he had been too incensed to fully register the danger he had survived. As he reached across to remove his seat belt, he felt his heart racing and he almost blacked out. Wiping away a trickle of saliva that was dripping down his chin, he noticed he was breathing very rapidly now, and realised he was experiencing a panic attack. Desperately fighting to control his hands, he fumbled to open the door. He needed to get out of the car and breathe in some fresh air before he choked to death, but somehow his limbs no longer moved freely.

By the time he managed to clamber out of the car he was breathing in shallow painful gasps. Reeling, he almost lost his balance when he pushed the car door closed. He nearly lost his footing again as he staggered up the drive. It was dark, and he swore as he made his way towards the house. Any movement on the path was supposed to trigger the security lights, but they did not come on. That was one more problem he would have to sort out. Unless he took matters into his own hands, nothing ever got done. His wife was a useless lazy cow who left everything to him. She had never been any different.

If she even noticed the lights weren't working it would never occur to her to have them fixed. She would just tell him about it, if she remembered, and wait for him to sort it out, as she did with everything else.

The house looked a long way off, and for an alarming instant he was confused about where he was and where he needed to go. At the same time, the ground seemed to rock gently with each dizzying step, as though he was on a boat at sea. Beside the front door, one of the downstairs windows was shimmering brightly in the darkness. Stumbling, he made a conscious effort to place one foot in front of the other, but he didn't seem to be making any progress in his long walk to the house. Everything around him seemed to be spinning and he couldn't control his limbs. With a jolt of fear, he understood that this was more than a panic attack. He was ill. He had been working too hard. As soon as he got inside, he was going straight to bed, and he would take a couple of days off to rest until he recovered. Not only that, he was going to insist Anne summoned the doctor. He was no good to anyone like this. The front door hovered ahead of him, tantalisingly out of reach.

He wasn't sure what happened, but one minute he was staggering towards the house, fumbling in his pocket for his key, and the next he was staring at a patch of moss on the path. His nose stung where he had hit it on a paving stone, and one of his hands smarted from breaking his fall, jarring his elbow painfully. Pain stabbed his shoulder as he turned his head slightly and saw the moon quivering crazily above him. He was vaguely aware of an irregular whine which seemed to be coming from his chest. Every time he inhaled, a sharp pain in his throat and chest worsened. He suspected he was having a heart attack. Understanding that he had tripped and fallen, he was afraid to move in case he had seriously injured his head which was pounding horribly. He felt sick. He tried to shout, but heard only a faint whimper. Perhaps he had suffered a stroke. Terror threatened to overwhelm him as it occurred to him that, if he didn't get medical assistance soon, he might die.

'Help,' he murmured, 'I'm not well. I've fallen over. I can't move. Someone, help! Anne! Someone! Help me, please! Help!'

But his voice was barely audible, and the words he uttered were no more than an incoherent mumble. He could not lie there waiting to pass out. Before he lost the power to move or speak at all, he had to summon help. He could hardly believe that he hadn't thought to use his phone straight away. His hand shook as he felt for it in his pocket. It wasn't there. Dismayed, he recalled taking it out of his pocket to check his emails while he was in the car. He must have left it lying on the passenger seat. He was alone and helpless, barely a foot away from his own front door, and no one was going to come to his aid. As though to complete his misery, it began to rain.

Painstakingly, he began to drag himself along the ground in what he thought must be the right direction, although he could no longer remember where he was going. In the darkness, and the rain, he squirmed his way along the path. Faint light from a street lamp was suddenly blotted out and in the dim light of the moon he vaguely made out a figure standing above him.

'Help,' he whispered. 'Help me.'

With a groan, he watched the other person lean over him, closer and closer, before vanishing into the darkness that was consuming everything. After that he felt nothing at all, only a coldness creeping over his limbs and body, dragging him down, down, into terrifying blackness.

'No, no,' he cried out, 'I'm not ready to die,' but his voice made no sound in the silence closing in around him.

# 16

HAVING WEPT HELPLESSLY FOR half an hour, Geraldine pulled herself together, showered, and made herself some dinner. By the time she finished eating, she was feeling calmer. On reflection, it seemed to her that the odds were stacked against Ian taking Bev back. For a start, the baby was probably not his. It was far more likely that the real father was Bev's boyfriend in Kent, and that he had only been interested in a casual affair. Not ready for any serious commitment, he had most likely tired of being saddled with a crying baby, and either he had asked Bev to leave, or else she had stormed off in a rage. Whatever the reason for the break-up, she had gone running back to Ian, hoping to find refuge with him. Geraldine couldn't blame Bev for seeking a secure home for herself and her baby, but she should never have lied to Ian over something as important as the identity of her baby's father. That level of deceit was unforgivable.

Even if the baby *did* turn out to be Ian's, his marriage to Bev must still be over. How could he live with her as his wife again, knowing he could never trust her? It was unthinkable that he would take her back, however beautiful she was. Plenty of fathers didn't live with their children full-time. And if discovering he had fathered a child was no reason for him to resurrect his marriage, then it need not prevent him from resuming his relationship with Geraldine. So she resolved to be optimistic. If her hopes were ultimately disappointed, she told herself she would be no worse off than she had been before Ian moved in with her. But she knew that wasn't true. Her disappointment was already sharper than a physical pain, and no doctor could prescribe a palliative for this suffering.

Lying in bed later that night, she was unable to sleep. Thinking about everything Ian had said, she was startled when her phone rang. Hardly daring to hope he was calling to say he was on his way back to her, she answered. Her disappointment was fierce when she heard a constable speaking to her from the police station.

'To be honest, I wasn't sure whether to call you,' he said, 'but the duty sergeant said you went to see David and Anne Armstrong earlier, so we both thought you'd be the best person to speak to her, even though it's late.'

'What's this about?' she asked. 'You do know it's past midnight?'

Despite her snappy response, Geraldine was pleased to be given something to take her mind off her own disappointment.

'We had a call from Anne Armstrong,' the constable explained. 'We thought you might want to know, seeing as you've seen them and spoken to them about their missing granddaughter.'

'What does she want at this hour?' Geraldine asked, with a sudden hope that the baby had turned up.

'She said her husband went out to the car wash five hours ago and never returned, and she's worried something's happened to him. She's tried his phone repeatedly, but he's not answering.'

'The car wash?' Geraldine repeated, not yet catching the drift of the call. 'So this isn't about the missing baby?'

'No, it's nothing to do with the baby. At least, I don't think it is. She called to say her husband went out to the car wash and he never came home.'

'Very well,' Geraldine said. 'Leave it with me for now.'

'Yes, Sarge. Thank you.'

Geraldine should have been thanking the constable for offering her a distraction from her own thoughts. She was too distressed to sleep much that night anyway. First she phoned around the traffic police and the local hospitals, but she could find no trace of David having been involved in a car accident. It was gone two o'clock by the time she finished, but she had not heard that David had turned up, so she called Anne who confirmed that her husband had still not come home. Geraldine offered to go round to the house, and Anne agreed straight away.

'I'm just so worried,' Anne said. 'After everything that's happened, do you think he might have been attacked again? This time they may not have used eggs. What if he's been stabbed? He only went out to the car wash. Why hasn't he come home? Something must have happened to him.'

Urging Anne to remain calm, Geraldine set off, and before long she pulled up outside the Armstrongs' house. There were two cars parked in the drive. A quick check confirmed that one belonged to Anne, the other to David. Whatever had happened to him, he had either driven home from the car wash, or else had not left home at all. Geraldine got out of her car and closed the door gently so as not to disturb the neighbours at half past two in the morning. Walking up the drive in the faint moonlight, she almost tripped over a body lying across the path.

She had found David.

Crouching down, she could discern no vital signs. Talking on her phone before she had fully straightened up, she reported the discovery and decided to wait for the assessment team before informing Anne that her husband was lying on her doorstep, dead.

'Do you want to request the assessment team?' the officer on duty asked when Geraldine spoke to him.

'Yes, the likelihood is he died from natural causes, but he'd been receiving death threats so we need to take a closer look before moving the body.'

After the hate mail and the attack on his car, there was a strong chance the councillor had been murdered.

'I can't see much out here because there's very little light from the street,' she added. 'All I've got is my torch. In any case, we need a medical examiner to check him over and that can't wait till the morning.'

'Very well, I'll get things in motion.'

Geraldine squatted down beside the prone figure to wait for the homicide assessment team, and within ten minutes her colleagues arrived.

'I'll go in and talk to the widow,' Geraldine said.

Anne opened the door as soon as Geraldine rang the bell.

'Thank goodness you're here,' she said. 'I've been going out of my mind with worry.'

'Let's go inside where we can talk more comfortably,' Geraldine replied quietly.

Geraldine had frequently spoken to those close to a murder victim while they were still ignorant of the devastating knowledge. Probably the most difficult part of Geraldine's job was sharing such news. What made this death particularly macabre to report was that Anne's husband was lying right outside her house. Hoping to guide Anne back into the house, Geraldine repeated her suggestion and took a step forwards. As she did so, the homicide assessment team vehicle reached them, and a medical officer arrived.

Anne looked startled. 'What's going on?' she demanded. 'What are all those cars doing out there?'

'Shall we go inside?'

'No, no, I want to know who all those people are. What are they doing on the path? Please, tell them to leave.'

'Not yet,' Geraldine replied. 'Those are police officers and they're here doing their job. I have some difficult news for you. Shall we go in and sit down?'

'No, no, what's happened? Tell me what's happened.'

Geraldine would have preferred to talk to Anne when they were both sitting down indoors rather than standing on the doorstep, but there was no help for it.

'I'm afraid your husband's dead,' she said softly.

# 17

ANNE LET OUT A low moan and lowered her head, hiding her face in her hands. Suppressing a flicker of compassion for the bereaved woman, Geraldine was careful to keep her own feelings in check. Difficult though it was, she could not allow emotion to distract her from her observation of Anne's response to the news that her husband was dead. She watched her closely, aware that anyone was a potential suspect in a murder investigation, and a spouse was always of particular interest. For a few minutes it was impossible to observe Anne's reaction as she kept her face hidden in her hands. At last she looked up. Although her eyes looked slightly red, they were dry.

'I'm so sorry. Are you all right?' Geraldine asked, despising her fatuous question.

However many times she found herself in this position, it was always difficult to find something appropriate to say; there were no suitable words.

'All right?' Anne repeated angrily. 'Of course I'm not all right. How can I be all right? You just told me my husband's dead. Where – where is he? Where...' She broke off, shuddering. 'I'm sorry, I'm sorry, I shouldn't have snapped at you like that. I'm not myself. I can't...'

'Not at all. It's perfectly understandable. Now, shall we go inside and sit down?'

'I want to see him. Please, I want to see him. Where is he?'

Geraldine shook her head. 'I'm afraid you can't see him just yet.' She hesitated. 'We need to find out what happened. The doctor should be with him now, and then we'll have to examine the scene, and depending on what we find, there may be a case for further investigation. But we'll keep you fully informed at every stage –'

'I want to see him. He's my husband. Where is he?'

'Very well, but please try not to disturb him.'

'Disturb him? What do you mean, disturb him? You just told me he's dead.'

Geraldine hesitated. 'Anne, I know this must be very difficult for you to hear, but we know your husband was recently the victim of several attacks, probably politically motivated. We have to explore the possibility that his death may not have been due to natural causes.'

Anne's eyes widened in alarm. 'What are you talking about?'

'You showed us an anonymous letter threatening his life. Have you given any thought to who might have sent it?'

Anne's features twisted in dismay. 'How should I know? I'd like to help but – where is he?' she burst out. 'I want to see him. I want to see David. Where is he?'

Geraldine stepped back and gestured to Anne to join her outside. There was no need to lead her down the drive. The medical examiner had completed her examination and the assessment team were conducting their preliminary review of the scene. Before anyone could confirm that the team suspected David might have been murdered, Geraldine saw that a common approach path had been established, and the area around the body was already cordoned off. A sergeant was on the phone, talking rapidly. Finishing his call, he walked over to Geraldine and brought her up to speed with what was happening. He told her there was nothing yet to suggest that David had died from anything other than natural causes. However, in view of the recent hate mail he had received, and the verbal and other threats to which he had been subjected, Eileen had insisted on scene of crime officers examining the site and a post mortem, before the body was released for burial.

In the few moments while Geraldine was listening to her colleague, she lost sight of Anne. Turning away from the constable, at first she thought Anne must have gone back inside the house, but then she caught sight of her, kneeling on the ground beside the body. Geraldine went over to her.

'Anne,' she said softly, 'I'm sorry, but you need to come away from there.'

Weeping uncontrollably, Anne allowed Geraldine to help her up and accompany her back to the house where they sat down facing one another.

'Would you like me to call someone?' Geraldine asked.

Anne had stopped crying. Now she looked up, and stared around as though dazed. 'Call someone?' she repeated blankly. 'Who should we call?'

'Do you want someone to come and sit with you?'

Anne shook her head. 'No, no, there's no one I want to see. There was only David. He was everything to me. You don't understand. How am I going to manage without him? He did everything for us, for me. He looked after me. He was my life, my whole life.'

'Are you able to answer a few questions?'

Anne shook her head again. 'I just want to be left alone. Please.'

'Of course. Perhaps we can talk tomorrow.'

'Talk? What is there to talk about?' Anne stood up. 'I need to make arrangements,' she said, speaking very fast. 'Where is he? What's happening? We can't just leave him lying out there. I need to call an undertaker. They'll know what to do. You know about these things. Have you got the number of an undertaker? I want the best one in York. But will they even be open now? It's –' she glanced at her watch. 'It's the middle of the night! No one's going to be open, are they? Or do they run a twenty-four-hour service? In any case, we need to bring him inside. We can't leave him out there. Your people can carry him in, can't they? But where should I put him?'

'You don't need to do anything just yet,' Geraldine replied. 'We'll take care of everything for now. We won't be bringing him in here. We need to take a look at him.'

'Take a look at him? Take a look at him?' Anne's voice rose in a shriek. 'What do you mean? I need to see he's properly treated. I have to arrange a funeral, a decent send-off. I need to do that for him. I'm his wife. Oh God, how am I going to tell Jessica? With all that she's going through.' She began to cry.

Geraldine let her cry uninterrupted for a while and at last Anne quietened down.

'I'll send a constable to speak to Jessica first thing in the morning,' Geraldine said. 'We don't need to wake her up, do we? Someone can go round there as soon as it's light. You don't need to tell her yourself, unless you want to.'

'No, no,' Anne replied. 'I don't – I can't... not in the state she's in. Oh God, this is all so awful. I can't believe it's happening.' She turned to Geraldine with a wild glare. 'You don't really think someone did this to him, do you? How did he die? Tell me. I need to know.'

Geraldine shook her head. 'I'm afraid we can't say anything until the pathologist has examined him.'

'You mean – does that mean you're going to do an autopsy?' Anne looked horrified. 'No, please, you can't. Please, don't touch him. He's dead. Leave him in peace. Let me bury him properly, as he is now. Please.'

Geraldine let out a faint sigh. 'I'm sorry,' she said. 'I know this is difficult for you, but we do need to establish what happened. The likelihood is he suffered a stroke or a coronary, but if there's more to his death than natural causes, we have to find out.'

'I don't believe anyone killed him,' Anne replied with sudden conviction in her voice. 'Not David. You couldn't be more wrong if that's what you think. He wasn't murdered, I know he wasn't. I mean, he had political opponents, of course he did, everyone in politics does. But no one hated him, not like that, not in a personal way, and not enough to kill him. I know. I know. People like David don't get murdered for their politics here in England. Not someone like David. Oh, I know he made out he was terribly important, but you mustn't be taken in by that. It's just not true. He was leader of the local council, for goodness sake. He wasn't the president of some global corporation. Please, leave him be.'

'I wish I could,' Geraldine replied, 'but the wheels are already in motion and in any case it's not up to me. My senior officers have considered the situation carefully, and we can't overlook what's happened until we're satisfied he wasn't the victim of another attack, which turned out to be fatal. Whether accidentally as seems most likely, or deliberately, we need to be sure he wasn't killed by his enemies.'

'David didn't have any enemies, not real enemies. Please, you have to leave him alone.'

'I'm sorry. We'll speak to your daughter first thing in the morning, and a family liaison officer will be here soon to keep you informed of what's happening. And I'll come and see you again tomorrow to see if there's any other support you need.'

'Please,' Anne begged tearfully, 'please don't let them mutilate his body. Please, let me bury him intact.'

There was nothing Geraldine could say to comfort the distraught widow and she left soon afterwards, feeling wretched. Only when she climbed wearily back into her car did it strike her that she hadn't thought about Ian once since receiving the call from the police station. There was nothing like death to take her mind off life.

# 18

THE POLICE STATION WAS buzzing with suppressed tension the following morning. Sipping a mug of strong coffee and picking at a plate of fried eggs on toast, Geraldine did her best to shake off her despondency. Her mood did not improve when she went to an early briefing Eileen had called and saw Ian across the room. He looked unshaven and Geraldine's personal disappointment was immediately lost in concern for his wellbeing. She had always thought that his wife, Bev, was self-centred. Geraldine's opinion was not entirely unfounded, although coloured by jealousy. Bev was blonde and undeniably beautiful, with dainty elfin features that gave her a childlike appeal. Her looks contrasted with Geraldine's strong striking features, short black hair and unfathomable dark eyes. Ian had been unable to devote himself to his wife to the exclusion of all else, and she had resented being married to a police officer dedicated to his work. Now Geraldine could only hope that he would not be cajoled into taking her back. Ian had admitted to Geraldine that he had never really loved his wife. He had been infatuated with her since they had met at school, but he had come to recognise that they had never developed a mature adult relationship. Even so, they had been together for a long time.

With a sigh, Geraldine turned her attention to what Eileen was saying.

'SOCOs found vomit on his jacket and on the seat of his car. So it looks as though he was going out when he fell ill and collapsed. He was apparently attempting to return to the house. His wife said he was going out to the car wash and didn't return home, but it looks like he never got there, and probably didn't even leave the drive.'

'Why didn't he phone her to come and help him if he was ill?' a constable asked. 'Or call an ambulance?'

'His phone was found in his car.'

'That was unlucky,' someone said.

'Perhaps,' Eileen replied. 'But let's not start jumping to conclusions before we even know what he died of. There could be an innocent explanation, but the body has gone for a post mortem. We'll discuss this again when we have more information. And now, what about Jason Colman?'

Ariadne shook her head. 'We've been following up every possible lead and there's still no sign of him anywhere, and we haven't come across any mention of a stag party being held the weekend he disappeared. All of the friends we know he was in contact with have now been traced and questioned and no one has any idea where he is. There's no sign of him on any CCTV at the airport or at any mainline station. It would be impossible to travel on public transport with a baby without leaving any trace at all, so we don't think he can have gone anywhere by train or bus. No taxi firm has any record of a pick-up from his house or anywhere nearby, and no driver has recognised his photo as a recent fare, and his car has not been moved. If it had, we would have a sighting,' she added, as though she was worried her team might be accused of failing to spot him. 'We'll widen the net, but so far there's been no trace of him. It's like he just disappeared.'

'Along with the baby,' a constable muttered.

'Sooner or later we'll find them,' Eileen said. 'Now let's get going.'

Geraldine drove Ian to the morgue. He didn't look at her as they set off and she hesitated, wondering whether to speak to him. After they had grown so close, it felt strange to be uncomfortable in his company, uncertain what to say to him.

At length she broached the topic that had been uppermost in her mind since Ian's wife had returned. 'How's Bev?'

'She's tired,' he replied tersely.

'Is the baby sleeping through the night yet?'

'He's only three months old.'

Geraldine noticed his voice soften slightly when he spoke about the baby, and something seemed to tighten in her stomach. She took a deep breath.

'I'll take that as a "no" then.' She paused before posing the question she really wanted to ask. 'Have you had a paternity test?'

'Not yet.'

'Why not?'

'Bev doesn't want me to.'

Geraldine spoke sternly. 'Ian, it's not her decision. If she wants you to support her and the baby, you have a right to know if he's yours or not.'

He muttered that it was none of her business.

'So you think you can just breeze into my life, move into my flat, and then simply bugger off again whenever you fancy, without even bothering to establish whether there's even a reason, just because that's what Bev wants? What about what *I* want? Have you stopped to think about –'

'Please, Geraldine,' he stopped her, in an anguished tone, 'I didn't ask her to come back.'

'Nor did I,' she retorted angrily.

Geraldine did feel sorry for Ian, but he wasn't the only person whose happiness had been snatched away by Bev's unexpected return, waltzing back into his life as though she still had a claim on him.

'She walked out on you, Ian,' she reminded him. 'She went

to live with another man and told you the baby was his.'

'I know what she did.'

After everything that had happened, Ian was back with Bev and her baby, while Geraldine was left on her own. Somehow Geraldine was being punished, although Bev was the one who had behaved badly. She drove the rest of the way in silent fury.

When they arrived at the morgue April, the blonde assistant, opened the door for them.

'Ian,' she smiled a welcome. 'We haven't seen you for a while.' She paused, seeming to register his strained expression, and reached out to put a hand on his arm. 'Is everything all right?'

'Everything's fine,' Geraldine replied shortly, when he didn't answer. 'We're here to see David Armstrong.'

She had never before objected to April's flirting with Ian, but now it irritated her, forced as she was to conceal her own feelings.

'Yes, yes, I know,' Avril replied, looking slightly put out. 'You know the way. Jonah's expecting you.'

The pathologist, Jonah Hetherington, raised a bloody glove in greeting and grinned.

'Two of you,' he said, smiling at Ian and giving him a mock bow. 'To what do I owe this honour, Detective Inspector? It must be the VIP status of our visitor here.'

He nodded at the body lying on the table.

'Do you know the cause of death yet?' Geraldine asked, returning Jonah's smile.

'He was knocked out by a combination of alcohol and pills,' Jonah replied cheerfully, as though he was commenting on the recent good weather.

'He was drugged? Are you sure?' Ian asked, sounding surprised.

Jonah raised his eyebrows. 'I wouldn't make such a bold statement without evidence.'

'So what's the exact cause of death?' Ian asked.

'He appears to have lost consciousness and choked on his own vomit.'

Geraldine stared glumly at the corpse lying on the table like a pale walrus. The dead man's face looked composed, as though he might open his eyes at any moment and begin to bully them all.

'Come on, Sergeant,' she imagined him saying. 'Can't you see I'm dead? And what are you doing about it? I want a full report on my cause of death by tomorrow, or I'll be speaking to your senior officers about your lackadaisical attitude. Don't you know who I am by now?'

'But that's not the whole story,' Jonah continued. 'The actual cause of death was not as innocent as him choking on his own vomit, unpleasant though that would undoubtedly have been. Someone wanted to make sure.' He pointed at discolouration around the dead man's mouth and nose. 'Something was pressed down hard over his face to prevent him breathing. He was suffocated, although he would most likely have died anyway without medical assistance.' He shrugged. 'Whoever killed him might as well have left him alone. The chances of his wife coming out and finding him in time to save him were slim.'

'Perhaps she *did* come out and find him,' Geraldine said quietly.

'Can you identify the pills he was given?' Ian asked.

Jonah nodded. 'It's a common drug, cetirizine. It can be bought as an over the counter medication usually taken for allergy relief, and one of the side effects is drowsiness. He evidently ingested more than the advised dose, resulting in confusion, drowsiness, and possibly difficulty breathing.'

Geraldine thanked him and Jonah smiled at her. 'Any time. It's always a pleasure to see you.'

Geraldine thanked him again as she said goodbye, but Ian merely grunted as he turned to leave.

'The inspector's in a good mood,' Jonah hissed in a stage whisper.

Geraldine nodded but she didn't answer. Taking the hint, Jonah didn't pursue the topic.

'See you again,' he said, 'but not here too soon, I hope. Ian, I keep telling her it would be nice to meet under other circumstances.' He turned back to Geraldine. 'We really have to stop meeting like this.'

'Come on, Ian.' Geraldine smiled at Jonah. 'We've got to go. Places to visit, people to question and all that.'

# 19

STRUGGLING TO GET THE buggy down the steps outside her house, Ella cursed as the back wheels caught on the edge of a step, nearly tipping the whole damn thing over. A woman who was passing stopped and called out to her.

'You've got your hands full. Do you need any help?'

Ella ignored her. She had deliberately chosen to go out just after sunset when she thought there wouldn't be many people about and she was less likely to be observed. Out of the corner of her eye she saw the woman glare at her before turning to walk up the steps of the house next door.

'You can mind your own fucking business,' Ella muttered.

Reaching to open her door, the woman paused and turned. 'What's that? Did you say something?'

'If I did, I wasn't talking to you,' Ella replied without looking round.

The pushchair safely through the gate, she hurried down the road, wheels bumping over the uneven pavement. Several of the street lights were not working but she didn't mind that. It was easier to avoid attracting attention in the dark. The last thing she wanted right now was nosy neighbours prying into her affairs. As she was passing across the badly lit space between two working street lamps, she heard footsteps behind her and involuntarily quickened her pace and, as she did so, the footsteps speeded up too as though someone wanted to keep pace with her. Without slowing down, Ella glanced over her shoulder but she couldn't see anyone behind her. Whoever

121

had been walking behind her must have disappeared into a house.

Shrugging off her momentary unease, Ella continued briskly on her way, telling herself she had been an idiot to worry. Just because someone else happened to be walking along the street at the same time as her was no reason for her to be jittery. She had done nothing wrong. In any case, whoever had been walking behind her probably hadn't even noticed her. But as she pushed the buggy round the corner at the end of her street, she heard the footsteps again, quite distinctly. They didn't seem to be getting any closer, yet when she looked round, no one was there. Doing her best to reassure herself that she was worrying needlessly, she kept going, regretting her decision to go out at a time when the streets were likely to be deserted.

With the small shop on the next corner in sight and an occasional car speeding past along the well-lit street, Ella relaxed. Up ahead she saw an old woman shuffling out of the shop clutching a couple of carrier bags, another woman went in, and a man passed her on the other side of the road. No one was going to confront her in full view of so many people. All she had to do was fill the bottom of the buggy with much needed cigarettes and booze, and get back home without being challenged.

She did her shopping quickly, avoiding meeting anyone's eye, but when she did glance up, no one was paying her any attention. Leaving the shop, she made her way as quickly as she could back along the main road. Turning into her own dark street she hesitated but the pavements were empty and there was no sound of footsteps. All the same, she walked as swiftly as she could and reached home without any further interference. She hurried back inside, this time struggling to negotiate the buggy up the steps. Eventually she abandoned her attempt to wiggle it over the doorstep, instead lifting the baby and all her shopping out into the hall, before yanking the empty buggy inside. Shoving everything back into the buggy without bothering to do up the straps, she pushed it into her front room.

It was just as well she lived on the ground floor or it would have been impossible to take everything upstairs in one go, and if she left her shopping behind in the hall some arsehole was bound to nick it. She had learned from experience not to leave anything unattended in the common area of the house where she rented a dingy apartment. One day she was going to tart her place up. She wouldn't know where to begin, but she had seen a paint and wallpaper shop in York, and intended to go in there and ask. She was definitely going to do it, before the baby was old enough to crawl around and get her fingers in everything, but Ella hadn't yet had the time, or the energy, to start on her home improvements; plus she needed to save up money to buy paint and brushes. Jessica had not been to see her for a couple of days, and she was running low on cash. Before she had finished stashing her purchases out of sight in the kitchen cupboards, the baby began to cry, its tiny mewling building to a crescendo. It was hard to believe that such a puny creature could make so much noise.

'Oh fucking hell,' Ella grumbled. 'Can't I get a moment's peace?'

The noise was impossible to ignore and the baby wasn't going to let up. Ella warmed a bottle of milk, went into the living room, and put her cigarette down. It was only half smoked so she stubbed it out, leaving the unsmoked half for later. She had only just got settled feeding the baby when the doorbell rang.

'Oh fucking hell, what now? You'll have to wait,' she yelled at the window, 'I'm feeding my baby.'

The doorbell rang again, sounding somehow insistent this time. Ella thought she knew who was calling.

'All right, all right, hang on, I'm coming!'

Still holding the baby, she went to open the door.

'How are you?' Ella asked, leading the way into the small living room.

'Can I hold the baby?' Jessica replied without even pausing to acknowledge Ella's greeting.

'Of course, of course. Come on in,' Ella said, 'and hello to you too,' she added under her breath. 'And how are you today, Ella? It's nice to see you, Ella.'

Short of slamming the door in Jessica's face, there was nothing else she could do.

'Do you want something to drink? I've got some coke.'

'Have you been smoking?' Jessica asked, frowning and screwing up her nose.

'Me? Oh no,' Ella answered. 'I told you I don't smoke. Someone was here, er – fixing the oven, and he lit up. Of course I asked him to put it out straight away. You don't smoke around babies, I said. Everyone knows that. Well, obviously he didn't know,' she concluded lamely.

Hoping Jessica would not find it odd that a man would smoke while fixing an oven, Ella avoided glancing at the half-smoked cigarette lying on a dirty saucer beside her armchair. It was lucky she didn't wear lipstick. That would have been a dead giveaway. As soon as Jessica turned her attention to the baby, Ella reached down and slid the makeshift ashtray under her chair. With a silent sigh of relief, she leaned back in her chair. Jessica was not looking at anything but the little girl lying contentedly in her arms. An elephant could have been sitting on the sofa without her noticing.

'So,' Ella said, 'how have you been?'

'Terrible,' Jessica admitted. 'This is just awful. I miss her so much. It's like a constant ache in my guts.'

'I can't begin to imagine how horrible it must be, but I'm sure it'll all get sorted and she'll be back with you soon.'

'I hope so,' Jessica muttered.

'I hope so too,' Ella echoed dutifully. 'What about your husband?' Ella asked, screwing up her eyes and watching Jessica closely.

If Jason returned, he might not agree to Jessica parting with so much money.

'What about him?'

'Have you heard from him yet?'

Jessica shook her head carelessly. 'He can snuff it for all I care,' she replied. Raising her eyes to meet Ella's, she added solemnly, 'Maybe he's already dead.'

Ella smiled nervously at her visitor, wishing she would go away.

# 20

HAVING DROPPED IAN BACK at the police station, Geraldine went to her next call.

'Is this about Daisy?' Jessica asked as she opened the door. 'Have you found her?'

She was trembling, and Geraldine thought she looked agitated rather than hopeful.

'No, it's not about Daisy. But I do need to talk to you and I'm afraid this can't wait. Can we go inside and sit down?'

'Why? What's this about? What's happened? Have you found Jason?'

'Let's go and sit down.'

Jessica nodded and led Geraldine to a small sitting room where they sat down on large soft armchairs. A few clothes were strewn around the room, some of them jumbled together in a plastic laundry basket.

'I'm afraid I have some bad news about your father,' Geraldine said.

Jessica looked surprised. 'My father? I thought you were supposed to be looking for Daisy.' She shivered. 'So, what's this about? What's happened to my father? Because I'm more concerned about my baby than my father's troubles. If he wasn't so hotheaded, people might –'

Geraldine interrupted her. There was no easy way to tell Jessica what had happened, and Geraldine had no words to soften the truth. 'I'm afraid your father's dead.'

Jessica looked at her as though she did not understand

what Geraldine had said.

'I'm very sorry,' Geraldine added.

Jessica continued to stare at her. 'Dead?' she repeated at last. 'Are you talking about my father?'

Briefly, Geraldine explained that David Armstrong had gone out the previous evening and failed to return. After Anne had called the police, her husband's body had been discovered outside the house. Geraldine was pleased Jessica was sitting down when she heard the news. Her face twisted with anguish and she began to tremble again.

'I don't understand,' she whispered. 'What's going on? What happened to my father? Why are you here? I mean, why are the police involved? What happened?'

'We're investigating the cause of your father's death,' Geraldine explained, speaking as gently as she could.

Jessica burst into noisy tears. As she did so, she dropped her head in her hands so that her face was hidden. Geraldine was a little frustrated by Anne and Jessica's tendency to hide their responses from view. She could often tell a lot from the expressions on people's faces.

'I'm so sorry you have to deal with this at the moment,' Geraldine said. 'I know it's a difficult time for you, but you have a right to know.'

'Where's Jason?' Jessica mumbled. 'Why isn't he here? What's happened to him?' She raised a tearful face to Geraldine. 'And where's my mother?'

Geraldine hesitated. 'She was too upset to tell you herself. The doctor's given her something to calm her down and I'm sure she'll call you as soon as she wakes up.'

Jessica looked up, her cheeks wet with tears. 'I ought to go round there and be with her.'

Geraldine nodded. 'She might be asleep, but I'm sure she'll appreciate seeing you when she wakes up.'

'How's she going to manage?' Jessica asked, echoing her

mother's words. 'My father did everything for her. She relied on him completely. We all did. He was always there for us.'

'Jessica, I know this must be very difficult for you, but I'd like to ask you a few questions.'

'Yes, yes, of course.' Jessica sat up and blew her nose, seeming to pull herself together. 'Even this is better than worrying about Daisy,' she murmured, almost to herself. 'I mean, I loved my father,' she added quickly. 'He's – that is, he *was* my father. He was a good father. He was good to me. But Daisy's my baby and I don't know what's happened...'

Geraldine interrupted quickly before Jessica could break down again.

'Did your father have any enemies?'

Jessica laughed harshly. 'Just about everyone he knew,' she replied. 'I mean, not me and Jason of course, we loved him; Daisy did too...'

'Who do you mean by "everyone"?'

Jessica shook her head. 'I mean, he had this knack for making people turn against him. That was the kind of man he was. He was – oh, I don't know – opinionated and full of himself, and he never listened to anyone else. He just bulldozed his way through life without paying attention to what other people wanted...' She broke off, perhaps afraid she had said too much. 'He loved us, his family, and he would have done anything for us. It was just everyone else. And he had political enemies.'

'Who were they?'

'I don't know. But there was stuff about him online, people complaining about his policies, and mum told me he was always being heckled at meetings. You'll have to ask her. But good luck getting any sense out of her.'

'What do you mean?'

'Just that she'll be a mess right now. I ought to go and see her.'

'We're doing everything we can to investigate the circumstances of your father's death –' Geraldine began when Jessica interrupted her.

'Never mind that. Where's Daisy? What's happening? What are you doing about her? She's only six months old, for fuck's sake, and she's been missing for nearly a week! Someone's taken her. Babies don't just disappear. Someone must have her. We have to find her. Someone must be taking care of her. She can't be... and where's Jason? He's taken her, hasn't he?'

'Do you believe Jason would take your daughter without telling you?'

Jessica shook her head. 'I don't know, I don't know.' She glared at Geraldine. 'I mean, you think you know another person and then it turns out you didn't know them at all. I don't even know where he is.'

'Did you and Jason have an argument? Could he have taken Daisy from you because he was angry with you? We need to know the truth, Jessica.'

'No, no. He can't have taken her away. He wouldn't do that to me. He loves me.'

'Jessica,' Geraldine said quietly, 'we're doing everything we can to find your missing daughter. In the meantime, your father has been murdered, and your husband has disappeared. Are you ready to answer a few questions about Jason? I need you to be calm now. Was there any bad feeling between your husband and your father?'

For a moment Geraldine thought Jessica was going to break down in tears again. Instead, she braced her shoulders and looked at Geraldine directly but when she spoke, her voice shook so much she was barely coherent.

'Listen, my father was a grown man who was stupid enough to put a lot of people's backs up. It's no secret he and Jason didn't get on too well, but there were a hell of a lot of other people who hated and despised him at least as much as we did, and it was only because he asked for it. So if he went and got himself killed, it shouldn't surprise anyone if I seem more upset about Daisy than about my father.' Her eyes hardened. 'If you ask me, my father got what he deserved. And a lot of people will say the same, because the truth is he was a selfish bully.' Her face crumpled in distress again and her eyes filled with tears. 'Daisy's just a baby. She's done nothing wrong. Why are we talking about my father? Please, do your job, and find my daughter.'

Geraldine assured her the police were doing everything they could to try and trace the baby, but Jessica just dropped her head in her hands again, weeping noisily. It was understandable that she was in a state about Daisy's disappearance, but Geraldine wondered if she had let slip more than she had intended, in ranting against her father.

'I think Jessica knows more than she's letting on,' she said when she returned to the police station.

'Surely this suggests a motive for Jason's disappearance?' Ariadne replied. 'If he lost his temper with his father-in-law, and killed him, perhaps without meaning to, it's quite likely he would have done a runner. And he might have taken his baby with him, afraid he might not see her again otherwise. Perhaps Jessica knows all about it and has arranged to meet him as soon as she can. They might have planned his disappearance together, and that's why you think she's hiding something.'

'The times don't add up,' Geraldine pointed out. 'Jason and Daisy both disappeared on Saturday, but David wasn't killed until Tuesday.'

The detective chief inspector nodded. 'All the same, we need to keep an eye on Jessica,' she said. 'I agree, there's something here that doesn't add up. It can't be coincidence that Jason's run off with the baby just around the time when David was killed. And you said Jessica wasn't too upset on hearing her father was murdered.'

'She was more concerned about Daisy, but that's probably understandable, given she didn't seem to have got on too well with her father.'

'Are you suggesting Jessica killed him? And she and Jason are in on this together?' Ian asked.

For a moment no one answered.

'Let's find out what's in David's will,' Eileen barked.

They were all feeling the pressure of a murder investigation on top of a missing baby in one family. David's position as a local dignitary made it more likely the media would seize hold of the story straight away, before the police even had time to investigate his murder.

# 21

JESSICA WAS VISIBLY ANNOYED when Geraldine returned to her house. She was reluctant to answer more questions and agreed to sit down with her only after Geraldine insisted.

'I need to be with my mother,' Jessica said. 'We've just lost my father and we still don't know where Daisy is. Don't you realise I'm here all on my own? Do you think it's easy being in the house by myself? I don't have time for this.'

'I'm afraid "this" is a murder investigation,' Geraldine replied, 'and we need to speak to everyone who was close to the victim.'

'We weren't that close,' Jessica muttered. 'I really don't have time to talk to you. I have to go and be with my mother.'

'So let's do this now, while we're both here,' Geraldine continued, ignoring the interruption. 'Otherwise we're going to have to ask you to come along to the police station to speak to us, and that will waste even more of your time.'

Pursing her lips, Jessica sat down, and Geraldine pressed on. She was slightly taken aback at the change in Jessica. No longer anxious and unsure of herself, she seemed quite assertive, almost aggressive in her attitude. But grief and worry could alter people's behaviour and no doubt Jessica had not been sleeping well since the baby had vanished. Her irascibility could be down to lack of sleep.

'Where were you on Saturday evening?'

'If you think you can pin this on me, you're going to end up wasting a lot of time. Yes, my father and I didn't always get on too well, but you've got no proof I laid a finger on him. Anyway, I expect I've got an alibi. When was he killed? Well? Go on, tell me when it was and I'll prove it couldn't have been me.'

Experience had taught Geraldine that unforced confessions were not uncommon, so she sat back and listened, but Jessica said nothing that might incriminate herself, or her husband.

'Were you aware of any bad feeling between David and anyone he knew?'

Jessica scowled. 'I told you, my father was one of those people who fall out with everyone. I don't think he meant to. I don't know that he even appreciated the effect he had on other people. He wasn't deliberately nasty, nothing like that, but he was –' she hesitated. 'He always thought he knew best.'

Geraldine watched Jessica carefully as she put her next question.

'You asked me when your father was killed?'

Jessica nodded, her expression solemn.

'He died yesterday evening, but –' Geraldine hesitated, unsure how much to reveal at this stage.

'Well, there you go then. I was here all evening. You can check our security cameras if you don't want to take my word for it. My mother insisted we had them installed all round the house. My father paid for it all,' she added with a shrug, as if to say she thought it an unnecessary expense.

Geraldine nodded and thanked her for her help. Her claim to have been at home all evening could be a deliberate deception, as could her apparent ignorance of the way David had been killed. The suggestion that the police check the security camera might be a bluff. In any case, Jessica could have slipped out of the back door of the house and walked crouching down to avoid the camera. All the same, she arranged for the camera to be removed so the film could be examined.

Driving back to the police station, Geraldine thought about how Jessica had spoken, as though being at home alone was something difficult. Although Geraldine had never struggled with her own company, having lived with Ian for only a few months, she no longer wanted to be on her own. But she was too busy to have time to worry about her own circumstances. That afternoon, Eileen had summoned the team together to discuss the toxicology report. The findings at the post mortem had already established that the threat to David's life had been serious.

'The victim was drugged before he was suffocated,' Eileen reminded them.

'It wouldn't have been difficult to give him the pills without his knowing. He then drank a couple of glasses of whisky on top of that before going out, intending to drive, if Anne is telling the truth,' Geraldine said.

'He could have taken the pills himself,' Eileen pointed out. 'He certainly knew he was drinking.'

'Are you saying you think he was intending to kill himself before he was murdered?' Ariadne asked.

Eileen shrugged. 'That's what we're going to find out. All we know right now is that he swallowed some chemical combination that caused him to fall unconscious and choke, before someone came along and took the opportunity to finish him off.'

'Did SOCOs find any evidence of cetirizine in the house?' Ian asked.

'The house hasn't been searched yet. I daresay we'll find them, but that won't prove anything. Even if he bought them himself, his wife might have handled the bottle. They are a common treatment for allergy relief, and he could have asked her to buy them, or to fetch the bottle for him,' Geraldine replied.

'What about the letter?' the detective chief inspector asked.

'Only David and Anne's prints were found on it so the writer was careful to avoid touching it with his bare hands.'

'Or her hands,' Ariadne added. 'His daughter described him as a bully.'

'We're checking her CCTV to try to establish whether she might have left the house on Saturday afternoon or evening,' Geraldine said. 'We might not be able to follow her journey very far once she left the house, but we could establish whether she was lying.'

'I wonder if he bullied his wife?' Eileen mused aloud.

Geraldine had been wondering the same thing. Anne would have found it relatively easy to drug her husband. She had the opportunity, and could easily have acquired the means. All that was missing was a motive.

'It can't have been easy, being married to a bully all those years,' Geraldine suggested tentatively.

'They were married for twenty-six years,' Eileen said. 'That's a long time, but she could have snapped.'

'Or perhaps she met someone else?' Geraldine asked.

Eileen gave her a sharp look, and Geraldine wondered if the detective chief inspector knew about Ian's situation. He was, after all, still technically married to Bev, who had a young baby.

'Anne was twenty-one when Jessica was born,' Geraldine said, forcing her attention back to Anne Armstrong. 'So she married quite young.'

'When she was twenty,' Eileen replied. 'Since then by all accounts she's been reliant on her husband for everything. Both she and her daughter said as much. I suppose if she married at twenty, she's never really had to look after herself. I wonder how she's coping?'

Geraldine declined an invitation from Ariadne to go out for a drink after work that evening. She dreaded being questioned about what was going on in her own life. While she was doing her best to continue as though nothing had happened to disturb her equilibrium, she suspected her colleagues knew more about her affair with Ian than they were letting on. Several times she had caught Ariadne giving her quizzical glances and once or twice her friend had appeared to be about to say something but had then looked away in apparent confusion. For the first time in Geraldine's life, her independence weighed her down, but the only person she could imagine sharing her home with had returned to his wife. With a sigh she forced herself to dismiss Ian from her thoughts and began reading over her notes on Jessica.

# 22

WHILE GERALDINE HAD BEEN visiting the morgue and questioning David's family, a team from the Visual Images, Identifications and Detections Office had been studying CCTV near David's home, in an attempt to identify any vehicles registered to Jason or Jessica, or any other known associates of David, who might have been in the vicinity at the time of David's death. The following morning a constable contacted Geraldine with information about a person of interest.

'I've been searching for the man Anne alleged threatened her husband in the car park.'

Geraldine nodded to indicate she knew who the constable meant. 'He said it wasn't over, and someone was going to stop David –'

'Look,' the constable interrupted her.

As she pointed at the screen, a group of people appeared, crossing a car park on foot, led by a tall thin man. Just before they moved off the edge of the screen, they caught up with David and his wife who turned to face them. David looked somehow puffed up and angry, while Anne was clearly frightened, her shoulders hunched and her eyes darting around nervously. She tried to hustle her husband towards the car but he stopped and turned to face the people who were pursuing him. The camera didn't pick up any of the words that were exchanged, but it was clear they were shouting at one another. The tall man shook his fist at David in a threatening manner before they all moved out of sight of the camera.

'His image isn't very clear here, but we managed to pick him up on his way into the hall. It's definitely the same man. His clothes, his gait, all identical.'

The film froze, showing a gaunt face gazing directly at the camera.

'It's a good resolution,' the constable said. 'We had to enhance it, but you've got to admit it's pretty clear. You could pick him out of a crowd.'

'Now all we've got to do is find out who he is,' Geraldine said.

The constable smiled. 'Our image recognition software has found a match.'

She pulled up another screen. Geraldine leaned closer to read the details: Jonathan Edwards, forty-two-years old, divorced, school librarian.

'He's a bit aggressive for a school librarian.'

'A former school librarian,' the constable corrected her. 'He lost his job last year. These details need to be updated.'

Eileen was more interested in the identity of the heckler than Geraldine thought his actions warranted.

'We know his anger's personal,' Eileen said, with something approaching glee. 'He may blame David for the loss of his job and he's following him around heckling his speeches. Could he be our killer?'

Geraldine frowned, wondering how a stranger could have introduced cetirizine into the dead man's diet. It seemed unlikely.

'All he did was shout out at a few public meetings,' she said. 'How was he supposed to have persuaded David to swallow pills?'

Eileen frowned. 'Let's speak to him,' she said shortly.

Jonathan Edwards rented a ground-floor bedsit in a converted house off Holgate Road. It was ten in the morning when Geraldine rang the bell and she wasn't sure she would find him at home, but after she had been waiting on the doorstep for a few moments a man's voice called out, asking who was there.

'Is that Jonathan Edwards?'

'Who wants to know?' he replied.

When Geraldine introduced herself, her response was met with silence. Too late, she was afraid she might have made a terrible mistake, and Jonathan might actually be guilty. If so, she had just alerted him to police interest in him. The house was terraced but even so there might be another way out. She was summoning backup when she heard the faint scrape of a lock turning, the door opened a fraction, and a pair of dark eyes squinted at her standing with the sun at her back.

'What do you want?'

'I'm sorry to disturb you, but we need to ask you a few questions. Can you open the door so we can talk?'

'Wait there while I throw some clothes on.'

The door shut. Geraldine had barely had time to wonder how long she was going to be left waiting on the door step again when the door opened and a long, narrow face peered out at her.

'Good morning, Detective Sergeant,' he said, politely enough. 'My name's Jonathan Edwards. What's this about? If my landlord sent you then I can only repeat what I've already told him, that I do not watch television at three in the morning, and in any case I fail to see how this is a matter for the police –'

'This has nothing to do with your landlord,' Geraldine hastened to reassure him.

Jonathan's lugubrious features relaxed slightly and his narrow shoulders drooped forwards. 'What's the problem then?'

He didn't invite her in. Conscious that he was a potential

suspect in a murder investigation, Geraldine was happy to remain standing outside.

'I'd like to ask you a few questions,' Geraldine repeated. 'It's about David Armstrong.'

She watched Jonathan's face closely as she spoke. His cheeks flushed slightly on hearing David Armstrong's name, but his expression didn't alter.

'The Tory councillor?'

Geraldine nodded.

'Well, I'm glad you lot are finally starting to sit up and take notice,' Jonathan said with a brisk smile. 'You are aware that you could be next.'

'I'm sorry? The next what?'

Although the words could be construed as a threat, Jonathan hadn't sounded hostile. Unexpectedly, he gave her a disarming smile.

'Look, Sergeant, Armstrong's been attacking local libraries, and even agitating to close schools in the area. He sees every public service as nothing more than a drain on funds which he's keen to keep for his own purposes, whatever they might be. Something to bolster his own position no doubt, and of no material benefit to the community. A sop to local businesses, and a revamp of the council offices. It's as clear as the nose on your face to anyone who bothers to examine what's going on. If you ask me, you ought to be watching your backs. Once the schools and libraries have been decimated, you can be sure the police won't be very much further down the list. I'm telling you, it won't be long before he reaches you.'

'The list? What list?'

'Armstrong's list,' he replied impatiently. 'His list of proposed cutbacks. Don't tell me you still don't get it? David bloody Armstrong and his cronies on the council are chipping away at any services that don't make money. That's all they're interested in: profit, profit, profit. Never mind essential services. Never mind protecting basic human rights. They don't care because they can afford private health cover and they can pay to send their children to fee-paying schools. The schools and libraries are first to go, because they're soft targets, but you'll be next. As for what's happening in the health service, it's – well, it's criminal. Literally. David Armstrong and his stooges ought to be locked up.'

'I'm not here to engage in political debate,' Geraldine replied, when he appeared to have run out of steam.

'Why are you here then, if not to help raise public awareness of these savage cutbacks?'

'I'd like to invite you to accompany me to the police station so we can ask you a few questions,' she said.

Jonathan took an involuntary step back but he made no move to close the door. Even in his evidently dawning alarm, he was intelligent enough to realise that would be pointless.

'Why?' he asked. 'What do you want with me?'

Geraldine gave what she hoped was a reassuring smile. 'It's just possible you can help us with an investigation,' she replied. 'We'd like to chat to you about your associates.'

'My associates? Oh, very well,' he replied, surrendering with a shrug of resignation. 'If I have to come with you, I might as well come now. It's not as if I've got a job to go to.'

# 23

GERALDINE AND IAN SAT down facing Jonathan across an interview table.

'You don't mind if we record this conversation, do you?' Ian asked.

He leaned back, affecting a casual pose, while Jonathan fidgeted in his chair, his voice rising in agitation as he fired a series of protests.

'Do I mind? Yes, I bloody well do mind. What is all this? Am I being arrested? If so, I demand to know on what grounds. You can hardly charge me with disturbing the peace. Heckling at a public meeting isn't a crime, nor is disagreeing with someone in a position of power. At least, it wasn't a crime last time I looked. I wasn't aware we were living in a police state yet. I demand to know what's going on.' He glared at Geraldine. 'You said I was just coming here for a chat. You said nothing about a formal interview. Do I need a lawyer?' He paused for breath. 'I refuse to say anything until I have a lawyer. All I will say is that I'm entitled to hold what political views I choose, and I've broken no laws. I take it David Armstrong is behind this?'

Geraldine glanced at Ian before replying. 'In a manner of speaking, yes.'

'This is outrageous,' Jonathan cried out. 'This really is the last straw.'

Geraldine and Ian had allowed him to talk freely, but he let nothing incriminating slip. Finally he sat back in his chair, folded his arms, and was silent. Geraldine had a fleeting impression that he might be enjoying the attention.

'We're not interested in your political views which, as you have reminded us, do not break the law,' she said quietly. 'We're investigating the unlawful killing of David Armstrong.'

'Unlawful killing? You mean he's dead?'

Geraldine nodded. 'Yes, David Armstrong was murdered.'

'Well, well, bloody hell.' Jonathan shook his head, frowning. 'I'm not going to pretend I'm sorry to hear it, although I probably shouldn't say that out loud. Still, it's not like I ever kept my feelings a secret. No, I can't say I'm the slightest bit sorry.'

'A man has been murdered,' Ian said, emphasising the final word in the sentence.

'He was asking for it,' Jonathan muttered.

Geraldine studied him. His face was pale and solemn, and he showed no signs of surprise.

'Are you saying you think he deserved to be murdered?' she asked.

A wary expression crossed Jonathan's face. 'That's not what I said,' he replied cautiously. 'I mean, no one deserves to be killed, do they? All I'm saying is that he was a nasty man with repugnant ideas who should never have been put in a position of power.' He paused for a second. 'You probably know that he was instrumental in cutting back the school library service? And you probably also know that I was a librarian, responsible for a group of schools, and now I'm on the scrap heap, and teachers are expected to do the job now, on top of everything else they do. So these days the job doesn't get done at all. That's *his* doing, David Armstrong. It's not just my job that's gone; it's the opportunity for children to be introduced to new books, not that the schools can afford new books.' He scowled. 'But of course I don't think he should have been murdered, and I'll thank you not to put words in my mouth.

If you ask me whether I think he ought to have been locked up for what he did, then yes, I do. He deserved whatever punishment the law could throw at him. But no one deserves to be murdered. We're not savages, although it's sometimes hard to believe. We do live in a civilised society. We've done away with the death penalty. But, what I am saying is that I'm not surprised someone went for him. I'm not the only person whose life he's ruined. I used to have a worthwhile job and I worked hard; and look at me now, living in a rented room on the bread line. How is that justice? You tell me.'

'I'd like you to think very carefully, Jonathan. Is there anyone you know who might have hated David Armstrong enough to kill him?'

Jonathan snorted. 'Only everyone who ever had the misfortune to have any dealings with him,' he replied.

'But anyone in particular?'

'No.' He shook his head. 'I'm telling you, it could have been anyone. And now, I refuse to answer any more of your questions until I have a lawyer present.' He paused, and then either curiosity overcame his caution, or he was more calculating than he appeared. 'How did he die?'

'I'm afraid we're not at liberty to disclose any details,' Ian replied.

'Well, I'm not saying another word without a lawyer.'

Clearly the implications of what they had told Jonathan had finally sunk in, and he began fidgeting nervously with the edge of the table. He must have realised by now that he might be suspected of having committed the murder, or at least of being involved in it in some way. But if it was possible his anxiety was prompted by the prospect of being unjustly accused of murder, it might equally well be due to guilt, and fear that the police would discover the truth.

Ian and Geraldine had no option but to wait for a duty solicitor to arrive.

'Am I being arrested?' Jonathan demanded, in a tone that sounded almost triumphant.

'We simply want to ask you some questions. Whether or not you're arrested on a murder charge remains to be seen,' Ian replied.

The duty brief arrived after a couple of hours, a twitchy young woman with mousy hair who sat listening in silence throughout most of the interview.

'Where were you on Tuesday evening between seven and midnight?' Ian asked.

Jonathan shrugged. 'I can't remember,' he muttered. 'Probably at home.'

'Were you alone?'

Jonathan glanced at the lawyer. 'Given that I can't remember where I was, it's hard to answer that.'

'My client has stated that he doesn't remember where he was on the evening in question,' the lawyer added unhelpfully.

'Tell us about your relationship with David Armstrong,' Geraldine said.

'There was no relationship. I didn't know the man.'

'You were witnessed heckling him in public and verbally assaulting him in a car park,' Ian pointed out.

'Yes, I know who he is – who he was,' Jonathan replied. 'I didn't meet him in any personal way. I just disagreed with his policies and everything he stood for: middle-class privilege, private wealth, and social injustice. It was nothing personal. We clashed on points of principle.' He glanced at his lawyer. 'That's all. I detested him in an impersonal kind of way, like I detest most of the politicians in government and on the council. But just because I find their policies abhorrent doesn't mean I intend to go around killing them.'

'Yet you focused your attacks on David Armstrong alone,' Ian pointed out. 'He was the target for your aggression.'

'Hardly aggression,' Jonathan said. 'I might have raised my

voice a few times, but that's what you do when you heckle at a public meeting. There's no point if other people can't hear what you're saying. And surely the whole point of such meetings and so-called consultations is to give members of the public a chance to air their views?'

Ian leaned forward. 'Did you ever visit Mr Armstrong at home?'

Jonathan shook his head. 'Absolutely not. I don't even know where he lives. We weren't exactly on visiting terms.' He smiled grimly. 'Not what you might call friends.'

'What about the letter you sent to his home?' Ian asked.

Jonathan looked puzzled. 'I never wrote him a letter. How could I when I don't know where he lived.'

'Do you know his widow?' Geraldine asked suddenly.

For the first time, Jonathan looked startled. 'His widow?' he repeated. 'What about his widow?'

Geraldine sensed that she had somehow rattled him, although she wasn't sure why. Before she could continue, Jonathan spoke again.

'I do know his widow. That is, I know who she is. She used to accompany him to his public meetings, although goodness knows why. It's not like she was on the council or anything. It seemed as though she just went along because she was his wife.'

Geraldine nodded. She had seen images of David Armstrong arriving at meetings in libraries and church halls, with his wife at his side. She was clearly keen to be seen to support him. Geraldine wondered for whose benefit she was demonstrating her loyalty to her husband.

'How do you know who she was if you didn't know them personally?' Ian enquired.

'She went to meetings with him,' Jonathan replied. 'I saw her there. And anyway, you've only got to look him up online to see them together.'

'So you admit you looked him up online?'

'What if I did?'

'Why would you do that?'

'How else was I going to find out where he was next appearing in public?'

'You admit you were stalking him?'

'I wasn't stalking him, I just needed to find out where he was speaking so I could attend the meetings and express my opposition. It's what we do in a free society. We do still have free speech in England. And yes, I admit, I tried to get other people who were opposed to his policies to come to the meetings as well and voice their opinions with me. The more people we could get to heckle him, the better. We needed to show people that there is another way.'

'By throwing eggs at his car?' Ian asked. 'Risking causing a serious traffic accident?'

The lawyer shook her head, indicating that her client shouldn't answer, but Jonathan ignored the silent warning.

'It wasn't just me. And yes, that was stupid, but it was done in a fit of anger because he refused to listen to our demands.'

'A fit of anger,' Ian repeated thoughtfully, 'in a man who admits he deliberately set out to orchestrate a hate campaign against David Armstrong?'

Jonathan sighed. 'You're not listening, are you? It was nothing personal. I was never attacking Armstrong himself; it was his policies we were protesting about. If he'd backed down and stopped closing public services, I'd have cheerfully clapped him on the back and bought him a pint. But he didn't.'

'And now he's dead,' Geraldine said.

'Yes, now he's dead,' Jonathan agreed in a flat voice. 'But that had nothing to do with me. Look, all I did was shout at him a bit. It was harmless enough. He didn't even take any notice.'

'Was throwing eggs at his car another harmless gesture?' Ian asked.

Jonathan shrugged.

'My client has admitted it was a foolish action which he now regrets,' the lawyer responded. 'If Mr Armstrong did drive dangerously as a result of my client's actions, that was Mr Armstrong's choice and not my client's responsibility. At no time did my client seek to coerce Mr Armstrong into driving the car after my client and his associates had thrown eggs at it.'

They warned Jonathan that he could still be charged with harassment and released him, with instructions not to leave York. They had no evidence to implicate him in the murder of David Armstrong, but he remained a potential suspect.

# 24

BEFORE THEY RELEASED JONATHAN, Geraldine and Ian asked him for a list of his political associates. It was plausible that one of them had been more active, and perhaps considerably more dangerous, than a man who vented his feelings in words and egg throwing. Jonathan had gathered together a group of irate left-wing campaigners who traipsed around after him, grumbling about social injustice. David Armstrong appeared to have been the main target of their resentment, but it wasn't clear whether that was because they were following Jonathan's lead.

'There could be someone else driving the campaign from the sidelines, winding up people like Jonathan who had a grudge against the victim,' Geraldine suggested.

'You're saying someone else could be "egging" the others on?' a constable said, chuckling at his own joke.

'I'm suggesting that Jonathan might not necessarily be the ring leader,' Geraldine replied. 'It might just be that he has the loudest voice and talks the most and so he's the one who's attracted the most attention. But perhaps there's someone with a serious grudge against David who was quietly organising these attacks and staying out of the limelight and allowing Jonathan to draw attention away from him, or her, whoever it is that's behind all this. After all, if David had an enemy who was planning to kill him, they would hardly want to draw attention to themselves, would they? And orchestrating a hate campaign against their intended victim by winding up disgruntled protesters like Jonathan would provide any investigation with a host of other suspects. And we still don't have any reason to suppose that his murder was politically motivated. It could have been a personal attack, which we're missing, concealed behind a smokescreen thrown up by the protests against his policies.'

Eileen nodded. 'At this stage, we need to consider every possibility. In the meantime, we've seen David's will, and it's fairly standard. His entire estate goes to his wife, but it's actually not that much. There's the house, of course, and his car, but apart from that all of his savings seem to have gone on supporting his daughter and granddaughter, and his political campaign to get himself elected. He's not exactly a wealthy man. His work pension ceases on death, and there's still a mortgage on the house, which isn't paid off when he dies. So no one is financially better off without him. Quite the opposite, in fact. Anne might end up having to get herself a job, or else sell the house and downsize. And David paid Jessica an allowance out of his own work pension, which she won't be getting any more. So the family certainly don't have a financial motive to be rid of him.'

A team of constables were tasked with investigating the list of names Jonathan had given them, cross referencing them with reports of politically motivated attacks, especially any that appeared similar to those carried out against David Armstrong. Several of Jonathan's associates turned out to be middle-aged women, aggrieved former librarians and retired school teachers, but one of the constables came across a potentially interesting name. Rod Browning was in his twenties and he had been involved in several violent protests while he was at university.

'He looks like someone we ought to question,' Geraldine agreed.

Although she wasn't convinced that Rod's history was

necessarily significant, she went to speak to Ian who was co-ordinating the investigation into Jonathan's associates. Geraldine knocked and opened the door of his office. When he looked up and saw her peering in, a wary expression crossed his face.

'What is it?' he asked, without inviting her to enter.

Ignoring his coldness, Geraldine went in. 'Naomi's come up with a possible suspect from Jonathan's list,' she said.

She was pleased that her voice was completely steady, while her feelings on being alone in a room with Ian were anything but calm.

'It's a young man with a history of violence. At university he was involved in a number of aggressive protests, causing damage to property, although no one was ever injured, except accidentally.'

The more she spoke, the more focused she felt on the case, and the easier it was to ignore the fact that she was alone with Ian. In that moment, she told herself, he was simply a colleague, and her senior officer. All the same, she refused to look directly at him for fear she would be distracted. His office was stuffy, and documents were strewn around untidily on his desk. When she glanced at him, she noticed that his hair was unkempt and he was unshaven. She looked away quickly.

'In any event,' she continued briskly, 'he was obviously a bit of a hothead when he was younger, and just the kind of person who might do something stupid.'

'Something stupid?' Ian repeated. 'You call murder "something stupid"?'

Geraldine was taken aback by the bitterness in his voice. Her glance brushed past his face; she caught only a fleeting glimpse of the desolate expression in his eyes. On the instant, her years of training seemed to slide away and she lost her grip on her professional detachment.

'Ian,' she blurted out before she could stop herself, 'you look exhausted. Do you need to take some time off?'

He scowled at her. 'Don't you dare suggest anything of the kind to anyone outside this room.'

Geraldine hastened to reassure him that she had no intention of sharing her opinion with anyone else.

'I can do without busybodies fussing around,' he added sourly. 'Look, Geraldine, I'm not going to pretend that I'm not in trouble –' he shook his head rapidly, like a wet dog. 'But it's my problem, and I'll work this out somehow.'

'It's not only your problem,' she replied, struggling to control her temper. 'This isn't just about you. It's about your wife, and the baby who may or may not be yours, and it's about me. What happens in your life affects me too, you know.'

Ian held up his hand. 'Enough, enough. Please, don't make this harder for me than it already is. I'm sorry, I know I'm being selfish, but I can't see any way out of this mess right now. I'll get there, I promise, but I need some time to work this out. I'm just asking you to be patient.'

'You know I'll wait,' she replied, slightly mollified. She hesitated before asking whether he had yet had a paternity test. 'It might help you to work out what you want to do. It must make a difference, to the real father as well as to you.'

As she spoke, Geraldine realised she was still clinging to the hope that Ian wasn't the baby's father after all. Until he took the test, there was no way he could be sure one way or the other. She wondered whether he was reluctant to find out the truth because deep down he really wanted the baby to be his, or because that prospect terrified him.

'Either way, you don't have to take her back,' she added miserably.

But Ian no longer appeared to be listening to her. With a sigh, she returned to her desk.

'I don't understand where the baby's being kept,' Ariadne said.

Still thinking about Ian and Bev's baby, Geraldine was startled.

'What do you mean, where he's being kept? What do you know about it?'

'She,' Ariadne replied, giving Geraldine a curious look. 'I mean, if Daisy *is* with her father, then how is he managing to keep her hidden? Surely someone would have seen them?' She shook her head. 'It's a terrible thing to say but, frankly, I don't see how the baby can still be alive.'

Geraldine nodded grimly.

'We have no idea what's happened,' Ariadne went on.

'Is it really coincidence that Jessica's husband has vanished, and her father's been murdered, both at the same time as her baby disappeared? She *has* to be the link. But how?' Geraldine replied.

'She's certainly unlucky,' Ariadne replied. 'She's like a character in a Greek tragedy.'

'I wonder,' Geraldine said, frowning. 'You know the saying: you make your own luck.'

'You mean you think she's responsible for killing her baby and her husband, and her father?' Ariadne asked, raising her eyebrows. 'Is there one word for a woman who murders all her male relations? Patricide combined with infanticide and mariticide?'

Geraldine shook her head. 'I don't really know what to make of it all. It's a mess, isn't it? But Jessica's at the centre of it. She has to be.'

# 25

ELLA LAY IN BED, trembling. She wasn't sure what had woken her up, but on the instant all her senses were alert, straining to see and hear in the silent darkness. She had an uncanny sensation, a kind of sixth sense, telling her she wasn't alone. Someone was lurking in her room, creeping closer to the bed, trying to avoid being heard. There was no doubt in her mind who it must be, because she always knew he wasn't far away. With shaking fingers, she reached for the torch she kept beneath her pillow. As she touched the cold smooth metal, she heard a noise, a regular tapping, nothing like the noise a baby might make. Her hand closed around the torch and she gripped it tightly. Cautiously she raised herself without making a sound, until she was sitting up. Hunched over on the bed she listened again, clutching the torch but not yet daring to switch it on. The tapping resumed, and she heard his footsteps shuffling along the corridor outside her room, coming closer and closer. She held her breath, listening.

At last she could bear it no longer. With a muted cry, she leapt out of bed, tripped on the threadbare mat, and knocked over a beer bottle as she fell, landing on her knees with a painful thud. She swore out loud. The bottle had been nearly empty but all the same the mat felt soggy beneath her bare knees. Too alarmed to worry about whether she had hurt herself, she clambered to her feet as quickly as she could, and stood with her back pressed against the wall, listening. A car roared past outside, but inside the building all was silent.

'What do you want?' she whispered. 'I know you're there.'

No one answered, but the tapping resumed. It could quite plausibly have been the plumbing, or creaking masonry, but Ella knew that this was more sinister than noises common to an old building. Someone was moving around her flat, and she knew who it was. Her whole body trembled as she switched on the torch. The feeble beam of light cast shadows up the walls which seemed to move towards her each time she shifted her position.

'I know you're there,' she repeated, more loudly. 'And you don't scare me,' she added untruthfully. 'You don't have that power. Not any more.'

She did her best to sound confident, but she was unable to stop her voice wobbling.

'You don't scare me,' she repeated. 'Really, you don't. No one scares me, especially not you. You're pathetic! So you might as well show yourself or, better still, go back to the hole you crawled out of. I don't want you here. Go away. Leave me alone. Leave me alone!'

Her voice rose to a shriek but still no one answered. Slowly she shone her torch all around the room. The narrow beam of light quivered up and down the walls and on past the closed door. The bolts were in place, top and bottom and she was alone in the bedroom, apart from the baby who was miraculously sleeping.

'All right,' she said, struggling to calm her breathing. 'Don't say I didn't warn you.'

Very slowly, without taking her eyes off the door, she reached under the bed and scrabbled around in the fluff and crumbs and empty cigarette packets until she found the knife which she kept there for just such an emergency. She could feel her heart thudding rapidly in her chest. Righting the beer bottle that she had knocked over, she grasped the handle of the knife, the blade pointing at the door, and straightened up. Her thoughts were whirling out of control as she tried to decide what to do. She was positive she had locked all the doors before going to bed. Knife in hand, she crept over to the door of her bedroom. The bolts were too small to hold the door against someone determined to smash it open, but they were strong enough to delay an intruder, giving Ella time to find her knife if he tried to break in.

Silently she slid the bolts across and flung open the door. There was no one in the corridor. She searched the living room but it was similarly empty. From the bedroom she could hear the faint sniffly sound that babies made when they slept. Apart from the occasional muffled drone of a car outside, there was no other sound. Having satisfied herself there was no one in the living room, she unbolted the door to the kitchen. Next, still brandishing her knife, she checked the front door. It was locked with the chain on, exactly as she left it every night. After that, she went around rattling all the internal bolts to check they had not come loose. The landlord didn't know about the bolts she had fixed to the doors, top and bottom, and so far he hadn't spotted them. If he did, he would probably make a stupid fuss, claiming it was a fire hazard to lock herself in her room like that, but she knew there were more pressing dangers. With all the doors bolted on the inside, it would be difficult for anyone to break in and creep up on her without being heard. Even so, she lived in fear of being burgled, or worse.

At last, satisfied that no one was prowling around the flat, she carefully bolted all the doors again. Afraid to put the bedroom light on, in case he saw the light under her door, she sat down on the bed and examined her injuries in the beam from her torch. One of her knees had a small dark mark on it, but the bruise on the other covered most of her kneecap and seemed to be spreading downwards. Now that she was able to stop and think about it, her knee hurt. Whimpering, she replaced the knife under the bed so that she could reach it without sitting up, stowed the torch under her pillow, lay down and pulled the covers right up to her chin, trying to ignore the pain in her knee. As soon as she closed her eyes, the silence was disturbed by the sound of a baby crying.

# 26

ROD BROWNING WORKED AT a health food shop in the city. Situated in Colliergate, between Kings Square and the Shambles, it was a picturesque shop, in keeping with the surrounding area. Leaving her car nearby, Geraldine walked along Colliergate to her destination. It was a mild sunny afternoon and, as she walked along the street, she began to enjoy her brief respite from work. For a moment she pretended that she was a tourist enjoying the sights of York, oblivious to the darker side of the city's life. More than anything, it was a relief to escape from the police station where she was at risk of seeing Ian, constantly aware that she was in the same building as him but unable to speak to him, except in a professional capacity. Their break-up would have been easier if they hadn't worked together. The irony of their current situation was that she and Ian had discussed the pros and cons of embarking on a relationship with a colleague at work before he had moved in with her, and they had both felt confident their relationship was strong enough to cope with any of the potential disadvantages.

'We're not teenagers,' Geraldine had said.

'And it's not as if we don't know each other,' Ian had agreed. 'We're hardly likely to surprise one other, after knowing each other for so long. What could possibly go wrong?'

As she walked, Geraldine tried not to think about those conversations, but by the time she arrived at the health food shop her good mood had evaporated. 'Yes, what could possibly go wrong?' she muttered to herself. It had never occurred to her back then to enquire what would happen if Ian's wife ever decided to return to him. Along with Ian, Geraldine had believed that Bev was happily settled with her former boss, and their baby. Now any certainty about Geraldine's own future with Ian had vanished. All she knew for certain was that the longer the situation continued, the less likely it became that Ian would ever ask Bev to leave. It was fair enough that he would want her back. She was his wife and he had loved her for a long time. There was no reason why he shouldn't want her back. Except that he had led Geraldine to believe he loved *her*.

Looking back over the time they had spent together, Geraldine couldn't recall him ever actually saying those words to her. He had once told her that he was 'in love' with her, but perhaps that wasn't quite the same thing. She had never even questioned how he felt about her, but had just assumed he felt the same as she did. Now she realised that she had behaved like a gullible fool. Ian had been on the rebound and desperate for comfort, and it was that need, not love, that had driven him into her welcoming arms. No doubt Geraldine's passion had soothed his smarting ego, but the moment Bev walked back into his life, his relationship with Geraldine had faded into the background. She had to accept that she had lost him or, rather, that he had never really been hers to lose. Their love affair had existed only in her mind, and she had been a blind idiot not to see exactly what was going on.

Somehow she had to swallow her bitterness and move on, but by the time she reached Rod's work place she was nearly in tears, despising herself and resenting Ian who had reduced her to a snivelling weakling. Her disappointment and rage threatened her ability to focus on the investigation, and she had to take a turn around the square to clear her mind before entering the shop.

'Can I help you?'

Geraldine smiled at the slim girl standing behind the counter.

'I'm looking for Rod Browning.'

'Rod?'

'Yes, I believe he works here?'

The girl nodded.

'Is he here today?'

The girl gave another nod. 'Yes, he's out the back.'

'Well, can you call him, or shall I speak to him there? Either is fine with me.'

'I'm sorry, I don't know,' the girl replied.

Geraldine felt her smile slipping. 'Shall I go and find him then?' she asked.

Without waiting for a response, she strode along the central aisle, between shelves packed with bottles and sachets, and brightly coloured boxes and packets, to the back of the shop. There was an internal door marked 'Staff only', with a keypad beside it, and no bell. Impatiently, Geraldine rapped on the door but no one came to open it. She knocked more loudly, and finally the door opened and a short, stocky man looked out at her. He had a pale freckled face and a mop of ginger hair that hung down past his ears, reaching the top of a bushy ginger beard.

'Yes? Who are you? What do you want?'

Geraldine introduced herself and explained that she was looking for Rod Browning.

'Yes, that's me. What's this about?'

He looked curious rather than concerned. Geraldine gave him a tight smile.

'Is there somewhere we can go where we can talk?'

With a nod, Rod ushered her through the door into a back office. The walls were covered in a coat of faded whitewash, and the bare floorboards were speckled with splashes of white paint. Although not large, the room felt smaller than its actual dimensions because it had no windows. There were a couple of plastic chairs and a table with papers and folders spread around in a disorderly jumble. Rod sat on one of the chairs and invited Geraldine to take the other.

'Now,' he said, 'what's this about?'

'What can you tell me about Jonathan Edwards?'

Rod hesitated. 'Jonathan Edwards?' he repeated. 'You mean – Jonathan? Jonathan Edwards?'

Geraldine didn't answer but watched him, waiting for him to speak again. As she had intended, he looked increasingly uncomfortable under her silent scrutiny.

'Yes,' he admitted at last, 'I know a guy called Jonathan Edwards. He's some sort of librarian, or he was. He lost his job in the cutbacks. We both did,' he added, becoming more animated. 'I used to do maintenance work in a school, odd job man, you know. But they laid me off, said the caretaker could do everything I did, fixing lights, patching things up, you know, changing fuses. There's always something to do, mopping up and tightening screws, replacing display boards. It was never-ending. There's no way the caretaker could do all that by himself. But they said the money had run out and they didn't have the funds to pay me any more, so they laid me off.' He scowled. 'So that's how I ended up here. It's not a bad job, actually, better paid than I used to be and I get to take home snacks and things when they're out of date. Not very out of date,' he added quickly. 'They're absolutely safe to eat, but we just can't sell them any more. It's not like most of the stuff here goes off anyway.'

'So you don't feel aggrieved about what happened? At the school?'

'No, not any more. I mean, sure I was pissed about it at first, who wouldn't be? But it's worked out OK. I mean, it was only a job. It's OK here. It gets boring, but in some ways I prefer it. Less pressure. They were constantly on at me to do something.'

'How did you meet Jonathan?'

Rod nodded. 'Jonathan, right. He was livid about losing his job. That's how we met, at a so-called job seekers' meeting. Jonathan's trouble is that he hasn't moved on. He's still banging on about how he was badly treated, unfairly chucked on the scrap heap. I know he's older than me, but he could have made more of an effort. I mean, look at me. I was laid off but I didn't give up. I found another job, and that's what he should have done.'

'You attended public meetings together where David Armstrong was speaking?'

'Oh yes, well, that was Jonathan's doing. He rounded us up, me and a couple of retired teachers who came along because they had nothing better to do, and it seemed like fun. I mean, it was all a bit of a laugh to begin with, but Jonathan started getting carried away, and that put me right off. Then I got the job here and so I'm not often available these days anyway.' He nodded towards the shop beyond the door.

Geraldine gave no sign that she was particularly interested when she put her next question.

'What exactly do you mean when you say Jonathan got carried away?'

'He's a nutter,' Rod replied. 'I had no idea how crazy he was when we first met. At first it seemed like – well, it's fair enough to challenge the council. We do still have freedom of speech and all that. Anyway, we all agreed that the council should be able to justify their policies, so we went around asking awkward questions at meetings. Then Jonathan started heckling the guy.'

'The guy?'

'Yes, David Armstrong. He's the leader of the council, and Jonathan seemed to blame Armstrong for everything that had gone wrong in his life. Anyway, Jonathan seemed to know whenever Armstrong was going to speak in public, and to begin with we went along to ask questions, challenging the councillor to defend his actions, that sort of thing, but then Jonathan began shouting out, trying to stop Armstrong from speaking at all, and the latest was –' he broke off, grinning sheepishly. 'Well, I'd rather not say any more.'

'You're talking about the egg throwing incident?'

'Yes. I wasn't sure if you knew about that. It wasn't me,' he added quickly. 'I mean, I was there, but I never threw any eggs at the car. It was a stupid thing to do anyway.'

'So what other plans did your friend Jonathan have lined up for David Armstrong? I'd advise you against withholding information from the police.'

Rod's grin faded at the severity of Geraldine's tone, and he gave her a sly glance that made her wonder whether he was being completely truthful.

'I haven't withheld information…' he stammered.

'What other plans did Jonathan have lined up for David Armstrong?' Geraldine repeated. 'How far was he prepared to go?'

Rod shook his head. His pale face peered anxiously at her from within its frame of ginger hair.

'I don't know,' he muttered. 'He never said anything about any plans. He just called me and told me where the next meeting was, and pestered me to join him. He was always on at me to join him in his campaign. But, to be honest, it got to the point where it all seemed a bit personal to me. I mean, I'm all for political protest – peaceful political protest is the sign of a healthy democracy. But Jonathan seemed to have it in for David Armstrong and, to be honest, I got a bit fed up with it. We weren't getting anywhere. How could we? I wanted to go bigger, you know, canvas our local MP. It's government policies that are doing the real damage. Compared to what's going on in parliament, our local council is irrelevant, but that's something Jonathan couldn't seem to get his head around.'

'Did you argue with him?'

'Not argue, exactly. We disagreed. But since I got the job here I don't really have that much time for Jonathan and his protests.'

'You were there in the car park when he threw eggs at David Armstrong's car on Tuesday,' Geraldine pointed out. 'That's only three days ago.'

Rod nodded, suddenly serious. 'Yes, and that's when I decided Jonathan had gone too far. I mean, a stunt like that could cause an accident. It was unacceptable.'

He sounded so earnest, Geraldine suspected he was putting on a show for her benefit. Neither of them mentioned David Armstrong was dead. It was even possible that Rod didn't know about it.

'Do you intend to see Jonathan again?'

Rod shrugged. 'I don't know. Like I said, I'm kind of busy these days, and between you and me, Jonathan can be a bit of a dick.'

# 27

'SO YOU THINK ROD Browning was over-egging it?' Eileen asked with a smile when Geraldine reported back to the team the following morning.

Geraldine chuckled. 'Something like that, yes. But as for whether he was telling the truth about the extent of his own involvement in the attacks, it's impossible to be sure.'

'It's not like you to be unable to see through subterfuge,' Eileen commented.

Geraldine shrugged at the compliment. 'Maybe it had something to do with his shaggy beard,' she said, adding that she hadn't been able to see his face properly.

'I think it may be time to have another word with Jonathan Edwards,' Eileen suggested. 'And what about the two retired teachers who protested with him? They might have something useful to add. They were there with Jonathan and Rod, weren't they?' She turned to Ariadne. 'Now, what about forensics? Have we come up with anything useful?'

They discussed the toxicology report in more detail. There was now no doubt about how David Armstrong had been killed. The composition of the drugs he had ingested had been established, and the likely brand of pill identified.

'It had to be someone he knew,' Geraldine insisted. 'Only someone he trusted could have persuaded him to swallow such a bitter concoction in sufficient quantity to kill him.'

'It wouldn't have taken much,' someone else said. 'It only needed to be enough to knock him out, or make him woozy, so his killer could suffocate him.'

'The killer might not have given him the pills,' Ariadne pointed out. 'He might have been discovered, semi comatose, quite by chance.'

'And a passing killer seized the opportunity to finish him off,' Geraldine added sceptically.

'Possibly, if the killer was following him,' Ariadne said, defending her speculation. 'It's plausible.'

Eileen nodded. 'The tox report suggests he ingested the pills and the alcohol shortly before he was killed, although they say it's impossible to narrow it down too specifically. But we do know he was fit enough to address a public meeting just a few hours before he was killed. All the evidence suggests he took the pills shortly before his death.'

'How quickly would they have taken effect?' Ariadne asked.

'Apparently the effects can be felt in as short a time as one hour,' Geraldine replied. 'So he could have taken the dose after the public meeting, all of which points to his wife.'

'She may have had the opportunity,' Eileen agreed, 'but what was the motive? We need to look into this further. And we need to examine the exact terms of his will. So come on, let's get going. Lots to do. Geraldine, you track down Jonathan Edwards' other associates, and Ariadne, can you find out whether David's widow is in any fit state to talk to us yet?'

Geraldine would have liked to interview Anne herself, as she seemed to be the most likely suspect, in view of the way David had been killed. But she had her instructions and she was soon on her way to see Alyson Read, a retired teacher who had accompanied Jonathan and Rod on most of their protests. Alyson was reportedly working in a charity shop not far from the police station, along Gillygate. Geraldine went in there on the way to Alyson's home and found her behind the counter. Alyson Read was a plump, comfortable looking woman of about sixty, with soft greying hair, kindly blue eyes, and a gentle voice. When Geraldine explained the purpose for her call, Alyson summoned her co-worker from the store room to watch the till, before leading Geraldine into the store room. Surrounded by piles of clothes and books, kitchen accessories and toys, Geraldine questioned her about Jonathan and Rod's protests against the local council, and specifically their targeting of David Armstrong.

'Oh, yes, the councillor,' Alyson replied. She frowned. 'I read somewhere that he died? Is that right?'

Geraldine nodded.

'What was it? Because it wouldn't surprise me to hear he had a heart attack or a stroke, or something like that. He always seemed so agitated and overexcited whenever I saw him. Of course Jonathan used to deliberately wind him up. The councillor was a horrible man, from what I could see, but even so, I'm sorry he's dead. I mean, sorry for his family. I didn't know him.'

'You went to the meetings where Jonathan heckled him.'

'Oh yes, that's right. But I never spoke to him. And I didn't shout out myself. I was just there.'

When Geraldine asked Alyson why she went to the meetings, her response was vague.

'My friend, Charlotte Stephens got me into it,' she replied. 'We both retired at around the same time and – well, Charlotte's quite political. I can't say that I'm all that bothered as a rule. Live and let live. But I don't approve of the way the council's been cutting services left, right and centre. Anyway, Charlotte dragged me along to the meetings with her, and to begin with it was fun.'

'To begin with? What happened after that?'

'Nothing, really. It became a bit boring, the same shouting every time, and always at David Armstrong, as though it was all his fault that people were losing their jobs.' She lowered her voice. 'Between you and me, I think Jonathan had it in for that man.'

'What about Rod Browning? Where was he in all this?'

'Oh, he just tagged along, a bit like me, really. He said that this shouting was all well and good, but we ought to be doing something more. Take action, was what he said.'

'What kind of action?'

Alyson shook her head. 'I don't know and if you ask me, that young man didn't either. It was all talk talk talk from the two of them. Like I said, it became boring after a while, but Charlotte enjoyed all the drama and we go – that is, we used to go for a coffee afterwards, just the two of us, and discuss it all.' She sighed. 'It sounds silly, but I lead a dull sort of life these days, and it was a bit of fun, you know. It made me feel young again, as if I was doing something useful.'

Geraldine thanked Alyson for her help and turned to leave.

'Oh, please, do ask me anything you like,' Alyson said, clearly eager to detain her.

'Thank you, but you've already been extremely helpful,' Geraldine assured her.

At least Alyson Read could be crossed off the list of suspects.

She found Charlotte Stephens at home. She was younger than Alyson, with chestnut hair and sharp brown eyes, and she too claimed not to have known David Armstrong. She said she had attended the public meetings more for the excursion than as a serious protest.

'I think it's shocking the way the council is forcing all these cutbacks,' she told Geraldine. 'It's so important to be well informed, and of course once you discover what's going on, I mean really going on, you have to express your opinion about it, don't you? You can't just sit around and keep silent when you disagree with what the politicians are doing. But Rod is right, it's the government we should be targeting, not the local councillors. I tried telling Jonathan, but he insisted we start at the local level. "Why don't we campaign against our local MP then?" I asked him, but he was set on targeting the leader of the council. I mean, he had a point, but I still think canvassing our MP would have made better sense. And it didn't have to be one or the other, did it? We could have gone for both. And now that poor man's dead.' She sighed. 'I wonder who Jonathan will be gunning for next.'

Geraldine thought that an unfortunate turn of phrase under the circumstances, but it seemed to confirm that Charlotte didn't know David Armstrong had been murdered.

# 28

A YEAR BEFORE DAISY was born, one of Jessica's neighbours had reported a disturbance at her house. After reading the report through carefully, several times, Geraldine set off to question the neighbour who had since moved to Leeds. The door was opened by a robust middle-aged woman.

'Are you looking for my daughter?' she asked, 'only she doesn't live with us any more. She's married now,' she added with a complacent smile. 'A lovely man –'

Geraldine interrupted her. 'I'm looking for Mrs Alice Whittaker.'

'That's me,' the woman replied, clearly surprised.

'I'd like to ask you a few questions about a former neighbour of yours. If you can spare a few minutes, I'd really appreciate your time, Mrs Whittaker.'

'Are you the police?'

'Yes.' Geraldine held up her identity card, and the woman squinted at it.

'I'm afraid I'm blind as a bat without my reading glasses, but, oh well, if you are who you say you are, you'd better come in. And please, call me Alice.'

Geraldine explained the reason for her visit and Alice nodded. 'Yes, yes, of course I remember,' she said. 'They were at it all the time. One evening I phoned your lot, because they were making a hell of a din. Honestly, I really thought he was going to kill her that time.'

'That time?' Geraldine repeated, keeping her expression

impassive. 'How many times did you hear them fighting?'

'He was always shouting at her,' the woman replied, 'and we used to hear her screaming the place down. They were terrible neighbours. Really terrible. You have no idea. They were one of the reasons we moved.'

'Did they know you reported them?'

'I don't know if they knew it was us. We debated whether or not to do anything about it, but in the end we decided enough was enough. We wanted someone to warn them to keep the noise down. It was a disgrace, the way they carried on. Talk about bad neighbours.'

'Do you know what they used to argue about?'

Alice shook her head. 'All we could hear was her screeching at him not to touch her, and him yelling at her not to do it again, but we never did find out what it was she was supposed to have done.'

Geraldine was not surprised to hear that the marriage had apparently been unhappy. The information seemed to confirm the suspicion that Jason had most likely run off with the baby, without a care for his wife's suffering. Having learned all she could from Alice, Geraldine returned to York and drove straight to Jessica's house.

'Sergeant,' Jessica greeted her, forcing a smile. Her face was flushed and her expression tense. 'I hope you have good news for me. I'm going out of my mind with worry about Daisy.' Her mask of composure slipped and she started forward in desperation. 'Please –' she cried out, and her voice broke. Taking a deep shuddering breath, she continued, 'Please find my baby.'

'I'd like to speak to you,' Geraldine said gently. 'Not about Daisy.'

'What do you mean?' Jessica scowled and looked as if she was going to shut the door, but Geraldine stepped forward smartly to prevent it closing, and followed her into the living room where Jessica slumped down on the floor, weeping, with her head in her hands. Magazines were scattered over the carpet, and on the table a plate of chips had grown cold. A scummy film had developed on a half-drunk cup of coffee which had spilt, leaving a damp brown pool that would probably stain the table.

'Jessica,' Geraldine said gently, sitting down opposite the weeping woman. 'Jessica, I've been talking to Alice Whittaker.'

'Who's Alice Whittaker?' Jessica asked.

'She used to live next door.'

'I'm not interested in hearing anything she has to say.'

'I'm afraid I'm going to have to ask you a few questions before I leave. Can you tell me what happened to cause Alice to call the police?'

Jessica let her hands fall from a face red and blotchy with crying.

'One time he nearly killed me,' she croaked. She glared at Geraldine with a strange intensity, her eyes swollen and bloodshot. 'He was going to kill me,' she repeated in a hoarse voice. 'If the police hadn't come when they did, he would have killed me. That's what he does, he kills people.'

Her breathing was fast, and it was clear she was becoming hysterical. She clambered unsteadily to her feet and swayed slightly before she sank down into the chair again.

'Tell me, where did he hurt you?'

Jessica shook her head and groaned. 'Here,' she said, pointing at her heart. 'And here,' she added, indicating her head. 'He screwed me up royally. You may not believe it, but I was happy before I met him. My life was normal. Normal! And now look at me.'

She dropped her head in her hands again. Geraldine waited.

'I'm sorry,' Jessica went on after a few seconds, speaking in a stronger voice, and seeming to pull herself together.

'They shouldn't have bothered the police. It was just a silly row. We were under a lot of pressure, worrying about – about everything. Bills, you know. Have you found her yet? Why haven't you found her? Why are you wasting time here with me, talking about Jason?'

She was becoming hysterical again, her voice rising to a shrill peak.

'We have a large dedicated search team looking for her,' Geraldine assured her. 'We're questioning everyone who might possibly have known you or your husband, and anyone who might have seen what happened. Where is your husband now?'

Jessica shook her head. 'He hasn't come back. I don't know where he is. And if he never comes back, that's fine by me,' she added, her voice hardening. 'I never want to see him again.' She glared at Geraldine. 'I'm going to change the locks on the doors. I should have done that a long time ago.'

'Jessica, does Jason know where Daisy is?'

Jessica shook her head. 'He said he only put up with me because of her. He wasn't interested in me. He's never cared about me. Now she's gone, he'll never come back, will he?' She burst out crying again. 'I want my baby, I want my baby.'

'Don't worry,' Geraldine assured her. 'We will find her.'

She hoped her words would prove true, but of course there was no way of knowing if the baby would ever be found and, if she was, whether she would still be alive. It was looking increasingly unlikely.

'Would you like to press charges?' she enquired gently.

Jessica looked puzzled. 'Press charges?'

'Against your husband. We have reason to suspect he violently assaulted you on more than one occasion. Jessica, I know you're under a lot of pressure, but whatever happens, you don't have to tolerate his aggression ever again. You shouldn't have to put up with that level of abuse. No one should. If you want him charged with assault, we can support you when he comes back, and make sure he never hurts you again.'

Jessica shook her head. 'No, no, I don't want to see him or think about him again. I just want my baby back.'

'Jessica, your husband attacked you –'

'No, no, he didn't. It was an accident. He never hurt me. That's a lie. It's a lie!'

Geraldine sighed. There was no reasoning with a woman who constantly altered her version of the truth, whatever that was.

'Very well.' Geraldine stood up. 'But please think about what I said. Once your daughter returns to you, do you really want her living with a violent man?'

'He'd never hurt Daisy,' Jessica whispered, seemingly horrified by a suggestion that must have already occurred to her.

'Jessica, you said you thought he was going to kill you. It happened more than once, didn't it? You just told me he would have killed you if your neighbour hadn't summoned the police to stop him.'

Jessica shook her head. 'No,' she whispered. 'I didn't mean it. It's not true. She's lying. I'm just angry with him, that's all. How could he go and leave me like this? He's my husband, and I don't even know where he is.'

'You said "he kills people". What did you mean?'

'Nothing, nothing, I didn't mean anything. I was just upset. It was all a stupid mistake. Please go, go away and leave me alone.'

'Jessica, we need to know where Jason is.'

'I don't know, I don't know. And if I did, I wouldn't tell you,' she added in a sudden burst of anger.

Ignoring Jessica's loud protests, Geraldine checked the house but there was no sign of Jason in any of the rooms.

There was nothing more she could do. Back at the police station, she discussed Jessica's erratic responses with Eileen.

'A typical domestic,' the detective chief inspector said with a sigh. 'The wife too scared, or too besotted, to press charges. If he contacts her, she'll probably warn him we'll be filing a report with all the details. There's already a history of his violence against his wife. Men like that think they can do what the hell they like behind closed doors. Of course, he'll deny having raised his hand against her. They always do.'

'Yes, and she'll probably continue to back him up, even though she'd be insane to protect him.'

'Yes, well, we're going to have to catch up with him soon and find out exactly what Jason Colman is playing at,' Eileen said. 'A violent man gone missing at the same time as his daughter disappears, leaving traces of blood on her sheet.' She sighed. 'It all seems to be pointing in one direction.'

'From what Jessica said, she has no idea where he is,' Geraldine replied, 'but we can't take her word for it.'

A team were still examining any CCTV cameras that might have filmed Jason after he left the house, but he seemed to have simply vanished. Officers were sent to question the other neighbours in the street. One way or another, they had to find Jason and question him about his missing daughter.

# 29

PEERING OUT THROUGH A gap between the curtains at her bedroom window, Jessica watched the police drive away, cursing her husband under her breath. This was all his fault. Admittedly, she had been a fool to put up with his behaviour. Ever since they were married, her life had descended into the realms of nightmare. Not only had he systematically abused her physically, mentally and emotionally, making her life a living hell, but he had threatened to take her baby away. Yet despite everything, she had been too frightened to report him to the police. She deplored her own cowardice, but she had always known that, if she betrayed him, he would kill her. What he might do to the baby was too horrifying to think about.

She used to pray he would attack someone else, beat another woman up, beat her to a pulp, beat her so badly that he would face a prison sentence when his victim reported him to the police. The more severe her injuries, the longer his sentence would be, because a stranger would have no reason to hold back in her allegations. But as far as Jessica knew, he had never lifted a finger against anyone else, only her. She wished she had never fallen in love with the man Jason had pretended to be and, most of all, she regretted having a baby with him.

She slumped down on the floor after the police had gone, listening to the faint hum of cars driving by. Eventually she clambered to her feet and went to study her reflection in the bathroom mirror. She looked terrible. Concealer and foundation would mask the blotches on her face, but even thick make-up wouldn't disguise her swollen eyes. If she could only stop crying, the puffiness around her eyes would recede, but they would still be bloodshot. Returning to the living room, she began clearing up the mess. It was slow going because she kept returning to the mirror in the hall to examine her face. After a while she gave up. Too tired to carry on, she let go of the handful of magazines she was clutching, letting them fall to the floor.

Having abandoned her attempt to tidy the house, she put the kettle on and made herself a mug of tea. She was relieved that the police had gone, but the house felt weirdly empty since their departure. She sat in the living room whispering to herself, 'I'm all alone.' Tears streamed down her cheeks. 'All alone, all alone, all alone.' The words seemed to repeat themselves in her head like a demented mantra. Although she had nowhere to go, suddenly she couldn't bear to remain in the house for another moment, and she hurried outside, slamming the front door as she left. After driving around aimlessly for a while, almost without thinking she approached Ella's lodgings. Visiting her friend and holding her baby was the only thing that gave Jessica any respite from her misery, however brief. Pulling into the kerb, she sat for a moment breathing deeply and trying to calm herself.

Ella took a very long time to open the door, and when she saw Jessica waiting on the doorstep, she appeared to hesitate.

'It's you,' she greeted Jessica fatuously. 'I wasn't expecting you today, but it's lovely to see you.'

Ella did not look very pleased. In fact, beneath her forced smile, Jessica sensed that Ella was nervous, although there was no need for her to worry. If either of them had cause to feel nervous, it was Jessica. She only wanted a chance to see her baby and hold her in her arms, just for a few minutes, to ease her aching loneliness.

'Well, you're here now so you might as well come in,' Ella muttered, glancing past Jessica's shoulder as though she was afraid someone else was with her, wanting to accompany her inside.

'Thank you. Thank you very much. I don't want to disturb you, but I just happened to be passing.'

Jessica watched Ella bolt the door behind them and tensed, hearing the faint sound of a baby whimpering.

'She's hungry again,' Ella said. 'She's always hungry.'

'That's good, isn't it?' Jessica asked with a stab of anxiety. 'It's healthy for babies to have a good appetite, isn't it?'

'Sure,' Ella replied, adding with an exaggerated sigh, 'it's costing me a fortune to feed her.'

Jessica didn't answer, but her hand went automatically to her bag. Ella followed the movement with greedy eyes.

'Come on, then,' Ella said with fake heartiness. 'You know I'm always pleased to see you, but I know you didn't come all this way just to visit me.'

As she shut her eyes and held the warm little body close, Jessica could pretend she was back at home with Daisy, but it was never long before these visits reduced her to tears, because she knew she would shortly have to drive home alone with no baby of her own snuffling or chattering in the back of the car.

'She's hungry all the time,' Ella said, gazing at Jessica anxiously. 'I've been buying shed loads of SMA, really a lot, and nappies seem to disappear so fast. And then there's the wipes, and I need more sheets for her cot, and another teething ring, and she should have toys to stimulate her development.' She paused. 'It's all so bloody expensive. I'm going to have to compromise on something, but I don't know what she can do without while she's so little.'

Her attempt at prompting Jessica to hand over yet more cash was clumsy, to say the least. Nevertheless, reluctant to upset her friend, Jessica pulled out her purse and counted out five twenty-pound notes.

'That should help, a little, at least for a few days,' Ella said, pocketing the cash. 'I try not to change her nappy too often, so as to economise, but she has to be fed. Now, I'd better put her back in her cot before she falls asleep on you.'

'I don't mind,' Jessica replied, with a quick smile.

But Ella was already lifting the small bundle out of her arms.

'Can't I hold her for a bit longer?' Jessica pleaded.

'I need more money,' Ella blurted out.

Frowning, Jessica took another two twenty-pound notes from her purse.

'That's all I've got,' she said, a trifle sharply.

'Thank you. Really, you have no idea what a difference it makes. Babies cost such a lot.' She broke off as Jessica began to sob.

Pulling herself together with an effort, Jessica stood up. 'I'd better be going, then. I'll come back soon.'

'Yes, come back, any time,' Ella said, 'but call first or I might be out. And don't forget to bring more cash next time, will you? You know I hate to ask, but the baby needs toys to play with. I can't be on hand to entertain her all the time, although God knows I do my best. And it won't be long before she starts crawling and then she'll need a playpen.'

Jessica sighed. 'I'll bring you a few things from home,' she said. 'Just on loan, until Daisy's back with me.'

'No, no,' Ella replied, sounding annoyed. 'No, please don't bring me anything from your house. That would make it seem as though you don't believe Daisy's ever coming back home. That's a terrible idea. You have to stay positive, Jessica. Just bring me more money, and I can get whatever I need.'

'All right, but I can't keep handing over great wads of cash. There's a limit to what I can afford.'

'Of course, that's understood, and there's no way I'd want to carry on like this for much longer. It's just that, while you're not having to cough up for Daisy, you have the money going spare, so it's not as if you can't afford to help me out like this, temporarily of course. I thought it might comfort you, coming to see the baby, but if you'd rather not come here anymore –'

'No, no, please, don't misunderstand me,' Jessica said quickly. 'You're right, you're right, I can afford it at the moment, of course I can. I'll bring you two hundred next time, all right?'

Ella's eyes narrowed. 'Two fifty would be better,' she said softly. 'Three, if you can manage it?'

# 30

EVERY YEAR SINCE THE death of their mother, Geraldine had visited her sister for tea on Celia's birthday. It was an obligation she fulfilled willingly. Although Celia put no pressure on her to continue the custom, Geraldine knew that her sister would be disappointed if she broke the tradition. The death of their mother several years ago had hit Celia far harder than Geraldine. Only after their mother's death had Geraldine learned the reason why Celia closely resembled their fair-haired mother, while Geraldine, with her black hair and very dark eyes, looked like the child of another mother. As it turned out, she was exactly that.

The shock of discovering she had been adopted by Celia's biological mother had been hard to deal with at first, but the passing years had softened her distress and Geraldine had come to terms, not only with her adoption, but with her adopted mother's failure to share the truth with her. She understood that the situation must have been tricky for her adopted mother who was dead now, and beyond question or challenge. Geraldine had forgiven her. It seemed the most sensible way to deal with her disappointment. The only alternative was to harbour a resentment which would help no one, least of all Geraldine herself.

Although she was involved in a murder investigation, the initial reports were in, a team were now questioning the Armstrongs' neighbours, the dead man's former work colleagues, and the other members of the council, and all the reports were being completed and cross referenced. That was a job for a huge team of constables who were working hard to get the records up to date.

Celia was used to Geraldine calling at the last minute to cancel arrangements and no longer even remonstrated when that happened, but there was nothing urgent for Geraldine to do that day and the traffic promised to be relatively light as it was Sunday, so she decided to stick to the arrangement she had made earlier in the month.

Initially, she felt as though a weight was slowly lifting from her shoulders as she drove away from York. Usually, the physical distance helped her to think clearly. The key to Daisy's disappearance lay with her father, although whether her biological father had known, or discovered the truth and returned to claim her or Jason had abducted her was unclear. Given Jason's disappearance, the likelihood was that Daisy was with him. But it explained nothing, because a man could no more vanish without trace than a baby could. It made no sense. If Jason was responsible, he must have been planning to disappear with Daisy for a long time. But without his passport, and with no trace of him anywhere in the country, his whereabouts remained a mystery.

For once, the long drive didn't help Geraldine to gain any helpful mental distance from the case she was working on, and she arrived at her sister's house feeling frustrated. Celia's household seemed like a shining beacon of domestic happiness compared to the experience of many people Geraldine met in the course of her work.

Celia's face lit up with pleasure when she saw Geraldine on the doorstep. 'You came.'

'I said I would,' Geraldine replied, returning Celia's smile.

'I know, but I was afraid something would turn up at the last minute to keep you in York. It so often does. I mean, I know you can't help it, but… anyway, you're here now so come on in. I'm so pleased you could make it, and Chloe's going to be really excited to see you.'

She flung her arms around Geraldine and gave her a hug. For an instant the warmth of human contact almost reduced Geraldine to tears. She had thought coming to see her family would take her mind off Ian, but Celia's embrace reminded her how much she missed him.

'How lucky you're not tied up on a case this weekend,' Celia went on.

'Actually,' Geraldine admitted, 'there is an investigation at the moment, but it's ongoing and it was no problem to get away for a day.'

She didn't add that she had been desperate to escape from York, and her work, and most of all from Ian. She hadn't seen Celia for a few months and had been waiting to tell her face to face about her relationship with Ian. Only now it was all over with Ian before she had even blurted out the news. Although she longed to unburden herself to her sister, she was glad she had not yet mentioned her brief romance to her. Celia's questions, and her sympathy, would probably have made Geraldine cry, and the last thing she wanted was to ruin her sister's birthday by sharing her misery.

'Geraldine, are you all right?'

'Sure. I'm fine, maybe just a bit tired, that's all.'

Before Celia could press her the baby began to bleat, and at the same time Geraldine's niece came out into the hall and let out a gleeful shriek on seeing her. Chloe was a teenager, and volatile in her moods. Sometimes she was sullen towards Geraldine, usually when her parents had refused to allow her to go out because her aunt was expected. But as long as she wasn't missing seeing her friends, she was always pleased to see Geraldine.

'It's not as if you don't get together with Abigail and Molly every day at school,' Celia had protested, half angry, half laughing, the last time Chloe had remonstrated in front of Geraldine.

'That's not the same,' Chloe had retorted furiously. 'That's *school*.'

But on Celia's birthday there was no clash of arrangements, and Chloe ran up to Geraldine and hugged her. Geraldine returned her niece's embrace with a smile.

'I've brought you a present,' she said.

'You shouldn't,' Celia scolded her.

'Shouldn't what?'

'You shouldn't spoil her.'

'No,' Chloe agreed earnestly, 'you shouldn't have brought anything for me. It's mum's birthday, not mine.'

'Oh, don't worry, I haven't forgotten her. I've brought a present for her as well,' Geraldine smiled.

Celia went off to change the baby's nappy, and Chloe and Geraldine followed her into the kitchen. For the next couple of hours Geraldine was preoccupied with holding the baby, and hearing about her niece's latest exploits and ambitions for the future. Chloe told Geraldine how she was aiming to be a professional footballer, while Celia listened, with an indulgent smile.

'That's this week's fad,' Celia whispered to Geraldine when Chloe left the room to try on the jeans Geraldine had bought her.

'It's a healthy sort of ambition,' Geraldine muttered, calling out loudly enough for Chloe to hear, 'I can change them if they don't fit.'

Chloe returned soon after, wearing the jeans. 'They're perfect!' she enthused. 'How did you know my size?'

Geraldine smiled.

'We do talk to each other, you know,' Celia said, grinning.

Just as they sat down to tea the baby began to whimper and Celia brought him to the table where he sat in his high chair, gurgling and curling and uncurling his tiny fingers. Watching Celia with her husband and children settled around her, Geraldine was struck by their contentment, which formed a stark contrast to Jessica's wretched family life. She hadn't thought about the case for a couple of hours and felt better for the break, and resolved to return to her work with renewed vigour the next morning.

'You *are* looking tired,' Celia said later, when she and Geraldine were finally alone together.

Chloe had gone to her room, allegedly to do some homework for school, and Celia's husband was putting the baby to bed.

'There's nothing to worry about,' Geraldine preempted her fussing. 'Work's been busy, and I haven't had much time to sleep in the last few weeks.'

'You could always call me in the night, as I'll probably be up with the baby,' Celia smiled. 'But the case isn't over?'

Geraldine sighed and shook her head. 'Not yet. I'm afraid this one's going to take a while.'

Celia gave her a shrewd look, her blue eyes troubled. 'Are you sure it's just work that's bothering you?'

Geraldine avoided meeting her sister's gaze. 'What else would it be?'

'True, I suppose,' Celia conceded. 'You know, it's high time you found yourself a decent man. There's more to life than work.'

Geraldine stifled a sigh. 'Not for me,' she muttered. 'Not any more,' she thought.

# 31

His dahlias had done well that year, but their colourful display at the back of the garden would soon be over. Lemon yellow, fuchsia and crimson, they flourished in front of the fence. In each of the far corners of the garden he had planted a tree, a fig and a small conifer, between which the dahlias were a riot of colour. They were, as his daughter said, his pride and joy.

'You can laugh at me all you like,' he had replied, 'but you have to admit they make a glorious show in the summer, and that doesn't happen by chance. It takes a lot of care and attention to produce a display like that.'

'I'm sure it doesn't happen by chance, and you're right, dad, they are lovely.'

More than a hobby to him after his wife died, maintaining his small patch of lawn and surrounding flower beds had become Roger's passion in life. So when he stepped outside on Monday morning to carry out his daily inspection of the garden and saw someone lying down among the dahlias, he was horrified. Where he would have been cautious as a rule, he now became reckless with fury. Had the intruder been sprawling anywhere other than right on top of the dahlias, Roger might have been more circumspect, but he had been nurturing those flowers for months. And now, after all those months of careful tending, the dahlias had been vandalised. Having called the police to report an intruder on the premises, Roger could control his temper no longer. Seizing his garden fork he waved it at the back of the intruder's head.

'Get up!' he roared. 'Get up, you filthy swine! Off my flower bed! Get up!'

He wasn't sure what he was going to do if the other man woke up before the police arrived, but he was momentarily too angry to worry about that. He shouted again, but the man on the ground did not stir.

'I said, get up!' Roger yelled.

Feeling a rush of blood to his head, he raised his fork, determined to confront the hooligan who had trampled on his dahlias. Lowering the fork slowly, he tensed to leap backwards if the man sat up suddenly and grabbed the prongs, but the man did not move. Roger poked him, tentatively, on his back, but still the man did not stir. Trembling, Roger raised the fork again, clutching the handle tightly in case the man leapt to his feet and tried to attack him. If necessary, Roger was prepared to bring his weapon down with all the force he could muster, heedless of the consequences. He was not a young man, but he wasn't old, and all the gardening he did kept him fit. Besides, his antagonist was trespassing. Roger had every right to defend himself from an intruder. He prodded the man's back again, but still the intruder did not react. Only then did it occur to Roger that something was seriously wrong.

The man was lying face down on the flower bed, and could be suffocating as Roger stood there shouting at him. Concern overcame his curiosity and he crouched down and hesitated, noticing a putrid smell, like a foul drain. Reaching out with one hand, he took hold of the man's arm. It felt soft and flabby under the sleeve of his jacket. With a grunt, Roger heaved the man on to his side, and drew back as the fetid stench intensified. The man's face was bloated, the skin greenish and blistered. His swollen tongue stuck out and his eyes stared at Roger, glassy and clouded. Stumbling backwards, Roger nearly tripped over the handle of the fork which had fallen from his grasp.

Afterwards Roger could not have said how long he stood staring down in shock, before he heard a siren. A moment later someone pounded on his front door. As though recalled from a nightmare, he turned and stumbled across the grass, yelling in a panic.

'I'm here! I'm here! Don't go away. For God's sake, don't leave! I'm coming!'

Two uniformed police officers stood on the doorstep. It crossed Roger's mind that they looked no older than his teenage grandchildren. He wished the police had sent someone more experienced to deal with the situation.

'Good morning, sir. We received a report of an intruder on the premises here,' one of the officers said pleasantly. 'Is everything all right, sir?'

'Yes, yes, that is no, no.' Roger stopped, aware that he was babbling. Taking a deep breath, he tried again. 'The fact is, there's a dead body at the bottom of my garden,' he blurted out.

The two police officers exchanged a rapid glance.

'Very good, sir,' one of them said, with exaggerated patience.

'Oh please, don't take my word for it,' Roger replied, miffed at their evident scepticism. 'Come and see for yourselves.'

As he led the two police officers round the back of the house and across the lawn to the back of the garden, Roger had a wild hope that he had imagined the body with its horribly decomposed face. Perhaps the man's skin had been discoloured with grass and leaves and mud, and he had recovered consciousness and done a runner, escaping over the fence, while Roger had been at the front door speaking to the police. But as they approached the flower bed he saw the body was still there, lying on its side, just where Roger had left it. He screwed up his eyes to avoid looking directly at the hideous sight of a dead body rotting into his carefully treated soil.

'Oh, heavens above,' one of the police officers said, backing away. 'What a sight!'

The officer who had spoken turned pale, and Roger was afraid he was going to throw up on the carefully manicured lawn. Meanwhile the other police officer was on his phone, talking snappily about what had happened. Roger paid little attention to what he was saying.

Having finished on the phone, the policeman turned to Roger. 'Now sir,' he said. 'Let's go inside and you can tell us exactly what happened here.'

Roger shook his head helplessly. 'Nothing happened. That is, what I mean is, I just found him lying here, dead. I don't know who he is – or was – or what he was doing here. How did the body even get here?'

The police officer looked around, taking in the fig tree and the spindly conifer.

'He must have climbed over the fence and then...' He looked back down at the body and frowned. 'And then... Mr Dexter, when was the last time you were in the garden?'

Roger frowned too. 'I came out about, I don't know, about half an hour ago, I guess. Maybe longer. I phoned you as soon as I saw the body, as soon as I realised he was dead. I saw it – him – almost straight away.'

'And before that? How long is it since you were out here before today?'

'I'm out here most days.'

'Were you out here yesterday?'

'Yes,' Roger replied. 'Like I said, I'm out here almost every day. Weather permitting, that is. Although if it's just drizzling I come out. There's always something to do,' he said, almost shamefaced about his dedication to his plants. Catching the drift of the constable's questioning, he added, 'The dead body wasn't here yesterday. It only turned up today.'

'Are you sure of that?'

'I'm positive. He – it's lying on my dahlias. There's absolutely no way I could have missed it. I'd have spotted it – him – straight away.'

Just then they heard knocking at the door, and the constable's phone buzzed.

'A team has arrived here to assess the site,' he said. 'We'll take it from here, sir. If you'd like to step away.'

All at once, Roger began to shiver. Nodding, he followed the constable across the grass to the house.

# 32

THE INITIAL RUSH OF excitement in the room faded when Eileen explained that the garden where a body had been found backed on to allotments, and scene of crime officers had found sufficient evidence to establish beyond any doubt that the body had been manoeuvred over the fence. It was highly unlikely the owner of the property had lifted a body over the fence into his own garden and then called the police himself to report it. So although a body had been discovered in a private garden, it seemed they still had not found the killer. The man who had discovered the body was still visibly shaken when Geraldine went to question him. He had already given a statement to the police at the scene, but he had been so shocked by his discovery that Eileen had asked Geraldine to visit him at his daughter's house shortly afterwards. After an hour or so, they hoped he would have calmed down enough to give a coherent account of what he had seen. It was important to speak to him as soon as possible after the event, before his memories became blurred, but the constable who had first spoken to him had not managed to get much sense out of him. In his seventies, and balding, Roger Dexter was a large man with a bushy moustache who bore himself with an air of injured authority, as though he was accustomed to being in charge of his circumstances and felt aggrieved to be involved in a situation over which he had no control. He was seated on a large plush armchair, clutching a tartan blanket. Despite the warmth of the room, and the blanket around his shoulders, he was shivering.

'I didn't know – I didn't realise – I thought –' he stammered when Geraldine asked him to tell her exactly what he had seen. 'I was so surprised – I went over because I thought a house burglar –' He broke off with a shake of his head. 'That is –' He drew in a deep breath and tried again. This time his words came out in a rush. 'I thought someone was trying to break in, because I could see there was a person at the end of the garden. My dahlias were completely crushed,' he added with a burst of indignation. 'As soon as I glanced in that direction I saw it – saw him.' He shuddered. 'I'm telling you, I had no idea he was dead. How could I have known? The fact is, I thought, when I saw him – my first instinct was to call the police and report an intruder, sleeping it off in my garden. It seemed unbelievable I know, but that was what I saw. At least, that's what I thought I saw. It never occurred to me that he might have had a stroke, or a heart attack, or whatever it was that did for him. But in any case, he was still trespassing on my property, regardless of what had happened to him. What was I supposed to do?'

'What did you do? Please try to remember exactly.'

'If I'd realised he was dead, I wouldn't have gone anywhere near him, I can promise you that. I would have gone straight back indoors and called the police. But I had no idea he was dead. How could I?' He looked at Geraldine anxiously. 'So I went over and yelled at him to get up.'

Geraldine frowned. 'Wasn't that a little rash, sir? He could have been violent.'

Roger nodded. 'You're right. It was stupid, I know, but I'm afraid I rather lost my temper. My dahlias, you see. He was damaging my dahlias.'

'You and your dahlias,' Roger's daughter said, entering the room and overhearing what her father said. 'I've put the kettle on, dad. Would you like a cup of tea, Sergeant?'

Geraldine declined the offer and turned back to Roger. 'What did you do then?'

'At first I thought he must have drunk himself unconscious, because he was just lying there. Drunk, or drugged, I didn't know what was happening, but whatever it was, I wanted him gone. I mean, it's hardly the place you'd expect to see a dead body, lying in your dahlias, in your own back garden, is it? Not that I know where you *would* be likely to see one.' He broke off with an awkward shrug. 'I'm sorry if I'm talking too much. It's my nerves. This isn't a situation I'm used to dealing with. Nothing like this has ever happened to me before.'

Once he had recovered from the shock of his discovery, Geraldine thought he would be busy telling everyone he knew about his experience that morning, but for now he was still reliving the horror. She thanked him. Clearly he had no idea that the victim he had found lying in his back garden had not been a house burglar struck down by alcohol or drugs, but a murder victim who had been dead for a while.

'Did you notice anything strange about the body?' Geraldine asked.

Roger shook his head, frowning. 'Like what?'

At that point his daughter came in with a tray. 'Here, dad,' she said to her father. 'Tea's ready. Are you sure you won't have a cup, Sergeant?'

Geraldine shook her head. 'No, thank you. I just need to ask your father a couple more questions and then I'll leave you in peace. Did you notice anything unusual at all at the scene, sir?'

Roger frowned as he took a cup in a hand that shook slightly.

'Apart from the dead body, you mean?'

Geraldine nodded.

'No, I can't say that I did. There was just that man lying there and to be honest I didn't look at anything else.'

'You mentioned in your initial statement that you attempted to move the body. Can you give me more details?'

Roger put his cup down on the low table between them and leaned forward.

'Oh yes. When I found him he was lying on his front, and I thought he might struggle to breathe in that position, with his face squashed against the ground, so I did my best to roll him on to his side into the recovery position. It's what I learned on a first aid course.' He paused, before confiding, 'I was tempted to leave him there to suffocate, but I thought better of it.'

'Dad, you would never have left him if you thought your intervention might save his life,' his daughter chipped in.

There was a hint of reproach in her voice. Perhaps she intended to remind him that he was talking to a police officer, and should be careful what he said.

Geraldine nodded. 'Yes, of course, I understand. Did you check for vital signs?'

'No, no. Nothing like that. I'm not sure I'd know how. In any case, once I saw his face, it was pretty obvious he was dead, even to someone like me who doesn't know about that sort of thing. And the smell –' He wrinkled his nose in disgust. 'He was – well, he was dead all right. Dead as my dahlias. I mean, there was no way he was still alive. It was horrible, horrible.' He shuddered at the recollection. 'Anyway, once I had him on his back I could see there was no way he was still alive and breathing.'

'Come on, drink your tea, and don't think about it any more,' his daughter said. 'Sergeant, I'm sure my father's told you all he can and we'd both appreciate it if you'd let him relax after his terrible ordeal so he can try and stop thinking about it. He did the right thing in calling you straight away and now he needs to be left to –'

'Just one more question,' Geraldine interrupted her. 'Please, this is very important. When you moved the body, was it easy to change the position of the limbs or was the cadaver stiff?'

'You mean had rigor mortis set in?'

Geraldine nodded. Members of the public were often well versed in the jargon surrounding murder victims, from watching murder mysteries on television, but they did not necessarily understand the full implications of the terminology. Around forty-eight hours after death, rigor would have given way to a flaccid state, and in any case, from the description of the corpse, putrefaction had already commenced, which meant the victim had been dead for more than a couple of days.

'No,' Roger said. 'He wasn't stiff or difficult to move at all. More kind of floppy, I'd say. When I tried to turn him over on to his side, into the recovery position, he rolled right over on to his back. That's when I saw his face and realised he was dead, so I didn't bother trying to shift his position again after that. I just moved right away from him – from it – and called 999. Do you know who he was? I mean, this man had nothing to do with me. I'd never seen him before. Not that I suppose I'd have recognised him if I had,' he added.

'Of course he had nothing to do with you, dad. He was obviously a burglar who climbed over the fence with the intention of breaking into the house and robbing you. If you ask me, you had a lucky escape. What if he hadn't collapsed and died before he got to the house? You could have been attacked!'

'Do you know who he was?' Roger repeated.

'Not yet,' Geraldine replied.

She did not try to explain that scene of crime officers had already established the victim had been killed elsewhere, and his body dumped over the fence some days after his death. There was no way that particular intruder could have attacked anyone.

# 33

HAVING SPOKEN TO ROGER Dexter, Geraldine went to his house, where the body had been discovered. One lane of the road leading to the allotments had been cordoned off, and constables were stationed around the open ground. Two forensic tents had been erected, one in an allotment beside the site where the body had been found, and the other in the garden itself, with a protective awning over the fence that divided them. The corpse itself was already on its way to the mortuary for a post mortem. Geraldine drove to the house and parked near the cordon that had been placed around the pavement outside. Pulling on protective clothing and shoe covers, she followed the common approach path along the side of the house and drew close to the spot where the body had been deposited.

There was a hollow in the flower bed, where a number of orange and yellow flowers had been flattened. Presumably the body had been left there in the early hours of Monday morning, under cover of darkness, when the allotments were deserted.

'Have we established who he was?' she asked a white-clad scene of crime officer who was crouching down studying the crushed vegetation.

He straightened up and shook his head. 'At the moment we're trying to work out how someone managed to get him over the fence,' he replied. 'We also need to establish how he was brought here, and where the killer went once the body had been successfully deposited.'

'And we still don't have any idea at all who the victim might be?' Geraldine persisted.

'Not yet. He had no means of identification on him, in fact, nothing in his pockets at all, and his face is hardly recognisable as human. If we have no match for his DNA on the database we'll be in the dark about who he is, unless someone reports him missing and we find him that way. What I can tell you is that he's been dead for at least a week, but he's not been here that long. We think he was dumped here some time last night, at a time when the roads round about would have been fairly quiet, and the allotments would have been deserted.'

'That ties in with what the householder said,' Geraldine agreed. 'Whoever left him here still took a risk though. Someone could have seen what was happening.'

A team of constables were questioning all the neighbours who had windows overlooking the allotments.

The scene of crime officer grunted. 'There was no moon last night and someone could quite feasibly have thrown a corpse over the fence at this point without anyone seeing, if they were quick about it. It would have been risky, but they must have worked out it could be done without anyone observing what was happening.'

'A calculated risk,' Geraldine muttered. 'So this was carefully planned.'

'It looks that way,' the scene of crime officer agreed. 'How long would it take to drag a body from the boot of a car, or a van, carry it across the allotments, run back to the vehicle and drive off?'

Geraldine didn't answer but she nodded. The scenario the scene of crime officer had suggested was plausible, and the body had certainly been transported there somehow.

Back at the police station, there was some speculation over whether the dead body could be Jason Colman.

'Yes, it's possible, but is there anything in particular that makes you think it might be him?' Ariadne responded to Geraldine's suggestion with a question.

'Admittedly there's nothing about the body itself to suggest it's Jason, but he's been missing for ten days,' she replied. 'This victim has been dead for over a week, so it fits from that perspective, and there's been no other reports of men missing recently in the area. It's by no means conclusive, but it's possible. At least we need to look into it. And if it *is* him, we need to find out how his body got there, and who was responsible.'

'And then we'll know who killed him,' a young constable piped up. 'But if it *is* Jason, why would he turn up now, out of the blue? He disappeared ten days ago.'

For a moment no one answered, then Geraldine commented bluntly,'He must smell pretty awful by now. That's as good a reason as any for removing him from wherever he was being kept.'

'Of course,' the constable muttered, looking slightly uncomfortable.

'You'll get used to it,' Geraldine said kindly.

'And if it's not Jason, who is it?' someone else asked.

Geraldine was fairly confident they had found Jason.

'There's only one way to find out,' Eileen cut in. 'And whoever it is, we need to establish the victim's identity as soon as possible and start to investigate. It can't be a coincidence if David's son-in-law is found dead less than a week after David himself was murdered.'

'And after his granddaughter disappeared,' Ariadne added. 'Don't forget the missing baby.'

'No one's forgetting the baby,' Eileen snapped.

Out of the corner of her eye, Geraldine saw Ian flinch. More than anything she wanted to speak to him and hear about what was going on in his life, but there was no time. While she dithered over whether to work her way around the room towards him, he strode away. Afraid of a rebuff, she was reluctant to try to see him in his office and instead returned to her own desk. There was certainly enough work there to keep her occupied. Even if the second victim's death had been an accident, which was possible, moving the body across the allotments and over the fence into a private garden had been a deliberate and carefully planned action.

'So it looks like Jason might have been murdered as well as his father-in-law,' Ariadne said, her usually cheerful expression dark.

Geraldine sat down at her desk without answering.

'I wonder if...' Ariadne's voice tailed off.

'If?' Geraldine prompted her friend.

'I was just thinking the two deaths must be related. It seems too much of a coincidence otherwise.'

'Hang on, let's not run ahead of ourselves,' Geraldine replied. 'We don't even know who the second body is yet. Jason could be the killer, and after drugging and suffocating his hated father-in-law he might have killed someone else.'

'Someone who witnessed him suffocating David outside his house?' Ariadne said, her eyebrows raised.

'All I'm saying is that there are any number of possibilities,' Geraldine replied. 'That's just one of them. It's also possible the body found this morning has nothing to do with David and his murder. Let's wait for the facts before we start drawing conclusions.'

Ariadne merely grunted, as if to say, 'All right, have it your own way, but you know as well as I do that we've found Jason.'

# 34

IT DIDN'T TAKE THE laboratory long to report that the body found near the allotments was indeed Jason Colman. DNA taken from his toothbrush confirmed the identification. For the second time in a week Geraldine drove Ian to the mortuary, where Jonah greeted them with an unaccustomed air of despondency. His ginger hair looked more wispy than usual, and his blue eyes seemed to have lost their habitual twinkle. His freckled face, always pale, looked positively sickly under the bright mortuary lights.

'You know how I like to solve your cases for you, Geraldine. I'm really sorry to have to disappoint you, but the time of death in this instance is really not at all clear cut.' He gave a resigned shrug.

'Can you give us an approximate time frame?' Geraldine asked. 'Even unofficially?'

Ian raised his eyebrows. Geraldine had spoken to Jonah on her own several times since Ian avoided viewing corpses whenever possible. By contrast, Geraldine had never felt squeamish around the bodies of victims, seeing them as an opportunity to discover information about the cause of their deaths, rather than the physical remains of a living, breathing person. Thanks to Ian's frequent absence from such viewings, Geraldine had developed a relationship of trust with Jonah who was happy to chat to her off the record. In fact his insights often suggested useful lines of enquiry.

'Due to the progression in the putrefaction I'd say he was

probably killed around two weeks ago,' Jonah replied.

'It can't have been more than ten days, eleven at the most. That's when he went missing,' Ian corrected him.

'In the light of that information, I'd hazard a guess that he was killed ten days ago,' Jonah replied promptly. 'You know this isn't an exact science, Ian, but I would say it was unlikely to be much less than ten days, due to the state he's in. So there you go, I was able to help you after all. That makes me feel a lot better. Not that it makes any difference to our friend here,' he added, prodding the body irreverently.

Ian watched Jonah's actions with a scowl of distaste, but Geraldine smiled.

'So we have a rough time of death. Can you do some more of your magic and say *where* he was killed?' Geraldine asked.

'Would you like me to give you the address?'

Geraldine grinned. 'Yes please, along with the name of the killer and where he or she is now.'

'I can tell you that Jason definitely wasn't killed where he was found. He was lying on his front when he was discovered, but fixed lividity shows he was lying on his back for a few days after he was killed.'

Jonah pointed to a large area of dark discolouration on the cadaver's back.

'In addition to which, insect activity in the body is in the very early stages, which might seem to contradict our estimated time of death.' He picked up a container. 'Look.'

Geraldine stared more closely, and was barely able to make out a few tiny white dots in the liquid that resembled floating grains of rice.

'The eggs indicate he was definitely outside exposed to the elements for less than, say, ten hours, confirming he was dumped there sometime on Sunday night. If he'd been there any longer than twenty-four hours, these eggs would certainly have hatched into maggots. But given that he was dead for longer than a week previous to being deposited in Mr Dexter's garden, he must have been left on his back in a protected environment, in a fairly well-sealed location where these little parasites couldn't get to him.' He gestured to the blowfly eggs. 'Someone was keeping hold of the body, storing it somewhere. Now why would anyone do that, I wonder?' He wrinkled his nose. 'Probably not to admire him. He's not a pretty sight, is he?'

'Presumably they were holding on to him until they thought it was safe to move him,' Ian said.

Geraldine wondered whether that suggested a period of reflection after Jason's death, meaning that his death had not been planned as carefully as the aftermath.

'How did he die?' she asked.

Jonah smiled. 'I thought you were never going to ask. Now here's something I can help you with, at last, with a fair degree of certainty.'

Turning to the body, he indicated a patch on the back of the head where the skin had been cut away to reveal a shattered area of the skull.

'Either he had a nasty fall,' he said, 'or someone gave him a hefty whack on the head with a heavy blunt object. I'm guessing he would have been knocked out and probably never recovered consciousness. At any rate, there are no signs of any defence wounds. He died of a haemorrhage, caused by the head injury.'

The three of them stared at the damaged skull for a moment.

'He was probably wrapped in a blanket before he was moved,' Jonah went on. 'We found wool fibres all over his clothes and exposed areas of skin. They've been sent for analysis but I can tell you they were a mixture of colours.'

'Could it have been a tartan blanket?' Geraldine asked, remembering the blanket Roger had been wrapped in.

'It could have been.'

Ian raised his eyebrows enquiringly. But the likelihood that Roger would have killed Jason, reported the body, and then gone to his daughter's house to wrap himself in the same blanket he had used to transport the body was so remote as to be barely worth following up. All the same, she resolved to send a constable to collect the blanket. They could not afford to overlook any possible lead. And once they found Jason's killer, they might also have discovered who had killed David.

Jonah had the body turned over and Geraldine heard Ian draw in his breath at the sight of the dead man's face. His skin was mottled green and purple and the eyes which bulged from his face would have been difficult to close.

'I know,' Jonah said, nodding at Ian. 'He would scare hardened fans of horror movies. So,' he continued in a matter-of-fact tone, 'I gather this one was related to the corpse you brought me just seven days ago? I have to say this is a very different kind of killing. I'd be surprised – don't quote me on this please, it's just a stray thought based on mere supposition – but I'd be surprised if they were killed by the same person.'

David's death appeared to have been premeditated. The pills might have been given to him without his knowledge. His wife, for example, could have made some excuse for his dinner tasting strange, or she might have mixed ground-up pills and put them into the whisky he drank. Jason's death, on the other hand, could have been accidental, even though it had been deliberately covered up. If Jason had been murdered, it must have been on impulse, because the killer had clearly not thought it through, and had taken a long time to work out how to dispose of the body, doing so only when the fetid odour became a problem. If David had been killed first, it was possible Jason might have been attacked because he had threatened to expose the killer, but it made less sense the other way around. The more she thought about it, the more confused Geraldine felt. But it was hard to believe the two deaths could be unrelated.

After thanking Jonah for his insights, Geraldine drove Ian back to the police station in silence. As soon as she reached her desk, she arranged for Roger's blanket to be collected and tested. The forensic team found no evidence that the blanket had been in contact with a corpse, and in any case the woollen fibres gathered from Jason's corpse were reported to have come from a red and blue blanket. Jessica and Anne's houses were searched but there was no sign of a red and blue blanket. Geraldine was not surprised. The blanket used to wrap the body could be anywhere by now, if it had not been destroyed. All the same, she felt a familiar frisson of disappointment. She wished the case could be as simple to solve as the murder mysteries she occasionally watched on television. Fiction tended to be reassuringly logical, while real life was convoluted and messy, and it was giving her a headache.

# 35

JASON WOULD HAVE HAD ample opportunity to remove Daisy from the house without telling anyone where she was. If he *had* taken the baby, his death took on an additional worrying dimension. There didn't appear to be any possible motive for him to have spirited his daughter away, with or without his wife's consent. Anne had denied there was anything wrong with Jessica, but she appeared to have been lying. Based on bloodstains found in the cot, Eileen had suspected the baby might have been killed and the parents had been covering up the murder. With the discovery of Jason's body, a new theory emerged, that he had been responsible for his daughter's death and Jessica had killed him as a consequence. Whatever the truth, it was beginning to look unlikely the baby would ever be found alive.

Jason and Jessica Colman's house had been subjected to a close forensic scrutiny. No evidence had been found to suggest that anyone other than Daisy's parents and grandparents had been in the nursery. Having excluded other possibilities, forensic evidence indicated that it could only have been a member of the family who had removed the baby from her cot. Jessica claimed she had woken in the morning to discover the baby had gone. If she was telling the truth, then her husband, mother or father must be responsible for abducting or killing the baby. But Jessica could have been lying when she said the baby had been stolen from her cot.

Over a week had passed since Daisy had allegedly

disappeared from home, and with every passing hour the likelihood that she would be found safe and well was growing more remote. The media had got hold of the story and were posting daily updates online, and the situation was being reported in the national news. On her way to speak to Jessica, Geraldine found a group of reporters waiting outside the Colmans' house, hoping to hear some news. A woman in a long black coat darted forward to intercept her as she approached the gate.

'Has the baby been found?' the reporter demanded in a strident voice. 'The public have a right to know what's happened.'

Geraldine strode past her without pausing to respond. She could just imagine the furore when they discovered that not only Jessica's father-in-law but also her husband had been found murdered. For now the media were focused on the missing baby, but that could change at any time. Meanwhile, the black-coated reporter pushed in front of her.

'Wait just a minute,' she cried out shrilly. 'You can't ignore us. We have our job to do, the same as you. Some of us have been standing here all morning, waiting for an update. What's happening in there?'

Geraldine manoeuvred her way past the woman and went through the gate, closing it firmly behind her. When the reporter pushed the gate open, Geraldine's patience finally ran out. She turned to face the woman, closing the gate between them again as she spoke.

'If you take one step on to this property, you'll be arrested for trespass, causing a public nuisance, and wilful obstruction of a police investigation, any one of which could cost your paper a fine.' She raised her voice so that the other reporters could hear her. 'Unless you want to find yourselves in trouble with the police, I suggest you go back to your desks, all of you, and wait for a press briefing.' She turned back to the reporter who had accosted her. 'Off you go.'

'We need to ask you a few questions first,' the reporter replied, standing her ground on the pavement, but not opening the gate.

Geraldine ignored her and marched up the path to Jessica's front door. Anne's car was not on the drive and when Jessica opened the door, it looked as though she was on her own. Considering what Jessica was going through, Geraldine shouldn't have been shocked at the change in her, but it was so marked, she was almost unrecognisable. Her blonde hair hung down in straggly greasy strands, her eyes were bloodshot, and her skin had lost its former healthy glow.

'Well?' she muttered urgently as soon as she saw who it was. 'Have you found her?'

Geraldine looked at her sorrowfully. 'I have some news for you,' she said, adding miserably, 'it's bad news.'

Jessica glared as though Geraldine was somehow responsible for Daisy's disappearance.

'Where is she?' she hissed. 'She's dead, isn't she? I'll never see her again.'

Aware of the photographers hovering behind her in the street, Geraldine motioned to Jessica to let her in. Realising they were being watched, Jessica darted back into the hall, out of sight, self-consciously smoothing her hair.

'I must look a mess,' she muttered.

'We haven't traced Daisy yet,' Geraldine said. 'We're still hoping to find her alive and well. But there's something else I need to tell you. Please, let's go and sit down.'

The last time Geraldine had seen her, Jessica had been threatening to change the locks on her doors to prevent her husband from entering the house. She had told Geraldine that if her husband never came back she would be happy. She never wanted to see him again. But the reality could prove very different, and Geraldine was prepared for Jessica to be distraught on learning of the death of her husband. She must have loved him once, enough to marry him and want to raise a child with him. Wondering whether such love ever really ended, Geraldine found her thoughts wandering to Ian. With a shiver, she forced herself to focus on the agitated woman in front of her.

'I want to ask you about your daughter,' Geraldine said, 'and also about your father. I'm so sorry, but we do need to see if there's anything you know that might help us. We're not convinced the two incidents are related, of course.'

Jessica nodded wretchedly. 'Do you think someone might have taken Daisy to get at my father?'

While she was talking she led Geraldine into the living room which looked even more untidy than Geraldine remembered it, with empty pizza boxes and dirty plates on the table. There was a smell of cheese mingled with beer and sweat. Jessica sat down, seemingly oblivious to the mess.

'There's nothing to suggest that might be the case,' Geraldine replied, 'but it is a coincidence, your daughter disappearing just before your father was killed. And there's something else.' She paused. 'I'm sorry, but there's no easy way to tell you this. I'm afraid Jason's dead.'

# 36

AFTER THE DISAPPEARANCE OF her baby, and the death of her father, it was hardly surprising that Jessica stared at Geraldine for a moment in complete shock.

'What do you mean?' she stammered at last. 'What are you talking about? What are you saying? What's that about Jason?'

'I'm afraid he's dead. We're going to need you to identify his body.'

'You mean you don't know if it's him?'

'I'm afraid it's definitely him. The DNA we took from his toothbrush establishes it, but we do need you to confirm his identity.'

Geraldine hesitated, wondering how well the pathologist would be able to clean up Jason's face before his wife viewed it. He had looked quite hideous when she and Ian had seen him lying on the table at the mortuary, with his lurid face and protruding eyes.

'My baby's been stolen,' Jessica replied in a tight voice, 'and my father's been murdered, and now you've come here asking me to identify my husband's body? So, my father's dead. We know that. My mother went to identify his body. There's nothing anyone can do for him now. And my baby's been taken, God knows where, and she could be crying for me right now...' she broke off, sobbing too violently to speak. 'Find her for me, just find her,' she mumbled through her tears. 'I don't want to hear about Jason, or about my father. I don't want to hear about people in my family who've been killed.' She paused and gasped. 'Did he – had Jason – was she there?'

Geraldine would have given anything to be able to reunite the bereft mother with her child, but her job was to investigate the murders of David and Jason. Taking a deep breath, she focused on the reason she had gone to see Jessica.

'I'm so sorry, Jessica. We haven't found Daisy yet, but we are doing everything we can to find her as quickly as possible. Do you know a man called Jonathan Edwards? He's about fifty, very tall and thin, and he used to work as a school librarian?'

Jessica shook her head, looking faintly bewildered. 'How can Jason be dead?' she muttered as though she had only just registered what Geraldine had told her. 'How is it possible? No, not Jason, not Jason.'

'Jessica, I need you to listen to me, very carefully. This is really important. Do you know Jonathan Edwards?'

Jessica shook her head.

'How about a younger man called Rod Browning?' Geraldine asked. 'He's about your age, and he has ginger hair and a ginger moustache and beard, and he works in a health food shop in York?'

Jessica shook her head again. 'I don't know these people,' she whispered. Her voice hardened as she asked, 'Have they got Daisy?'

Understandably she was only concerned about her missing child, although Geraldine did think she might have been interested in finding out who had killed her father and her husband.

'It's not that I don't care that Jason's dead,' Jessica said, perhaps realising what Geraldine was thinking. 'But he's gone, isn't he? There's no point in getting upset, not yet. We have to focus all our attention on finding Daisy.'

'There is a massive search underway,' Geraldine assured

her. 'We are going to find her. But my job is working on the murder investigation. That's important too. Whoever killed your father is still at large and could be a danger to others, as could the person who killed your husband.'

But it was clear that Jessica was barely listening to her. As Geraldine was preparing to leave, they heard the front door close and a woman's voice shouting, 'It's me.'

The door to the living room opened and Anne came in. Her expression changed to one of alarm when she saw Geraldine.

'What–?' she asked. 'What are you doing here? Is it – have you found her?'

'I'm afraid we've found your son-in-law's body,' Geraldine replied quietly. 'Jason's dead.'

'Jason's dead?' Anne repeated in surprise.

'And she's on at me about dad,' Jessica said through her sobs.

Anne heaved an exaggerated sigh. 'We've told you everything we know,' she said, her voice raised in anger. 'All we're interested in now is getting our baby back. As for that good-for-nothing husband of hers, we'll grieve for him as much as he deserves when we have Daisy back.' She pressed her lips together in an attempt to control herself, but tears filled her eyes. 'Please, just find Daisy,' she pleaded.

'I'd like to ask you a few questions before I go,' Geraldine replied, resuming her seat. 'Perhaps we could talk alone?' she added, glancing at Jessica who was sniffling into a handkerchief.

'I'll go and put the kettle on, mum.'

Anne looked as though she was going to remonstrate when Jessica stood up, but she thought better of it and sat down.

'Let's get this over with then,' Anne said. 'It might sound callous to you, Sergeant, but right now I'm more concerned to support my daughter than to find out who killed my husband. And I certainly don't care what happened to Jason. Is that a terrible thing to say? David's gone and past help. I'll mourn for him, of course I will. We were married for twenty-six years. You don't just write that off in a moment. We spent a long time together. But Jessica needs me right now and I can't afford to go to pieces. As for her husband, he was never much of a support to her. I'm sorry he's dead, of course, but I can't sit here and tell you I'm sorry he's out of her life.'

'What do you mean?'

'I mean that he only ever thinks – thought about himself. He's – he was a bully and a – well, let's just say he was a thoroughly nasty piece of work. She made a big mistake the day she married him. I wouldn't be surprised –' she broke off and dabbed at her nose with a tissue.

'What wouldn't surprise you?' Geraldine asked.

Anne glanced at the door and spoke hurriedly. 'I wouldn't be at all surprised to discover he took the baby away himself, just to spite her. I wouldn't put it past him, that's all I'm saying.'

'But what would prompt him to do that?'

Anne shrugged. 'To get back at her. I'm telling you, he's a nasty piece of work.'

Jessica came back carrying two mugs of tea. She gave one to her mother and kept the other for herself. Evidently Geraldine wasn't considered deserving of tea.

'Was your marriage happy, on the whole?' Geraldine asked her outright.

Jessica gaped and almost spilt her tea. She put her mug down carefully on the table before answering. Geraldine was aware she was considering what to say. Without answering the question, she turned to her mother.

'What have you been saying?' she demanded furiously. She turned back to Geraldine. 'My parents never liked Jason. They thought he wasn't good enough for me. But honestly, no one would have been good enough for them. Jason and I were happy enough, thank you. Don't believe a word my mother has been saying about him.'

Jessica seemed to have forgotten about her own attack on Jason. Now she burst into tears. With both Jessica and Anne in tears, Geraldine left. There was no point in pressing either of them for answers, although she had an uneasy feeling that she had somehow been hoodwinked, as though Jessica and Anne were both deliberately hiding behind Daisy's disappearance to avoid talking about their murdered husbands. But it was impossible to judge whether they were sidestepping the subject from grief or guilt.

# 37

NOW THEY KNEW WHY Jason had disappeared without trace, but they were no closer to discovering where he had been hidden away, or to finding his baby, or to working out who had killed him or his father-in-law.

'There are too many unanswered questions surrounding these tragedies,' Eileen said.

With the baby still missing, the team were all hoping desperately that there would turn out to be no more than two deaths in this sorry family.

'It all centres around Jessica,' Eileen said. 'Is she really an unfortunate victim in these crimes, or does she have something to do with all of it? Her baby, her father, her husband. She's the common link.'

'Along with her mother,' Geraldine pointed out.

Eileen nodded. 'True. They might even be in this together.'

It sounded unlikely, but nothing could be ruled out. Jessica and her mother had both been questioned, but as yet no evidence had been found that suggested either one or both of them could be guilty of any crime.

'Can a mother kidnap her own baby?' Ariadne asked.

Before Eileen could answer, her phone buzzed. Studying the screen, she frowned.

'Here's an unexpected development,' she said. 'I'll upload the message and we'll have him brought straight here for questioning.'

Johnathan Edwards had been stopped at Leeds Bradford

Airport, attempting to board a plane. Clearly he had not realised how serious the police were when they had told him not to leave the area.

'He thought he could just skip off,' Eileen fumed, but there was a distinct note of triumph in her voice.

The airport was about an hour's drive from York, and two hours later Geraldine and Ian faced Jonathan across an interview table, with a duty solicitor present. Geraldine entered the interview room behind Ian and took a seat without once glancing at her colleague, but consciousness of his presence at her side made it hard for her to focus on anything else. She wished that Eileen would stop partnering her with Ian. They had worked together on many cases over the years, and knowing one another as well as they did made them an extremely effective team. All the same, every time Geraldine saw Ian her breath seemed to catch in her throat, and she felt an urge to reach out and put her arms around him, drawing him close. She wondered whether she might speak to Eileen about it, but was reluctant to appear unprofessional. She had always prided herself on her refusal to allow personal problems to intrude on her work.

'You were caught attempting to leave the country,' Ian began the interview.

Jonathan scowled. 'I was going on holiday. I booked it months ago. It's not a crime to have a holiday, is it? Was I supposed to pay out all that money for nothing? Anyway, I've lost it now, because thanks to your intervention I've missed my plane. What happens now? Are *you* going to refund me the cost of my flight? And the cost of the night in Spain I'll have missed if I fly out tomorrow?' He was almost spitting with rage. 'This is an outrageous infringement of my rights as a citizen, to be prevented from leaving the country for a perfectly innocent purpose.'

'My client has not been charged with any offence,' the

lawyer said, fidgeting as she spoke. 'You are interfering with the rights of an innocent member of the public and we will be seeking compensation.'

Geraldine glanced at the same solicitor who had accompanied Jonathan at his previous interview. She looked about sixteen, although she was old enough to have qualified in her profession. Her mousy brown hair looked dull and she seemed lethargic, as though she was present only in body. She was young to be taking so little interest in her work and Geraldine wondered if she suffered from depression, or perhaps she had recently split up with her boyfriend. With a faint sigh, she returned her gaze to Jonathan.

'We asked you not to leave York,' she reminded him. 'Why were you attempting to leave the country? Surely you must have realised we would receive an alert?'

'I just told you,' he replied, his voice growing strident with irritation. 'I was taking a holiday. That's not a crime, is it? Well? Is it?' He leaned forward in his chair and glared at her.

'There's no need to raise your voice,' Ian said quietly.

'I'm not bloody raising my voice, but you don't seem to want to hear what I'm saying. I went to the airport because I was flying to Spain. I booked this holiday months ago and so I went. What's wrong with that? It's not as if I was trying to avoid being questioned. If you check my booking, you'll see it was made months before any of this happened. And you had me stopped and brought here like – like a common criminal.'

'We asked you not to leave York,' Geraldine repeated patiently.

'So you keep saying, but it's a free country and you haven't charged me with anything, which means I'm entitled to go away if I want to. Don't forget, it's taxes from people like me that pay your wages.'

Geraldine was sure that Ian was thinking the same as her, but neither of them pointed out that Jonathan was no longer paying income tax because he had lost his job.

'And before you say anything else, I'm going back to the airport tomorrow and going on my holiday. I'll send the bill for my rescheduled flight to your chief inspector.' Red-faced, Jonathan sat back in his chair and folded his arms. 'And we'll see what my friends on social media have to say about that!'

'About a possible suspect in a murder case trying to slip out of the country?' Ian asked softly.

'What? You can't say that – I'm not a suspect in anything. You haven't charged me with anything. I'm a free man. Innocent until proved guilty. Suggesting otherwise is slander. I don't even know what I'm doing back here. What the hell do you want with me?'

'You have to see that in trying to board a plane to Spain when we specifically asked you to remain in York means you've brought suspicion on yourself,' Geraldine replied. 'We are bound to question what you were doing, where you were going, and why you wanted to leave in such a hurry.'

'I told you, I was going to Spain for a week, and I've already told you, I booked it months ago. I was going on holiday.'

'So you say.'

'You can see my ticket. I fly back after a week. Only now it's going to be six days, isn't it?'

Ian shook his head. 'I'm afraid we can't let you leave the country until this case is cleared up.'

'You can't stop me,' Jonathan replied, but he didn't sound very confident. He turned to his lawyer. 'They can't stop me, can they?'

'I think you'll find that in a murder investigation, within reason we can do whatever we deem necessary or appropriate,' Geraldine said.

Jonathan shook his head angrily. 'No, that's not right. You had me here, you questioned me, you let me go, and that has to be the end of it. If you had anything on me, you wouldn't have let me go in the first place.'

'Things have changed slightly,' Ian said.

'How have they changed? What's happened to make you suspect me that you didn't know about before?'

'Your attempt to leave the country,' Ian replied drily. 'You must see that looks suspicious.'

'Oh for goodness sake,' Jonathan snapped. 'You're saying if I hadn't decided to go away you wouldn't have brought me back here? So what difference would it have made if I was at home or in Spain, seeing as I wasn't being questioned?'

Ian shrugged.

'All right,' Jonathan went on. 'Let's pretend I never went to the airport. Pretend I never bought a ticket to Spain. I'll go home and pretend none of this ever happened. How's that? It's not as if I can afford another flight anyway. So I won't go away. Some stranger gets himself killed, and I'm not allowed to have a holiday. Listen, I solemnly promise to stay in York until you find the real culprit, even of it means throwing money away, all the money I spent on my trip. And now I'm going home.' He stood up.

'I'm afraid that may no longer be possible,' Ian said.

'What? Nothing's changed since the last time I was here, and you couldn't find any evidence I was guilty then. You didn't even charge me. Don't you see? Nothing's changed since then.'

'But you tried to leave the country,' Geraldine told him, 'and that changes everything.'

The solicitor spoke up for the first time. 'My client has given his word that he won't try to skip the country again –'

'Skip the country?' Jonathan repeated. 'Skip the country? What kind of language is that? I was going on holiday. I thought you were supposed to be on my side.'

'I'm afraid we're not sure we can trust him,' Ian told the

solicitor. 'We'll continue this tomorrow. Interview terminated by DI Peterson at four forty-five pm.'

He nodded at a constable standing by the door who approached the suspect.

'If you'd like to come with me, sir.'

'What? Where are you taking me?'

'You're going to spend a night with us here and then we can continue this discussion in the morning,' Ian said. 'I'm afraid we have to stop now. We have other matters to attend to.'

Realising what was going to happen, Jonathan began to protest loudly.

'No, no, you have no right to do this. No! I refuse to go to a cell. Bloody hell, do something, woman!' He yelled at his solicitor.

'There's nothing I can do but I'll be back tomorrow,' she replied. 'And then you will have to charge him or let him go,' she added, turning to Ian.

'But what about tonight?' Jonathan insisted. 'I can't sleep in a cell. Oh, bloody hell, some holiday this is turning out to be.'

# 38

'WELL, WE NOW KNOW he has a temper,' Ian said to Geraldine as they walked away from the interview room.

'That's hardly a crime,' Geraldine replied. She laughed. 'If we're going to treat everyone who has a temper as a suspect, there won't be many people we won't have to interview.'

'It suggests he might have killed David in a fit of rage.'

'It no more points to him being a suspect than anyone else. He had good reason to be annoyed.'

'Well, of course it doesn't mean he's guilty, but it does make it seem plausible that he killed David Armstrong. We know that he had reason to hate him, and now we've established he has a temper.'

'And what about Jason?'

Ian looked sombre. 'You heard what the pathologist said. He doesn't think one killer was responsible for both murders.'

Neither of them suggested they go to the canteen, but they walked there almost without thinking. Before Ian's wife had returned to him, he and Geraldine had frequently gone to the canteen together to chat over a mug of coffee. Usually their discussions had centred on work, and this occasion was no exception. They sat down at their favourite corner table where they were able to converse without being overheard, and could watch their colleagues hurrying in and out.

'The pathologist was only voicing his opinion, based on limited information,' Geraldine said as she took her seat.

'Exactly. He was drawing conclusions from information which is incomplete,' Ian grumbled.

It wasn't the first time he had criticised the pathologist for being too free with his speculation.

'Yes, you're right, of course, but –' Geraldine hesitated.

'But what?'

For the first time since Ian had moved out of her flat, she looked up and stared directly at him. Their eyes met, and for a moment neither of them spoke. Knowing each other so well, it was difficult to hide their feelings from one another. Seeing the misery in his face, Geraldine wondered if her own feelings were as obvious to him as his were to her.

'Playing strictly by the book isn't always the most useful approach,' she murmured.

Ian frowned at her words. 'Geraldine, what are you talking about?'

She tried to explain that Jonah sometimes gave her useful insights that he would be unable to voice if he were to restrict himself to what he was allowed to tell her.

'The point is,' she concluded lamely, 'he gives me helpful details, off the record. He wouldn't be able to do that if he could only tell me what he's actually allowed to say.'

Ian scowled. 'He has no business saying anything he's not allowed to say.'

Clearly Ian disagreed with Jonah speaking so candidly to her. Geraldine wasn't sure whether Ian was being pedantic about the rules, or if he was feeling jealous of the friendship that had sprung up between her and the tubby little pathologist who, in any case, was happily married. The thought that Ian might be feeling possessive about her gave her an unexpected thrill, although it was just as likely he was asserting his authority as her senior officer, but she made no comment. The police station canteen was hardly the place for an emotional scene.

Leaving him in the canteen, gazing morosely at his mug of lukewarm coffee, Geraldine drove to the primary school where Jonathan Edwards had worked. The school was situated at the end of a cul-de-sac of square brick houses. Leaving her car beside a tall hedge at the end of the road, she rang the bell beside a gate in the high metal railings that surrounded the site. A woman's voice answered over a crackly intercom and Geraldine identified herself. Crossing a tarmac car park, she entered a two-storey flat-roofed building with large square windows. A sign by the door showed a name which was also displayed by the gate: Clifton Primary School. She pushed open a door marked School Office and a middle-aged woman looked up at her with a worried smile.

'How can we help you, Sergeant?' the secretary asked when Geraldine introduced herself.

Geraldine hesitated. She had come there to talk to the head teacher, but the school secretary might have useful information.

'Do you know a man called Jonathan Edwards who used to work here?' she asked as she stepped into the room and closed the door gently behind her.

The secretary's neatly permed brown curls bobbed around her ears as she nodded her head.

'He left us last year,' she said, adding tersely, 'cutbacks.'

'What can you tell me about him?'

'Has something happened to him?'

'No.'

'Is he in trouble?

'What makes you say that?'

'Only that you've come here asking about him.'

Geraldine smiled. 'He's not in any trouble as far as I'm aware, and I don't know that anything's happened to him. We're speaking to him as we think he might be able to help us with an enquiry.'

The secretary's worried expression cleared. 'Is there anything we can do to help?'

'No, thank you, I just wanted to make a few enquiries. We need to establish how reliable he might be as a witness,' Geraldine said, hoping her explanation sounded sensible. 'Did you find him honest?'

The secretary frowned at the question. 'I should certainly think so,' she replied, sounding slightly affronted. 'I don't think Mr Brice would have kept him here otherwise. Working with children we have to be scrupulous about our staff.'

The head teacher smiled sadly when Geraldine explained the purpose for her visit.

'He was a loss,' Gordon Brice said, nodding his head solemnly. 'Jonathan was a dedicated member of our staff here, and he did good work with the children. It's not easy encouraging them to read, and it gets harder every year. There are so many other sources of entertainment for them these days, mostly online. We do our best, of course, but the parents aren't always on board, and without their support we're fighting a difficult battle. We need all the help we can get. I have to tell you, Sergeant, these latest cutbacks have been disastrous. I don't think we'll ever fully recover.'

From what Geraldine heard, Jonathan had been quiet and hard working, liked by the children and the rest of the staff, although none of them had known him well. The headmaster seemed bemused and even faintly entertained at hearing how his former librarian had been a vocal opponent of the leader of the council, but his smile faded abruptly when he learned that David had been murdered.

'Murdered?' he repeated, frowning. 'And you're telling me you suspect Jonathan may have been involved? Surely not. No, I can't for one moment believe Jonathan would have had anything to do with – with the councillor's murder. No, Sergeant. That's not... it's not possible. Not Jonathan. He was a gentle, kind man. He worked with children!' he added, a note of outrage creeping into his voice.

'Even people who work with children have been known to commit terrible crimes,' Geraldine replied softly.

'Listen, Sergeant, Jonathan was a harmless man. A little odd perhaps, but harmless.'

'In what way was he odd?'

The headmaster sighed. 'Please, don't go getting the wrong impression,' he said. 'I didn't mean odd in a bad way.'

'What did you mean by it?'

'Just that he was the kind of man who struggled to relate to people, other adults, that is. He lived with his mother and I don't believe there was ever anyone else in his life. After his mother died, he told me he only lived for his work here. He was dedicated to the children.'

'Did you really know him?'

The headmaster shook his head, his kindly expression overshadowed by regret.

# 39

'SO HE WAS A loner,' Ariadne said, when Geraldine reported on her interview with the headmaster.

'That doesn't make him a criminal,' Geraldine replied. 'There's nothing wrong with being happy living on your own.'

She spoke more fiercely than she had intended.

Ariadne laughed. 'I was brought up with five brothers and sisters and as soon as I had the chance to live on my own, I grabbed it with both hands. Best thing I ever did!'

That evening, as she was thinking about Jonathan, the loner, Geraldine heard a ring at her bell. Checking the security camera, she was surprised to see Ian waiting at her door. She had given him a key to the flat when he had moved in, but since he had left her, she appreciated that he considered it would be inappropriate for him to use it. For a second she hesitated, her finger resting on the button that would buzz him in. Quelling an angry temptation to leave him standing outside, she pressed the button.

'Come on in,' she muttered, although she had turned away and he couldn't hear her. 'Come in and batter my feelings again, why don't you?'

She hurried to the mirror in the hall and glanced at her reflection. Her short black hair was neat enough, and she hadn't yet removed the minimal make-up she wore during the day to accentuate her large dark eyes, but tension was making her look disagreeable. She wondered if Ian would realise how nervous she was feeling. Taking a deep breath, she went to the kitchen, took two wine glasses from the cupboard, and opened a bottle of Chianti, red but light. She had just finished pouring two glasses when she heard her front door close and turned to see Ian standing awkwardly in the kitchen doorway. He looked flustered. His hair was sticking up as though he had just run his hand through it, a habit he had when he was feeling anxious, and his eyes darted around the room without resting on her.

Ian's unease made her suddenly feel very calm.

'Let's go and sit in the living room,' she suggested.

She set the two glasses and the opened bottle on a tray.

'I've opened a red,' and she lifted it up, pleased to see that her hand remained steady. 'Or would you prefer tea or coffee?'

She smiled at him, as though this was a casual social visit. Ian shrugged, muttering that he didn't mind what they drank, and she followed him into the living room, still holding the wine. Taking a seat, she set down the tray and pushed a glass across the table to him. Raising her own, she gave what she hoped was a gracious smile. If he had come to tell her their affair was over, at least she would know where she stood.

'Cheers,' she said and drank.

Tentatively returning her smile, Ian picked up his glass. She hoped he had not noticed how desperately she had gulped at her wine. As the silence between them grew uncomfortable, they both spoke at once.

'How are things at home?' Geraldine asked.

At exactly the same time, Ian stammered that he owed her an apology.

'What for?' she asked.

'Oh please, don't be disingenuous,' he replied with a touch of irritation, although she could tell he was trying as hard as she was to remain composed. 'I moved in here and then moved out with scarcely a word of explanation, and you want to know why I might think I owe you an apology. Let's at least be honest with each other. Did my moving in – and out – mean so little to you?'

'It didn't seem to mean much to you,' she snapped.

She pressed her lips together and stared at her wine, annoyed that he had stung her into betraying her feelings.

'I've taken a paternity test,' he told her.

Geraldine held her breath and waited, aware that this could change the course of both their lives. At the same time, she realised that it actually meant nothing to her. If Ian wanted to move back in with her only because he had discovered Bev's baby wasn't his after all, she would never know what might have happened if he had turned out to be the father of the child. Geraldine would never have stood by and allowed him to abandon his wife and child, but this way she would never know if he loved her enough to be prepared to give up everything to be with her. Struggling to hide her dismay, she sipped at her wine and refused to look at him.

'We get the result tomorrow,' he went on.

'So you still don't know whether Bev's baby is yours or not?'

'Not yet. I wanted to make a decision about my life – mine and yours – without knowing if I was the father. It seemed fairer to you. Otherwise you'd never really know how I feel about you.'

Geraldine nodded to show she understood, although she still wasn't quite sure what he was telling her.

'If the baby's mine,' he pressed on, with an air of desperation, 'I'll do everything I can to support Bev and my child, for as long as she needs me to. Despite the way she's behaved, I'm determined to do the right thing. But…'

He paused and drew in a deep breath. Geraldine felt as though the room was spinning around her. She put her glass down and stared at the dark red wine, willing him to take her in his arms and tell her that he loved her, and only her, no matter what.

'I'm not going back. I can't. The marriage is over.'

She waited.

'Are you listening?' he asked, a note of anguish creeping into his voice. 'Did you hear what I said?'

'What about this?' she asked, waving one hand around. 'You and me? I don't want to sound narcissistic, but how is your break-up going to affect *my* life? All you've told me is that your marriage is over, whatever happens with the paternity test. But you've broken up with Bev before. Actually, I think you're making the right decision not to go back with her, because the marriage wasn't working for either of you, and it would be a mistake to try and patch it up now just because of the baby. But of course it's not my place to comment on that,' she added, aware that she was talking wildly. 'And you still haven't told me what you're planning to do next.'

Now she was the one who was sounding desperate.

'Well, I haven't packed a case, but I was hoping to stay here tonight,' he replied. 'I left some of my things here, unless you've thrown them out.'

It was hardly the most romantic of declarations, but Geraldine felt tears of relief sliding down her cheeks.

'Your things are in a box. I was going to return them to you, if you asked for them nicely.'

Then, to her embarrassment, she burst into tears. Ian came around to her side of the table and put his arms around her and she cried noisily on to his shoulder.

'Oh bloody hell,' he said after a moment, 'I've just walked out on one hysterical woman and now I seem to have saddled myself with another one.'

Geraldine pulled away from his embrace and wiped her eyes. 'I'm not hysterical,' she replied, doing her best to stop her voice wobbling. 'I'm happy.'

Ian grinned at her. 'Oh, go ahead and cry if you want to. Now, where's that box?'

'It's in the bottom cupboard in the bedroom.'

At the door he turned. 'You know, if you had thrown my things out –'

'You wouldn't have come back?' she asked, struggling not to break down in tears again.

'Don't be so daft.'

He pulled a new toothbrush from his pocket, still in its wrapping. 'I came prepared. Anyway, thanks for hanging on to my things. Not everyone would have been so understanding.'

'I never gave up hope,' she said softly, and he smiled.

'Oh never mind my finding my things,' he said, coming back and putting his arms around her again. 'Now you've stopped snivelling, I can think of something else we can do.'

# 40

THE FOLLOWING MORNING IAN summoned Geraldine. He sounded gruff on the phone, and she felt apprehensive as she walked along the corridor to his office. When she arrived, he instructed her to shut the door before telling her that he had received the result of the paternity test. He paused for an instant and drew in a deep breath before telling her the baby was not his.

'After all that,' he added, with a sigh.

'How do you feel about it?' Geraldine asked.

As she took a seat facing him across his desk, she did her best to conceal her elation, knowing she would no longer have to share Ian with his ex-wife. Only their past connected them now.

'I don't know,' he admitted. 'Confused. I mean, I'm relieved of course, but a small part of me, a very small part, is bitterly disappointed. Can you believe that? It would have been awkward and complicated but –' he broke off and heaved a sigh. 'It's not as if I ever wanted to have a child, but... anyway,' he went on more briskly, 'I've had a lucky escape.'

'What's Bev going to do now?'

He shook his head. 'I haven't told her yet. I wanted to tell you first. But hopefully the father of her baby will take her back once he knows the baby's his.'

'Assuming the man she was having an affair with *is* the father.'

'Whatever happens, and whoever the father is, I'm not

responsible for her baby, or for her. To be honest, I want to wash my hands of the whole affair, and never see her or think about her again. We were married once, but it's over, bar the formalities of finalising the divorce. There's no reason why we should ever have anything to do with one another again. I'm free.'

Geraldine was watching him carefully as he spoke. 'You don't look very pleased about it. Are you sure it's over?'

'If you mean the relationship between me and Bev, then yes. Absolutely. I couldn't be more certain. You of all people should know that. But – well, I thought I might be – I thought I was a father. Bev told me categorically that the child was mine. Geraldine, I thought I had a son! That's something, isn't it? It's a huge deal. And now I discover she was lying, just because she wanted to come back to me. I suppose she thought my job was better paid and more secure than his. I'll get a good pension. That would have interested her, especially now she has a child to consider.' He pulled a face. 'I can't say I blame her altogether.'

'Ian, she lied to you and manipulated both you and the father of her child. She can't just pick and choose who she wants to select as the father, and then change her mind whenever she feels like it. Parenthood is a biological fact. She tried to put you off taking a paternity test, but you, and the father, and above all the child, you all have a right to know the truth. It would probably come out at some future time anyway, and imagine how painful that would be, for everyone involved. Another man is the father, Ian, not you. She tried to conceal that from him as well, and I dare say it's important to him too. She was deceiving both of you in the most despicable way imaginable. And you think that's justifiable on the grounds that you earn more than him? Really?'

'Yes, I know, I know. You're right, of course you are. It was despicable behaviour. But – well, I thought her baby was mine and, even though I never wanted it in the first place, I can't pretend I'm not disappointed to discover that it's not mine after all. I'm sorry, but that's just how I feel.'

Geraldine nodded. 'I do understand. I'd be feeling just the same if that happened to me.'

Ian smiled. 'That was never going to happen to you. You're a woman. You can't possibly imagine what it feels like. I feel – cheated. I can't really explain, but she managed to persuade me that this was how it was always meant to be between us. A family. It had begun to feel somehow inevitable. Oh well, it's over and that's that.'

'I know it's not the same thing at all, but I felt angry and betrayed when I discovered the woman I had believed was my mother had lied to me all my life. These emotional relationships are complex and painful. You're right to want to move on, but you can't sweep all this under the carpet and pretend it never happened.'

While she was talking, she was thinking about Jessica, and Daisy's unknown father.

'I wonder who the father is?' she said aloud.

'Whoever the father is, Bev's baby is nothing to do with me any more,' Ian replied.

'No, I meant –' Geraldine broke off in confusion.

Ian had just told her his momentous news, and she was thinking about the case they were working on.

'What?' he asked.

She frowned. 'I was thinking about Jessica and the missing baby.'

Before she could apologise, Ian smiled.

'I know you're just trying to take my mind off my own problems,' he said. 'And you're right, because we have a job to do. We can continue this later, but for now, let's get back to work. What's on your mind, Sergeant?'

'I was just thinking about this kind of situation and the

emotional turbulence it causes, and the anger and resentment it can set off. And I was wondering whether anyone else knew that Jason wasn't the father of Jessica's child.'

'You said she didn't know about it herself.'

'Let's just assume for a moment that she was lying. I'm not convinced she's a hundred per cent reliable and, in any case, as you said, a woman with a child might convince herself it's justifiable to behave badly if she thinks it's in the interests of the child. So let's imagine that Jessica *did* know Jason wasn't the father of her child. Who might she have told? Jason? Her mother? Her father? The biological father of her child?'

Ian nodded slowly. 'Jason might have fatally injured the baby in a fit of anger on learning he wasn't the father. Or Jessica and the father might have been keen to conceal the truth.'

'By stealing the baby and killing Jason to prevent him from telling anyone? It seems a bit extreme.'

'I wonder who the biological father is,' Ian said, repeating Geraldine's question.

So far Jessica had insisted she didn't know the identity of the father, but she might break down and give them a name if she thought that would help them to find Daisy. It was too late to question David, but no one had yet asked Anne if she knew anything about Daisy's father. It was a tenuous lead. Anne probably believed Jason had been Daisy's father, but it was worth asking her, just in case she knew the truth. Jason had been killed at around the time Daisy had disappeared, so there was a possibility that Daisy's father had come to abduct her and killed Jason for trying to stop him. How that tied in with David's murder was as yet unclear. Perhaps Jessica had told David about her affair with Daisy's father. If the unknown father had taken Daisy, he might have silenced David to prevent him from betraying his identity to the police. As Geraldine and Ian discussed the theory, it began to seem vaguely possible.

'It's all very murky and confusing,' Geraldine said doubtfully, 'but it's as plausible as anything else we've come up with, and it could connect the two murders and the disappearance of the baby.'

'The absent father might be the missing link,' Ian agreed.

Even Eileen conceded it was worth looking into. 'We can't afford to rule anything out, however unlikely,' she said.

# 41

THE FOLLOWING MORNING, EILEEN held an early briefing to go over the reports that had come in since the previous meeting, even though there was nothing new to discuss. They seemed to be doing a lot of talking, without making any progress. Every member of the team appeared frazzled so that for once Geraldine felt completely out of place with her colleagues. She was afraid her happiness would be obvious to everyone. Various officers put forward their theories about the case, each one vaguely plausible and all different. Ariadne suggested that Jason might have abducted Daisy after a violent argument with his wife.

'Perhaps he thought she was unfit to look after a baby. Her own mother described her as emotional, didn't she?' Ariadne concluded. 'And the neighbour told us Jessica and Jason had violent arguments.'

'Anne told me Jessica's "not what might be called level-headed",' Geraldine said, recalling the notes she had made at the time. 'She said Jessica's "very emotional, very difficult and highly strung", and she used the words "unreasonable" and "hysterical" to describe her. And that was a mother talking about her own daughter whose baby had just been abducted.'

'It's a pretty damning opinion,' Eileen remarked. 'Although family members aren't always the kindest judges of one another.'

'If that's what her adoring mother thought of her, Jason might have thought the same about Jessica and decided to take Daisy away from her,' Ariadne said.

A constable suggested Jason might have taken Daisy after learning he wasn't her biological father.

'Why would he want to abduct her because he *wasn't* her father?' Geraldine asked.

'To punish his wife?' Ian suggested with a bitterness probably only Geraldine noticed. 'For six months he helped take care of the baby, never questioning that she was his. He worked hard to support his family. Then he discovered he wasn't the father of the child he had been led to believe was his own daughter. What better way to be revenged on his wife than to take her baby away from her?'

Others dismissed the idea of Jason being responsible for the disappearance of the baby, and thought he might have been murdered because he had witnessed her being taken by her biological father.

'Perhaps he disturbed the father in the act of stealing the baby, and had to be silenced,' another sergeant suggested.

'None of this establishes who took the baby, or why,' Eileen pointed out irascibly. 'We can theorise until we're all blue in the face, but we need evidence to show us what happened.'

The most credible explanation was still that the baby's biological father had found out about his daughter and had come to the house to claim her, and Jason had then been killed trying to stop the real father from taking Daisy away.

'That makes a kind of sense, but where's the evidence to support it?' Eileen repeated, sounding anything but pleased about the way the discussion was going. 'From no leads at all, we're suddenly swamped with theories, and awash with a variety of vaguely plausible suspects. We need to know what happened to that baby. We need proof of what went on. And we need to find her soon.'

David and Jason appeared to have been killed by different people, which meant that, although the victims were closely related, their murders could have been carried out independently of each other. The situation was further complicated by Jason having been killed at around the time Daisy had gone missing.

'We're going to have to treat these three cases as separate crimes and look into each one rigorously and quite independently. If in the course of our investigations we discover a link between them, so much the better. But let's not assume anything, please. Evidence before speculation. And Daisy's disappearance must take precedence over everything else,' Eileen concluded. 'To that end, we need to do everything possible to find out the identity of her father, and we need to speak to him urgently.'

She didn't add that perhaps Daisy was alive and well and being cared for by her biological father, although everyone in the room must have been nursing that hope.

As soon as the briefing finished, Geraldine went to speak to Anne who, predictably enough, denied knowing that Jason was not Daisy's father.

'That's a preposterous suggestion,' Anne replied indignantly on being told the truth.

Sloppily dressed in a faded tracksuit, her hair greasy, she was mourning for her husband, or else pining for her granddaughter. Perhaps both. Geraldine couldn't help feeling sorry for her, despite her attempts to retain professional distance from Anne's circumstances.

'I'm not saying Jason wasn't a good father,' Geraldine said hurriedly. 'But we have to pursue every possible avenue in our efforts to find Daisy, and DNA evidence proves that Jason wasn't your granddaughter's biological parent.'

Anne glared at her. 'Well, I think you should concentrate on looking for whoever killed my husband and not start fabricating nasty stories about my daughter. I'd like you to leave now, please.'

'I'm only telling you the situation –'

'Please leave my house.'

Annoyed with herself for having mishandled the interview, Geraldine returned to the police station. Somehow, since Ian had come back to live with her, she seemed to be losing her grip at work. Resolving to be more careful, she sat down at her desk.

'You're looking cheerful,' Ariadne said. 'Do you fancy having lunch later?'

'Sure,' Geraldine replied, although she would have preferred to eat with Ian.

As it happened, Ian came over as Geraldine and Ariadne sat down together in the canteen.

'Do you mind if I join you?'

'Not at all,' Ariadne said, moving her tray aside to make room for him at the table.

Geraldine nodded and smiled happily at him.

'So,' Ian said, as he stabbed at his food, 'I read your report, Geraldine. You didn't get very far with Anne Armstrong, did you?'

Geraldine shook her head. 'I'm inclined to think Jessica believed Jason was Daisy's father. There was no reason why either of her parents would have suspected otherwise. Anne did seem genuinely shocked when I told her Jason wasn't Daisy's father.'

They chatted about the case, but until they came up with some new leads, there was nothing much more to say. Back at her desk, Geraldine scanned through some reports of women Jessica might have encountered. There was a list of women who had attended the same antenatal class as her. All of them had been questioned, but not one had kept in touch with her. Geraldine glanced through a list of mother and baby classes in the area. Jessica's name did not appear on any of the lists. She looked at the names of women who were looked after by the same health visitor. Without holding out much hope of learning anything new, she decided to speak to her the next day. But first, she had an evening with Ian to enjoy. The aroma from the kitchen was making her mouth water and she realised she was ravenous.

'This must be how normal people live,' she said, when Ian served her a steak he had cooked.

He raised a quizzical eyebrow. 'Normal people? What the hell does that mean?'

She laughed, embarrassed to admit that she had always felt isolated from other people. The sensation of living behind a glass wall probably had something to do with her subconscious sense of distance from her mother. Growing up, she had been aware that her fair-haired sister closely resembled their mother, while she herself had looked and felt different to them. Learning of her adoption had helped to explain her feelings of alienation from her mother, but she had discovered the truth too late to try to change their relationship. Since her mother's death, Geraldine had at least been able to strengthen her bond with her adopted sister, Celia, but she felt closer to Ian than she had ever done with anyone else. The feeling was almost too precious, so that sometimes she woke in the night, caught up in her terror of his leaving her again.

'I don't know what I mean by normal,' she prevaricated. 'But I can tell you this steak looks perfect.'

# 42

GERALDINE WAS DETERMINED TO investigate Jessica's contacts further, so with that in mind she went to see the health visitor again. Mary Spinner was at home that evening, and she invited Geraldine into her house and offered her some tea.

'Do you know whether Jessica was close to any other young mothers?' Geraldine asked when they were seated on chintz armchairs in Mary's neat little front room.

'No one that I was aware of,' the health visitor replied stiffly. 'She seemed to want to keep herself very much to herself. She was a strange girl, really.'

This sounded promising, but when Geraldine pressed her for an explanation of her remark, Mary just repeated that Jessica kept to herself.

'She was only interested in her baby,' she added. 'In fact, I'd say she was quite obsessed with her baby. Of course, that's not uncommon in first time mothers. But –' she hesitated. 'She didn't appear to have anything else in her life. I mean, she had a husband, and she saw a lot of her parents, although it didn't sound as though they got on that well. She was very introverted; I suppose that's what I'm trying to say. Introverted to an unusual degree.'

'Would you say she was depressed?'

'No, I wouldn't say so. Not that I was aware of, anyway. But I did encourage her to get out and about and meet other mothers. It's never a good idea to be isolated with a new baby, especially a first one. I suggested several groups to her, but she seemed very resistant to socialising.' Mary frowned and fiddled with a button on her pale blue cardigan. 'I tried more than once to persuade her to go to a mother and baby group. It would have been good for the baby as well as for her. But she simply wasn't interested. She told me she had friends, but –' she sniffed, 'I didn't altogether believe her. So I persisted and eventually she told me she had joined a group in a local church, but I think she said that just to placate me. Anyway, I decided it was best to leave her to sort herself out. Not everyone wants to be helped,' she added sourly.

'What church was it?' Geraldine asked.

Mary shook her head. 'I'm sorry?'

'You said she joined a group in a local church. Did she mention which church she went to?'

'I really can't remember. There are so many. I don't think she told me which one it was.'

'Are you sure? Please, try to remember.'

But the health visitor shook her head. 'No, I'm sorry. I have an excellent memory for these things, but I really don't think she gave me the name. She was very private like that.'

Geraldine spent the next day researching churches in the locality. Starting with the one closest to Jessica's house, she worked her way through the websites until she found one that ran a weekly mother and baby group. It was within easy walking distance of Jessica's house. Next she tracked down the organiser, who agreed to meet her at the church that afternoon. There was a sign outside the church: 'Parent and baby drop-in session with toys and tea in a welcoming, safe environment. Come in and chat to other parents every Tuesday 11am-1pm'.

The organiser of the group was called Mandy. A confident, well turned-out woman in her twenties, she had a shrill voice and a forceful manner. Geraldine noticed she was holding a folder under her arm.

'Yes, I run the mother and baby group,' Mandy said. 'Is there a problem? Only any complaints should strictly speaking come to me in the first instance, and I'm not aware of anything that could require police intervention. We're all volunteers running the group –'

'No, no, there's been no complaint. Nothing like that,' Geraldine hastened to reassure her. 'We're interested in having a word with a woman we believe came to your gathering here, at least once. We're having difficulty tracing her, and we're hoping you might be able to point us in the right direction.'

Mandy frowned, but she didn't remonstrate. 'Well, come in, and I'll show you the hall where we hold our meetings. But I'm not sure I can do more than that.'

Once they were inside, Geraldine showed her a photograph of Jessica.

'Do you recognise her?'

Mandy frowned. 'Yes, I think I may have seen her here a couple of times, but I never spoke to her. She wasn't exactly sociable.'

That sounded like Jessica.

'She was with another oddball – sorry, another mother who didn't seem to want to talk to anyone. Why would they come here if they didn't want to join in? We're a very friendly group of women, and we're all in the same boat, stuck at home a lot of the time with our babies. Who wouldn't welcome the chance of a friendly chat?'

Geraldine felt a frisson of excitement, wondering who the other oddball was, and how well she had known Jessica. She kept her expression impassive as she asked for the other mother's name.

Mandy shook her head. 'Sorry, I don't know.'

'Do you keep a record of the people who come along?'

'No, only if they are regulars and want to be on our mailing list for notification about dates of meetings, and we have an

242

online second-hand toy exchange. No one makes any money out of it,' she added quickly. 'Jessica and her friend didn't come often enough for me to ask if they wanted to be on the mailing list.'

Geraldine hid her disappointment.

'Can you describe her?'

'I can do more than that,' Mandy answered with a bright smile, clearly pleased that she was finally able to help.

Opening her phone, she scrolled through a long series of photographs until she found the one she was searching for.

'I've only got this one of them.'

Studying the screen, Geraldine saw an image of a group of smiling women. Two women were sitting to one side of the group, away from the others. One of the pair was Jessica. The other was a skinny blonde girl with a frightened expression.

'Can you send me a copy of this?'

Mandy hesitated.

'I only need the image of those two women.'

'I suppose I could crop it –'

'No, please don't alter the image in any way. There's a chance we may be able to isolate one section and enhance it sufficiently, if you send it in its original format.'

When Mandy continued to hesitate, Geraldine added, 'If you don't feel comfortable sending me the image, I can take your phone and –'

'You can't take my phone!'

'Or you can bring it to the police station yourself. My car's outside and I can drive you there right away. This needs to be done as soon as possible,' she added. 'A child's welfare could be at stake,' she added vaguely, 'so we do need to have that image from you, one way or another.'

With a sniff, Mandy asked for the address where she could email the photo. With the image safely on her phone and forwarded to the Visual Images, Identifications and

Detections Office, with instructions about what she wanted, Geraldine thanked Mandy for her help and took her leave.

'Wait,' Mandy detained her at the door. 'What's this about? It's not got anything to do with that missing baby, has it?'

'No,' Geraldine lied.

It was the quickest way to extricate herself and she was in a hurry to track down Jessica's companion. The simplest course would have been to ask Jessica directly for details of the unknown woman, but some instinct warned Geraldine to pursue this without telling anyone outside the police team.

As soon as she was back in her car, she spoke to an officer in the Visual Images, Identifications and Detections Office. 'I just sent you an image. Are you clear about what I want? I'm interested in the two women sitting on the extreme right of the picture. There are two women sitting apart from the group, and it's the one on the very end of the row that I need to see more clearly. Can you do something with the image? I know it's a bit blurred. It was taken on a phone.'

'Leave it with us,' her colleague replied. 'I'm sure we can enhance it so you can see her clearly; enough to identify her anyway.'

# 43

THE TEAM AT THE Visual Images, Identifications and Detections Office were as good as their word. Soon after Geraldine arrived back at her desk, they sent her an image of Jessica and another woman seated beside her. Neither of the two women in the picture appeared to be talking, they both looked fairly glum and they were holding babies who looked around the same age. Geraldine studied the image of Jessica's companion, an emaciated girl with lank blonde hair which she had probably dyed herself, because the dark roots were uneven. She looked fragile, and could have been anorexic, with her stick-like limbs and painfully thin body. Her face was covered in pimples and she had an unhealthy appearance. Geraldine wondered whether she might be a drug addict. Her large pale eyes were her only attractive feature. At a first glance it was difficult to see what smartly-dressed Jessica might have in common with the thin girl, other than their babies possibly being the same age, and the fact that they were both somehow isolated from the group of women who were chatting a few seats away.

Geraldine wasted no time in organising a team to question every midwife, hospital and local doctor's surgery in the vicinity, hoping to discover details of Jessica's companion. Armed with the photograph, Geraldine set off to speak to some local gynaecologists herself. She showed the photograph to every member of the team attached to the maternity unit at the hospital in York, explaining that she was looking for a young woman who had given birth around six or seven months earlier.

Whoever she asked returned the same answer. 'I'm sorry, I don't recognise her.'

'Mothers do sometimes look a bit different when we see them in here,' one of the gynaecologists added, with an apologetic smile. 'They're not always at their best, in terms of grooming.'

The other members of Geraldine's team had similar responses to their enquiries. It seemed that Jessica's friend had not given birth in York. They would have to widen the net if they were going to find the unknown woman who had befriended Jessica. But when Geraldine showed the photograph to Jessica's health visitor, she finally received a positive response.

'Oh yes, I know who that is,' Mary said at once. 'It's —' she broke off and paused, frowning.

Geraldine waited, hiding her impatience.

'Yes, it's coming back to me. Her name's Ella,' the health visitor said at last.

'Ella?'

'Yes.'

'What's her other name?'

'Just a minute.'

Mary went and fetched her laptop.

'Ella Wilson.' She read out an address. 'I never forget a face, but names do sometimes escape me. I see so many of these young mothers,' she explained apologetically. 'And when I haven't seen them for a while, it's easy to forget their names.'

'When did you last see Ella?'

'I haven't seen her for at least three months.'

'Why not? Has she moved?'

'Well, I wouldn't know about that, because I haven't seen her.'

'But why not?'

246

Mary gazed at her solemnly. 'I haven't seen her since her baby died. It was a terrible tragedy. A cot death. There was nothing anyone could have done. These things happen – rarely, thank goodness. Of course, the poor woman was in a state. I tried to arrange some support for her, but she didn't want to know. She sent us away with very firm instructions not to bother her again. I tried a couple of times, but she always turned me away. I had to accept there was nothing more I could do for her, and I haven't seen her since.'

'Are you sure she lost her baby?'

Mary gave her a strange look. 'Of course I'm sure. It's not the kind of thing you can forget. The poor woman was distraught. But, like I said, she didn't want any help, at least not from me or any bereavement counsellor. I did try. Such a tragedy.'

'A cot death?' Geraldine repeated.

'Yes, although Ella wasn't exactly what you might call a fit mother,' Mary replied. 'She refused home visits and she smoked, although she emphatically denied it, and I'm sure she drank, and the baby was small for her age, and always sickly looking without actually being ill.'

Geraldine didn't wait to hear any more. There was only a slim chance Ella might know where Daisy was, but it was still a chance. With Ella's address stored on her phone, she logged a report and went to find Jessica's friend. She waited for a few minutes on the doorstep but there was no answer so eventually she gave up and left, intending to return in the evening. If she still didn't find Ella at home, she would return very early the following morning and keep trying until she tracked her down. Calling at the police station on her way, she went home to wait for Ian.

He was slightly less excited about Geraldine's lead than she was.

'Well done for managing to trace a friend of Jessica's,

but, really, so what? I'm not quite sure what you expect this woman to be able to tell us,' he said. 'It's not as if we're still looking for Jessica. We know where she is and we've heard everything she has to tell us. Is Ella likely to add anything that might help us find the missing baby, or work out who killed Jason? I'm sorry, but I can't see where you're going with this.'

Geraldine did her best to hide her disappointment at Ian's lukewarm response to her painstaking detective work.

'We don't know what Ella might have to tell us,' she pointed out. 'We haven't spoken to her yet. But it's possible Jessica might have confided in her and told her something that can help us resolve this case. We have to try anyway.'

'Yes, of course. I'm not for one moment suggesting you shouldn't follow it up. I'm just not quite sure why you're so excited about it.'

'I'm not excited,' Geraldine lied. 'That is, I am, but I don't know why. Like you said, she probably won't have anything useful to tell us.'

'By saying she probably won't, you mean you think she possibly might,' Ian said, smiling at her. 'Well, let's hope your instincts are right and she can tell us something we don't already know.'

Geraldine had an uncomfortable feeling that Ian was privately laughing at her optimism. She didn't mind. If he was right, and she was allowing herself to indulge in a vain hope, they would have lost nothing. But there remained a slim chance that Ella might be able to add a tiny piece to the puzzle that was currently perplexing them all. That evening, after supper, she drove back to Ella's house but once again there was no answer when she rang the bell. She waited around for a while and then went home to Ian who was reading a history book while he waited for her.

'Don't stop reading on my account,' she said.

'I was just passing the time until you returned,' he replied. 'Shall we have a nightcap before we turn in?'

'Sounds like a good idea.'

They went out on to her balcony and sat facing the river in companionable silence. The night was peaceful and, for a while, Geraldine forgot about the grim details of the case they were working on, as she gazed at the moonlight glinting on the water, pleasantly conscious of Ian sitting beside her.

# 44

THE FOLLOWING MORNING, GERALDINE got up early, leaving Ian in bed.

'Where are you going?' he demanded sleepily. 'It's Saturday. You're not working today.'

He reached out and grabbed her by the arm as she sat on the bed to put on her socks. She laughed as he tugged her gently towards him, and was tempted to climb back into the warmth of his embrace.

'I want to follow up on a possible lead,' she replied.

'You and your leads,' he mumbled, as he nuzzled her neck. 'What is it this time?'

'Ella.'

'Oh yes, the woman who befriended Jessica,' he murmured sleepily. 'Can't she wait?'

Thinking that Ella was more likely to be home early in the day, Geraldine resisted Ian and set off. Ella lived on the ground floor of a dingy house in a row of terraced properties near the Holgate Road. When Geraldine rang the bell, no one answered the door. She peered in the window, trying to see through a gap in the grey net curtains, but the flat appeared to be deserted. It was not yet eight o'clock in the morning, so she supposed Ella was not yet up. Whatever the reason, she wasn't answering the door, so Geraldine drove to the police station to do some work and returned two hours later. Once again no one opened the door when she rang the bell and rapped on the door. She tried tapping at the window, but the place appeared to be empty.

The following day, when she arrived to try again, a neighbour from the flat upstairs flung open a window and demanded to know who was calling. Geraldine explained she was looking for Ella.

'Ella? Are you talking about that skinny girl who lives downstairs?'

'Yes. I don't suppose you happen to know when she'll be in?'

The woman shook her head, 'I haven't seen her around for a few days.'

'When did you last see her?'

'I don't know. Last week, maybe. Did you say you know her?' The neighbour glared suspiciously down at her.

Geraldine decided it was time to introduce herself. The woman upstairs looked startled, then slammed her window shut. As Geraldine was wondering whether to ring the bell for the upstairs flat, the front door opened and she saw Ella's neighbour, arms akimbo, squinting inquisitively at her. Wearing a towelling dressing gown, she looked as though she had just got out of bed.

'What's she done?' she demanded.

'I'm afraid I can't discuss that with you.'

'Listen, I live here and if there's something going on I have a right to know. That woman lives right underneath me and if the police are coming here I want to know why. What's she done?'

'Would you like to go inside so we can talk more discreetly?'

The woman grumbled loudly but did not move to let Geraldine enter.

'Well?' she demanded. 'You haven't told me what this is about yet.'

Standing on the doorstep, Geraldine explained that the police thought Ella might be able to help them with an enquiry, adding vaguely that they were investigating one of Ella's acquaintances. Geraldine was keen to keep the neighbour talking, in case she had anything useful to add to what little the health visitor had told her about Ella.

'Who's that then?'

'I'm afraid I'm not at liberty to say any more than that. I probably shouldn't even have told you that much, so please keep this to yourself,' Geraldine added, lowering her voice.

She hoped her masquerade of sharing confidential information might encourage the woman to speak more freely to her, but the woman merely grunted.

'Do you have any idea where Ella might have gone?'

'I told you, I haven't seen them for about a week, and that's all I know.'

'Who else was living here with her?'

'No one.'

'You just said there was someone else in the flat.'

'No, I didn't.'

'You said "them"?'

'Just her and the baby,' the woman explained.

'Baby?'

'Yes, she's got a young baby about six months old.'

Geraldine felt a tremor of foreboding. 'When did you last see them?'

'Oh, I don't know.'

'Was it more recently than, say, several months ago?'

'I just told you, I saw them a few days ago.'

Geraldine spoke very deliberately. 'And you're sure you saw Ella, the woman who lives here, and her baby? Was it just the two of them? There wasn't anyone else with them?'

The neighbour stared at Geraldine in surprise. 'No, it was just the two of them. And she had her baby with her. I know what I saw, and it's her baby all right.'

'Are you sure it was her baby you saw with her?'

'Unless there's another baby living with her that cries all night every bloody night –'

The woman broke off and an expression of alarm spread over her face. Perhaps she too was thinking of the reports in the media about a missing baby.

'No, that's fine,' Geraldine hastened to reassure her, worried that the neighbour might be in contact with Ella and alert her to the fact that the police were interested in the identity of the baby she was looking after. 'It's not her or her baby we're investigating, but someone else we think she might know. Can you tell me where I might find her?'

'I just told you, I've no idea. Like I said, I haven't seen her for a few days.'

Not since Ella decided to disappear with the baby she had abducted, Geraldine thought.

She handed the other woman her card. 'Thank you, you've been very helpful. If you see Ella, please don't tell her we were here asking for her. I don't want to frighten her off.' She forced a smile in an attempt to reassure the neighbour. 'This is merely a routine enquiry, but if you could give me a ring to let me know when she comes home, that would be really helpful.'

From the expression on the woman's face, Geraldine guessed she was more likely to warn Ella the police were looking for her than contact them, but she had to try.

'You did what you could,' Ian reassured Geraldine when she went straight back to the flat and told him what had happened. 'And now, it's the weekend and time you took a break from the case. You'll only get yourself worn out and frazzled, and a tired officer isn't a good officer. Come on, let's get a coffee, and perhaps we can go for a drive.'

'A drive? What are you talking about? Where are we going to drive to?'

He shrugged, smiling. 'I don't know. I thought we might

go out for lunch somewhere off the beaten track. Just spend a few hours together –'

'Ian, you're not listening to me, Ella's done a runner –'

'Geraldine, she's not at home. You can try again on Monday, but she probably won't know what happened to Jessica's baby. Why would she?'

'Ella's neighbour saw her with a baby just a few days ago, and the baby has been crying there at night. Ian, Jessica's health visitor told me Ella's baby died three months ago –'

Ian's jaw dropped. 'Come on, then,' he snapped, grabbing his phone. 'What are we waiting for? Let's get to work. Once we're sure the health visitor's story checks out, we'll start a full-scale hunt for Ella and the baby she's taken with her.'

# 45

An URGENT SENSE OF purpose pervaded the police station which buzzed with people talking on the phone, typing furiously, and hurrying along corridors. A message had been sent to all UK airports and mainline stations, bus depots and taxi companies, anyone who might be able to intercept a young woman seeking to move around with a baby.

With the hunt for Ella underway, Geraldine went to speak to Jessica again, to find out whether she might know where Ella might be. She found her at Anne's house.

'Where is she?' Anne cried out, once they were all seated. 'Where's my granddaughter? We need you to find her.'

Geraldine refrained from mentioning that the police had a lead which suggested Daisy was alive and well. It would be too cruel if she was mistaken in her suspicions of Ella, and the baby she was caring for was not Daisy after all.

'We're still looking for her,' Geraldine said. She turned to Jessica. 'We'd like to talk to you about a woman called Ella.'

Jessica shook her head as though she didn't understand. She went very pale and her lips moved wordlessly.

'When did you last see Ella?' Geraldine asked, very gently, as though she was speaking to a frightened child.

'Ella?' Jessica echoed faintly. 'Who's Ella?'

'Yes, who's Ella?' Anne demanded. 'What has she got to do with any of this? Has she taken Daisy?'

'You have a friend called Ella,' Geraldine said.

'I don't know anyone called Ella,' Jessica replied.

Licking her lips nervously, she returned Geraldine's level gaze with a hostile glare. Geraldine held out a blown-up photograph of Jessica and Ella sitting together. The images had been enhanced and both faces were very clear.

Jessica nodded. 'Oh yes, Ella,' she whispered. 'I remember her now. We met at the church.'

'Why did you just tell me you didn't know her?' Geraldine asked.

'I forgot,' Jessica answered. 'I mean, I remember her, but I didn't know she was called Ella. She must have told me her name, but I forgot. I scarcely knew her. I only met her...' she hesitated. 'I only met her a couple of times. It was at a mother and baby group in a church,' she added by way of explanation. 'We were sitting next to each other and our babies were about the same age, so we talked a bit. But not much. I don't really know her.'

After listening carefully, Geraldine asked Jessica whether she knew where Ella lived.

Jessica shook her head.

'We weren't close. We weren't what you might call friends. I just happened to bump into her at the group and we started chatting about our babies, as you do. That's all there was to it. I haven't seen her for months. We didn't fall out or anything, but I stopped going to the group. It wasn't for me. I don't know if she kept on going. We never kept in touch. I only saw her there twice, I think, and we only spoke to each other once.'

'You didn't hear from her again?' Geraldine asked.

Jessica shook her head and began to cry.

Anne stepped in. 'What is all this about, Sergeant? What's this woman Ella got to do with us? All we're interested in is finding Daisy.'

'We all want to find Daisy,' Geraldine replied softly.

'Yes, well, Jessica's answered your questions, and told you she hardly knew the woman you're asking about. So can we please focus on what matters. You can see how upset my daughter is. So never mind anything else, what are you doing to find my granddaughter?'

She gave an anxious glance at Jessica who was crying hysterically.

'I'm sorry, but we don't yet know where Daisy is,' Geraldine said. 'But any friend or acquaintance of Jessica's may possibly be able to help us. We need to question them all.'

'She was never my friend,' Jessica mumbled through her hands. 'I hardly knew her. Where's my baby?' Her voice rose to a wail. 'I want my baby. I want my baby back!'

'Where is she?' Anne shouted, rising to her feet and seeming to lose her temper. 'Where's Daisy? We need her back. If you know where she is, you have to bring her back to us right now. Or I'll go and get her myself. Where is she?'

'That's what we're trying to find out,' Geraldine replied. 'That's why we're keen to speak to everyone who ever met Jessica, in an attempt to find out where Daisy could be. Jessica, do you have any idea where Ella might be?'

Jessica shook her head.

'Did she ever mention any other friend to you? A boyfriend, perhaps? Did she tell you the name of the father of her own baby, or say anything about him? Anything at all that might help us to trace him? She could have gone to him.'

Jessica was crying too hard to answer.

'Sergeant,' Anne said, 'my daughter has already told you she knows nothing about this woman. Now can we please focus on finding Daisy?'

'It's possible Ella may be able to help us,' Geraldine replied. 'Until we find her, we can't be sure she can't help us.'

'Why aren't you out looking for her then? What are you doing here, pestering my daughter like this?'

Geraldine hid a spasm of irritation. If this interview was challenging for her, it was even more difficult for the missing baby's mother and grandmother. Recently widowed, their situations were truly awful, while Geraldine was just trying to cope with the familiar frustrations of her work. Quietly she explained that a major manhunt was under way, but still all the police really knew so far was that Daisy was missing.

'We're conducting an extensive search.'

'So what you're saying is, you have no idea at all where Daisy could be,' Anne snapped.

'Not yet, no. But we want to speak to anyone who met Jessica, and find out whether they have anything that might help us.'

Anne sniffed. 'Grasping at straws,' she muttered.

'Perhaps, but we're hoping that, sooner or later, one of those straws will lead us to Daisy,' Geraldine said.

# 46

SOMEONE HAD BEEN RINGING the bell, but Ella had stopped opening the door. She didn't want to see anyone. If she hadn't run out of supplies, she would never have gone out again. Now that she had left the flat, she knew she couldn't go back. Turning away from the counter in her local corner shop, she filled her basket with nappies, wet wipes, packets of SMA and jars of baby food before hurrying back to the counter to pay. Pulling her hood further down over her eyes and praying the baby wouldn't make a noise and draw attention to them, she handed over the cash, grabbed her change and fled. She was still feeling shocked and shaky from seeing her own face staring back at her from the front page of a local newspaper. Luckily the young man behind the counter didn't appear to have looked at it, or at least didn't recognise her beneath her hood.

A steady drizzle was falling, but Lily was well protected beneath her rain cover. In fact, she was probably fast asleep because she was so quiet, no doubt lulled by the soothing motion of the pushchair. As she limped hurriedly along the street, cursing her aching knee, Ella turned over various possibilities in her mind. There was only one person she knew who might be relatively unaware of the details of the news story about a missing baby. Without having seen any of the photographs splashed all over the front pages of local newspapers and no doubt shown on the news on television, Christine might have no idea that Ella was being chased by the police. There was no reason why she would suspect the unlikely truth.

The bus dropped Ella and Lily about a mile from her schoolfriend's address. By the time Ella found the house she was looking for she was tired, her knee was throbbing and her shoulders ached from pushing the buggy. A lamp in the narrow porch lit up the front door, and she found the bell easily. If Christine turned her away, she would have nowhere else to go; nowhere she would be safe, that was. Daylight was fading fast as she rang the bell a second time, praying that Christine was at home.

She breathed a cautious sigh of relief when Christine opened the door on the chain, eyes scanning the air in front of her with rapid irregular movements in a way that Ella remembered. She used to join in the mockery of her blind classmate when they were at school together, and now she found herself automatically rotating her own eyes to mirror Christine's wandering gaze.

'Christine,' she blurted out, and paused.

'Yes? Who is it?'

'Christine, it's Ella, from school.'

'Ella?'

In the light overhead she saw a faint frown flicker across Christine's face.

'Yes, you remember me, Ella Wilson. We were at school together.'

'Of course I remember you.'

There was a bitter timbre in the blind girl's voice. It was hardly a warm greeting.

'What do you want, Ella?'

Ella decided it was best to be as honest as the truth would allow.

'I – I need your help,' she said simply.

Christine began to close the door. As if she realised this

was a critical moment, the baby woke up and began to howl.

'Is that a baby?' Christine asked, halting in surprise.

'Yes, she's mine and we have nowhere to go and it's raining,' Ella said quickly. 'If you don't let us in I don't know where else we can go at this time of night, in the dark and the rain.' The baby was crying more loudly. 'She's called Lily,' Ella added.

Too late, it occurred to her that she should have given Christine a different name. The police would know she had a baby called Lily, and they were looking for her. But as she had hoped, Christine seemed oblivious of the police interest in her new visitor, and barely seemed to register the baby's name.

'Oh well, you'd better come in then,' she said, releasing the chain and opening the door. 'At least until the rain gives over.'

'Do you live here by yourself?' Ella asked, and then kicked herself for putting a question that sounded so suspicious. Christine might think she had come there to rob her. 'It's just that my baby is very wary of men,' she added quickly. 'She won't settle if there's a man in the house.'

Remembering the back story she had fabricated, Ella was already laying the groundwork. But, more importantly, she had to know if anyone else lived in the house. If so, they would almost certainly have seen her face plastered all over the news.

'You're all right, there's no need to worry,' Christine answered, taking a step back to allow Ella to enter the house. 'It's just me here. I have a friend who drops by every week to check I'm all right, and there are plenty of people I can call on if I need anything, but I manage fine on my own. I've always been independent. School taught me how to cope on my own,' she added.

If Christine felt bitter towards Ella for the years of bullying she had endured, she didn't show it.

'I'm sorry if we gave you a hard time,' Ella said cautiously, feeling her way.

She didn't want to set off an emotional row. She just wanted somewhere safe to stay, with someone who would not have seen her picture in the news.

'Oh, that's all water under the bridge now,' Christine assured her, a trifle too heartily for Ella's comfort. 'We were children then.'

'Yes, but we still should have known better.'

The baby let out a loud cry and Christine frowned. 'Is she all right?'

'She's hungry,' Ella replied, thinking, 'We both are.'

'You'd better come through and feed her and then we can have a chat and catch-up and you can tell me what you're doing here.'

Christine led her into a living room and gestured to an armchair. 'I think you'll be comfortable there?'

Ella realised that Christine was expecting her to breast feed the baby. She wanted to. She had tried. But her milk had disappeared a while ago, and nothing she had done had caused it to return. Those days were over.

'I need to heat up some milk,' she said. 'Is there any chance you could hold her while I prepare a bottle?'

She took what she needed from her backpack as quickly as she could and found her way to the kitchen. Lily meanwhile was screaming loudly. Hurriedly fumbling with the teat, Ella ran back into the living room. She didn't want Christine's neighbours to hear the baby crying and become curious. The baby stopped crying as soon as her lips fastened on the teat.

'People might think it was the television,' she said, unintentionally voicing her thoughts aloud.

'What's that?'

'Oh, nothing.'

'Would you like some tea?' Christine asked and went to put the kettle on.

'Are you sure you can manage?' Ella called after her.

Christine grunted and didn't bother to reply. By the time she returned with a tray of tea, Ella had finished feeding and changing the baby, who was contentedly gurgling in her arms.

'Do you want to hold her again?' she asked. 'She's happier now.'

Christine held out her arms and Ella carefully passed Lily over, keeping her own hands beneath the baby until she was sure Christine was holding her securely. Glancing at Christine's happy expression, Ella began to relax for the first time since she had seen her photograph in the local paper. She hadn't stopped to read the article, but she could imagine what it said. Only when Christine switched the television on did she rouse herself from her pleasant doze.

'Can we change the channel?' she asked, worried that the news might pop up after the quiz programme Christine had put on.

'What would you like to watch?'

Christine turned her head in the direction of Ella's voice, her eyes moving rapidly as though she was annoyed.

'I'm sorry, did you want to watch this?' Ella asked. 'Only Lily prefers cartoons.'

Christine's expression softened and she held the remote control out in Ella's direction. As she switched channel, Ella thought about what had just happened. There was no reason why Christine would be pleased about Ella turning up out of the blue like that, asking to stay, but she definitely enjoyed holding the baby.

'She likes you,' Ella said. 'She won't stay with most people. I can't believe she isn't crying.'

'What happened?' Christine asked quietly. 'Who are you running away from?'

Ella heaved a loud sigh. 'It's my husband,' she lied. 'He's always been bad-tempered. He can be violent. I kept meaning to leave him but then Lily came along and he promised to be different. But he didn't change. People never do.'

She glanced apprehensively at Christine, afraid she had reminded her of their time at school together.

'Not once they're adults anyway,' she amended her statement. 'Anyway, I was afraid he might hurt Lily, so I ran away.'

Christine frowned, considering what she had heard. Ella held her breath.

'You ought to report him,' Christine said at last, in a decided tone of voice. 'You can get the police to issue an injunction against him.'

'What does that do?'

'It means he isn't allowed to come anywhere near you and if he does he can be arrested. You can't let him near the baby. And you shouldn't let him hit you, for that matter.'

'I know; you're right. He kept promising he would change, and I kept giving him another chance, and another one. But with Lily it's different. If he lays a finger on her, he could kill her. She's so tiny. I had to get her away from there. I had to bring her somewhere he wouldn't find me. So you mustn't tell anyone we're here, not until I've figured out what to do.'

'You did the right thing,' Christine said. 'We'll keep her safe. No one's going to hurt her. We won't let them.'

'I can't believe she's settled so readily with you.'

Christine let out a grunt of contentment as she felt the warm bundle resting in her arms. Smiling, she stroked Lily's tiny fingers and Ella congratulated herself on having had the wit to find a safe haven, while outside the police continued hunting helplessly for her.

# 47

WITHIN HOURS, DNA EVIDENCE found at Ella's flat had been confirmed as a match for Daisy. They knew who had taken Jessica's baby, but now Ella had vanished.

'It can't be that easy for a woman to disappear with a baby,' a constable said.

Several other officers agreed.

'Assuming she still has Daisy with her,' Geraldine muttered, voicing everyone's worst fear.

Panicking and alone, Ella might have realised the game was up. On her own she might be able to avoid attention, but with a young baby to care for wherever she went, her chances of escaping detection were slim. Clearly she was deranged to have kidnapped a baby in the first place, which meant her plans might be erratic at best, and certainly unpredictable. If she had decided to ditch Daisy, after leaving her flat off Holgate Street, there was no way of knowing what she might have done with the baby. The outlook for Daisy was not looking positive, and the longer Ella remained at large, the more of a danger she was going to pose, whether to Daisy, or to anyone else, including possibly any other baby she chanced to come across. At the risk of causing widespread panic, Eileen decided to give a statement to the media. It was a tricky subject, and Geraldine was concerned about what the detective chief inspector was planning to say, and how sensibly the media would report the story. Lurid headlines of a baby snatcher would not help the investigation.

That evening Geraldine and Ian watched the local news headlines at home. The first item involved a fight outside a pub where two drunken youths had ended up in hospital. That was followed by a brief mention of David Armstrong, whose death was considered newsworthy since he had been a public figure of some standing. After that, a photograph of Ella appeared on the screen.

'Police are looking for a young mother who might be in trouble and in urgent need of medical assistance,' the presenter said evenly. 'She goes by the name of Ella, although she may be using a false identity, and she is believed to be travelling with a baby. If anyone knows where she is, please contact your local police station without delay, or call the number displayed on the screen.'

It was a neat way of asking for information, without focusing on the missing baby at the heart of the investigation. There was no point in mentioning Daisy by name. Ella was probably using a false name for herself and Daisy, if she still had her.

Geraldine would have liked to work on finding Daisy. Even though a murderer – possibly two – could be on the loose, the missing baby seemed more urgent a case. But there was not much she could do. A massive hunt was now under way, with numerous officers drafted in from surrounding forces to help with the door-to-door questioning, the search of the area surrounding Ella's lodgings, and the scrutiny of hours and hours of closed circuit television film from local stations and bus stops. So far no positive sighting had been made, but the search was not going to be called off until every inch of the vicinity had been explored.

Meanwhile, Geraldine was sent to speak to the Armstrongs' doctor. The surgery was not far from the police station. It was a lovely day, and she would have liked to walk there, but she couldn't afford to spend the time so unproductively. She arrived at the surgery and went straight up to the reception desk, where a couple of people were waiting.

'Hey, there's a queue,' a disgruntled patient called out.

Without acknowledging the complainant, Geraldine held up her identity card to the receptionist and asked to speak to the relevant doctor.

'Do you have an appointment?' the young woman behind the desk replied.

Geraldine sighed. When she had first been promoted to the rank of detective inspector, she had quite enjoyed parading her position. These days it just felt dreary. She wasn't sure if that change was due to the response she received from the public, who seemed increasingly hostile towards the police, or if it was because she herself had become less excited about her role since her demotion. Probably it was a combination of the two. Now she held up her identity card again, right in front of the receptionist's eyes.

'Kindly take your eyes off your screen for a second and look at this, and then I'd like to speak to Dr Merrill as soon as his current appointment finishes.'

The receptionist frowned and began to trot out her practised response. 'I'm afraid you'll have to wait your turn –'

'Listen,' Geraldine said quietly, 'I don't want to have to charge you with wasting police time and obstructing the course of an investigation into a serious crime, but I should warn you that's the way this conversation seems to be heading.'

The receptionist glared at her. 'I'll call the practice manager,' she said. 'Please take a seat.'

'So you're still asking me to wait? Listen, I need to speak to Dr Merrill as soon as possible, and neither you nor your practice manager is going to cause me any further delay. As soon as the patient who is with him right now leaves his consulting room, I want to speak to him.'

'I'm calling the police,' someone shouted out.

Geraldine turned round. 'Yes, please do that,' she replied loudly, holding up her identity card. 'And please tell them that I need the nearest patrol car here right away, so that two uniformed constables can close the surgery until we've finished our enquiry.' She turned back to the receptionist. 'Or you can tell Dr Merrill I'd like to speak to him right away. It's up to you.'

An older woman came bustling out of a door behind the reception desk.

'What seems to be the trouble?' she asked.

Once again, Geraldine held up her identity card and lowered her voice. 'I need to speak to Dr Merrill, and your receptionist seems to think it's your practice policy to obstruct the police in conducting an enquiry into a serious crime.' She flipped open her phone. 'You have my location. I need a couple of uniformed officers to help me out here with a situation, and we'll need to charge a couple of ladies with obstruction –'

'No, no, wait!' the practice manager cried out in alarm. 'There's no need for any of that. Of course you can see the doctor right away. This way, please. And please, cancel that request. This is all a misunderstanding.' She turned and glared at the receptionist.

Muttering 'Cancel that' into her unconnected phone, Geraldine followed the manager along the corridor to a consulting room. As soon as a patient emerged, the manager ushered Geraldine into the room.

'This is a detective sergeant,' the woman said, anxious to smooth over the disagreement. 'She would like to ask you a few questions.'

'Are you a patient?' the doctor asked.

'I'm here in a professional capacity.' Geraldine turned to the manager. 'I'd like to speak to the doctor alone.'

Mumbling under her breath, the manager left.

'I'm part of the team investigating the death of a patient of yours, David Armstrong,' Geraldine explained.

'Oh yes, of course. Please, take a seat. How can I help you, although I have to tell you I've already been questioned at length and have nothing further to add to what I've already said.'

'I appreciate you have patients waiting and won't take up much of your time,' Geraldine said as she sat down. 'What we need to know is: did you recently prescribe any drugs containing cetirizine to David or Anne Armstrong?'

The doctor frowned. 'Cetirizine can be purchased over the counter for allergy relief,' he replied. 'It's not necessary to have a prescription.'

He turned and consulted his computer. After a moment he turned back to Geraldine, frowning.

'Thirteen years ago, David Armstrong was admitted to hospital suffering a severe reaction to a drug containing cetirizine. It's unusual to experience such a severe reaction, but by no means unheard of. He had somehow contrived to take an overdose, as a result of which he was no longer able to tolerate it in any significant quantity.'

Geraldine drew in a deep breath. 'And his wife would have been aware of that?'

'Well, he was admitted to hospital,' the doctor replied gravely. 'Of course, you may not be at liberty to share the implications of this with me, but if there's anything else I can do to help, please don't hesitate to ask.'

Thanking him, and with his assurance that he would not mention the subject of their discussion to anyone, Geraldine left. She was aware of the receptionist glaring balefully at her as she passed the desk, but she was too busy on her phone to react.

# 48

HAVING CALLED IN AT the police station to report her findings, Geraldine went home. While the hunt for Ella continued, Geraldine and Ian were focusing on looking into everyone who might have had any dealings with the two murder victims. Despite living and working side by side, Geraldine and Ian had not spent much time together since Ian had moved back in with her four days earlier. At the police station they focused on their individual allotted tasks, and when they were not at work they inevitably found themselves drawn into discussing the case. Geraldine didn't mind, but when Ian complained they were 'living and breathing work twenty-four seven', she wondered whether he was beginning to regret having moved in with her.

Over a late breakfast, as they discussed their plans for the day, she wondered how the conversation might have gone if they had not been investigating a double murder, and whether Ian was thinking the same.

'What do you suppose we might be doing today if we weren't both working?' she asked.

Ian's puzzled frown made it clear that he had not been considering the same question.

'We *are* working. We're always bloody working.'

'I know, but if we weren't on a case right now, what would you be wanting to do?'

He smiled, gathering her drift. 'We would still be in bed. Asleep,' he added quickly, seeing her grin. 'We'd get up late –'

'And go out for breakfast,' she interrupted.

'Somewhere out of town,' he said. 'We'd drive to a village and sit outside an old pub, quaffing beer.'

'Outside with all the smokers,' she said, 'drinking beer for breakfast.' She laughed. 'Maybe we should stick to work after all. Your suggestion doesn't sound too healthy.'

Ian laughed too. Watching him, she was gratified to see that he seemed to be recovering his usual good humour.

'No one has been back to question Jason's work colleagues after the initial flurry of activity,' Ian said. 'I wonder whether we ought to do some more digging?'

Geraldine grunted. Jason's colleagues had of course been notified about his death when his body was discovered four days earlier. They had been told that he was the victim of a fatal accident, but not that he had been killed and his body thrown over a fence. The details of his murder had not yet been made public.

'They must think it's a bit odd that he went missing for a week before his alleged accident,' she replied. 'And presumably they must know that his daughter's gone missing. It's been all over the news. Surely they'll have joined the dots by now.'

'All the more reason to go and speak to them to try and scotch any idle talk.'

Geraldine laughed at that. 'With his high-profile father-in-law murdered, his baby daughter missing, and his own allegedly accidental death, I think it's going to be impossible to prevent people spreading rumours. But you're right, we ought to try and keep a lid on things as far as we can.'

Ian stood up. 'Come on then, let's go and see Jason's work colleagues, and find out what they have to say about him.'

As they drove into town, Geraldine tried to pretend they were an ordinary couple going out for the day, not two detectives working a case.

'As soon as it's over,' Ian said, 'let's take a week off, go away somewhere, have a break.'

'That's exactly what I was thinking,' she replied with a smile. 'Where do you fancy going?'

In some ways they knew one another so well, yet she had no idea about the kind of places he liked to visit, or the sort of holidays he preferred.

'Somewhere interesting,' he replied. 'Historical sights, maybe ancient ruins to see, or beautiful architecture, but with empty stretches of beach as well, and not blisteringly hot and definitely not cold.'

She laughed. 'Sounds perfect. Probably not in England then.'

'And I want to meet your sister,' he added. 'I mean the sister you grew up with. I want to hear all about what you were like when you were younger, and see embarrassing photos of you as a child.'

They chatted all the way to their destination. Jason had worked for an estate agency in the centre of York. Geraldine followed Ian inside where a young blonde woman was sitting behind a desk. The desk beside her was empty. Behind her two middle-aged men were staring at computer screens. The young woman rose to her feet with a welcoming smile. Geraldine went over to her while Ian went to speak to the two men seated further back in the room.

'Hello, please sit down. I'm Alex. What are you looking for –'

'Thank you. We're not here to buy a property.' Geraldine cut off the agent's friendly patter, and held up her identity card as she spoke. 'I'm Detective Sergeant Geraldine Steel, and that's Detective Inspector Ian Peterson over there, talking to your colleagues.'

The young woman's expression grew sombre. 'I take it you're here about Jason?'

'Yes, I'm afraid you're right.'

The estate agent let out an impatient sigh. 'Will this take long? Only I've got a viewing in an hour.'

'We'll be as quick as we can. Did Jason have any enemies that you were aware of?'

'We didn't talk about personal matters. We were here to work.'

'How did he seem recently? Did you notice him looking stressed?'

'You mean before he left?' She paused. 'We heard he's dead. What happened to him?' Unexpectedly, her eyes glistened with unshed tears.

'Did you notice anything unusual before he disappeared?' Geraldine asked, ignoring the other woman's question.

Alex shook her head. 'I'm afraid not,' she replied. 'He was at work as usual and then he was off on the Friday because he was going away.' She screwed up her pretty face in an attempt to remember. 'He said he was going to a stag party; I can't remember where. Anyway, that was a couple of weeks ago and after that he never came back and now... well, he won't be back, will he?'

A single tear rolled down her cheek and she dabbed at it with a tissue. Geraldine couldn't help noting the contrast between Alex and Jessica. Geraldine and Ian compared notes in the car on the way back to the police station. Ian agreed it was perhaps interesting that Alex appeared so distressed on hearing about Jason's death. They wondered whether Jason and Alex could have been having an affair. But a little digging revealed that Alex had a boyfriend, and they could only conclude that Jason had been well liked at work, nothing like the cruel and violent man he seemed to be at home. No one working at the estate agency had been able to shed any light on what had happened to him.

'Another one ticked off the list,' Ian said as they reached

the police station. 'And we're no closer to finding out why he was killed.'

Geraldine didn't answer but she felt more determined than ever to discover the truth behind Jason's murder. She had a feeling they might already know who had killed his father-in-law, although they had yet to prove anything.

# 49

FOR A SHORT TIME everything seemed to be going well. Even her knee was less painful now she could rest her leg. But Ella knew she couldn't stay with Christine indefinitely. Having arrived late on Friday afternoon, there had been little time for them to talk about much except practicalities like who was going to feed the baby, and where Ella and Lily would sleep. Christine had two bedrooms in her flat, the smaller of which barely had space for a bed. The original second bedroom had been partitioned into a small bathroom and a box room. Ella assured her hostess that she and Lily would be fine in the smaller of the two rooms, but Christine insisted on giving up her own bedroom for them. They spent more than an hour changing the bedding on Christine's bed and carting junk from the box room into the living room so that Christine could sleep in the small second bedroom where a bed was concealed beneath piles of clothes, obsolete kitchen appliances, boxes of washing powder and cleaning materials, old framed photographs, a hoover, an iron and ironing board which she admitted she never used, along with all sorts of random bric-a-brac she had gathered over several years of living alone in the flat.

'I don't like to throw anything away,' she explained. 'You never know when you might need something.'

Ella wondered what use a blind person might ever have for old photographs, but she merely grunted in agreement. Once she was settled in Christine's bed for the night, with Lily asleep in a makeshift cot on the floor, Ella began to make plans. Christine was evidently unused to living with a baby. She seemed to be enthralled with Lily, constantly enquiring what the baby was doing, and asking to hold her, but the novelty might wear off after a few disturbed nights. Ella had a feeling she had read somewhere that blind people had a very heightened sense of hearing. But more worrying was the thought that Ella could hardly insist that Christine keep her guest's presence secret. Ella had done her best to drum into Christine that she did not want her violent husband to be able to track her down, but Christine was bound to blab to someone. Even if Ella insisted she was sharing the news in confidence, it only took one person to suspect that Christine's unexpected visitor was the woman who was plastered all over the news for disappearing with a baby, and the police would be knocking on the door to investigate, and then everything would be over. They were bound to take Lily away from her, and that would be worse than the prison sentence she might have to serve.

Christine spent most of the next day holding the baby and giving her the bottle which Ella prepared, handing her to Ella only when her nappy needed changing. Ella tolerated Christine's hogging the baby. Not only did it help to cement a relationship between Christine and the baby, making Christine less likely to expose Ella, but it kept Christine indoors. If she went out, there was no knowing who she might meet and what she might say.

'What's she doing now?' Christine asked repeatedly.

Swallowing her irritation, Ella would reply with various fibs. 'She's looking at you', or 'She's following you with her eyes', and 'She's watching your lips really closely when you talk'.

Her lies were rewarded with a smile from Christine. Ella was not spinning her falsehoods out of an altruistic wish to make Christine happy. It suited Ella to persuade Christine to allow them to stay in her home as long as possible. But it was wearing, pretending to befriend Christine and having to be grateful to her all the time. However easy or difficult Christine proved to manipulate, there were other considerations. Sooner or later her neighbours were bound to notice there was a baby living in the house next door, and their curiosity might be aroused. Besides which, Christine had friends who visited her. It was going to be impossible to keep the baby's presence secret for long.

On Monday morning, the doorbell rang. Ella was instantly on her guard.

'Don't answer it,' she hissed.

'It's only Gina,' Christine replied.

'I don't want anyone to know I'm here.'

Christine laughed. 'Don't worry, Gina won't tell anyone.'

'If she finds out I'm here, I'm leaving and taking Lily with me. You won't see her – you'll never hold her again. You don't want that, do you?'

But it was impossible to dissuade Christine from opening the door. Having made Christine promise not to tell Gina about her new housemate, Ella took Lily upstairs. She cuddled her and fed her and soothed her, desperate to keep her from crying and betraying their presence upstairs. Christine's visitor seemed to stay for hours, but at last Ella heard the front door slam. She was glad she had invented her cover story about a violent husband who was hunting for her, without which it would have been very difficult to explain why she wanted her presence in the house kept secret. But she knew she couldn't continue to rely on Christine remaining silent about her visitors. Leaving Lily downstairs with Christine, she announced she needed a shower. With the water running, she crept silently along the landing to the box room where Christine was now sleeping, and searched until she found over two hundred pounds in cash stuffed in a wallet in a drawer beside the bed. Pocketing it, along with a pair of sunglasses belonging to Christine, she went downstairs.

Moving as quietly as she could, she made up a bottle of milk. While the kettle was boiling she filled two carrier bags with food that was ready to eat: apples, bananas, biscuits, cereal, cheese, bread, and a large bottle of lemonade. She also grabbed a handful of tea spoons which she dropped into one of the bags.

'I have to pop out to the shops,' she said, returning to the living room and putting the bags down as quietly as she could.

Fortunately, the baby began gurgling loudly, distracting Christine.

'You can leave Lily here.'

'No, she's been inside for long enough. She could do with some fresh air. It'll do her good to go out in the pushchair.'

'What if he sees you?' Christine asked.

'He won't. He'll be at work. We won't be gone long, I promise, but I have to get out for a bit. I haven't been out of the house all weekend, and nor has Lily.'

'I'll come with you.' Christine heaved herself to her feet.

'No, you stay here and get some lunch ready. We won't be long. Do you want anything from the shops?'

To Ella's relief, Christine subsided into her chair again and reached for her bag.

'Here,' she said, holding out her purse. 'Take some money and you can bring back the change. There should be more than enough there to get whatever you need for Lily.'

Ella opened the purse and removed fifty pounds in notes as silently as she could, before putting the purse down on a chair. 'Thanks, I'm sure that's way more than I need.'

Shoving the money in her pocket, she bundled Lily into her pushchair as quickly as she could, slipped the bags of food on the handles, put on the sunglasses and left. Visiting

Christine had bought her some time, but now she had to find somewhere else to stay where no one would recognise her. At least she had enough money to buy a store of jars of baby food and nappies to keep them going while she was looking for somewhere to hide out.

# 50

As she was on her way to the police station, Geraldine was summoned to an early morning briefing. There was an air of expectation in the incident room as they waited for Eileen. At last the detective chief inspector strode into the room and began to speak.

'We have had a report from a social worker that a woman with a baby answering to the description of Ella and Daisy has been traced. They were staying with an old school friend of Ella, a blind woman called Christine. Ella and the baby, whom she is calling Lily, have left, and Christine says she doesn't know where they went.'

'The baby Ella lost was called Lily,' Geraldine said. 'It has to be her. She must know we're looking for her, so she went to stay with a blind woman who wouldn't have seen her face plastered all over the news.'

'That's clever,' Ariadne muttered.

'Not clever enough,' Geraldine replied. 'No one can disappear completely without leaving any trace at all. You just have to know where to look, and who to ask.'

'Exactly,' Eileen agreed, with an approving nod at Geraldine. 'We need to question Christine and the social worker who reported this. So far Christine has refused to say anything, and the social worker knows only what Christine told her. Apparently the social worker found soiled nappies and empty jars of baby food in the house and questioned Christine about what was going on. But Christine is refusing to tell us where

Ella is now. She may not even know where Ella has gone.'

Geraldine was sent to speak to the blind woman. Christine lived alone, and when Geraldine arrived there was no one else with her.

'How do I know you are who you say you are?' Christine asked, reasonably enough, since she could not see Geraldine's identity card.

'Please call the police station and verify who I am, or you can invite a neighbour to look at my identity card.'

She waited on the doorstep while the blind woman checked her out. Finally Christine was satisfied, and reluctantly agreed to answer a few questions after Geraldine suggested she could accompany her to the police station if she did not want to talk to her at home. Christine did not invite Geraldine in, but at least she agreed to talk to her.

'You recently had a woman staying in your house,' Geraldine began.

'What's wrong with that?' Christine retorted, but she did not deny the statement.

'A woman with a baby.'

Christine's expression softened, while her eyes wandered past Geraldine and back again, seeming to circle her.

'The baby's only six months old. We need to put her welfare above everything else. She's just a baby. Did you hold her?'

Christine didn't answer.

'The baby was fine when she was staying with you, but we think she might be at risk right now.'

Christine's expression changed again, this time to one of alarm. 'Lily's at risk?' she faltered. 'How? What do you mean?'

'Ella told you she was the baby's mother, didn't she?'

Christine nodded warily.

'Christine's baby Lily died three months ago.'

'No, no, you're wrong. Lily's alive and well. I held her. I fed her. She's not dead. She was crying and kicking and –'

'The baby Ella brought to your house is called Daisy. Ella stole her from her mother, and is taking care of her as though she is her own. But she's not. And Daisy needs to be returned to her real mother. Christine, we're all very worried about the baby's welfare. Ella is homeless and we believe she is mentally unbalanced. She can't take care of a baby properly. She stole another woman's baby, and she has no money and nowhere to live.'

Christine shook her head and her voice hardened. 'She stole nearly three hundred pounds from me,' she muttered. 'She told me she was just going to the shops but she took so much with her, the pushchair, the baby, food for herself. She didn't mean to come back, did she? She was planning to go away for good.'

'She's stolen money from you, and a baby from someone else. Christine, Ella is a criminal and a dangerous person. You were lucky she didn't knife you in your bed.' Geraldine was exaggerating, but it was essential she turn Christine against Ella if the blind woman was going to help them find her. 'I know she's your friend, but –'

'No,' Christine replied. 'Ella was never my friend. She was just someone I was at school with. She turned up here out of the blue, and wanted to stay. I wouldn't have let her in only she had a baby with her, and it was raining.' She began to cry.

'You did the right thing, Christine. You probably saved little Daisy's life. But now you have to do the right thing again and tell us where Ella has taken her.'

Christine shook her head, still crying. 'I don't know where they went,' she sobbed. 'I don't know. Ella went out to the shop – she said she was going to the shop – and she never came back. She never came back. She took all my money and she left. I can't help you. I can't help you.'

'You already have helped us a lot,' Geraldine replied. 'I'd

like to send a team here to take fingerprints and samples of DNA, and search your house to help us find Ella.'

Christine nodded.

'And I'll make sure your social worker is here when they come.'

'Thank you.'

'If you can think of anything else, please call me straight away. I'll put my number on your phone so you can get in touch with me easily.'

Christine reached out with an involuntary movement. 'Ella told me her husband was violent. How did her baby die?' she asked, her voice barely above a whisper.

'It was a cot death,' Geraldine replied.

For an instant neither of them spoke. Then Geraldine thanked Christine and turned to leave. Just by telling Geraldine that Ella had nearly three hundred pounds in cash, Christine had helped the investigation. With enough money to take a train or a bus out of the area, it was unlikely that Ella would still be in the village. She might even have left York. As soon as she left Christine, Geraldine was on the phone widening the search for Ella and Daisy.

# 51

EARLY THE NEXT MORNING someone knocked at Christine's door. Pulling on her dressing gown, she went downstairs.

'Who is it?'

'Christine, it's me. I'm with Lily and we need your help. Let us in, please. We've got nowhere else to go.'

Christine frowned. 'Go away,' she said.

'Please, Christine, if you don't do it for me, do it for Lily. She needs your help. Please, she's freezing to death out here.'

There was a muffled sound of a baby crying. Christine dithered for a few seconds, then opened the door.

'Come on in then,' she said, 'but I'm calling the police.'

She heard Ella bustle inside, lift the pushchair over the step, and close the door. As Christine flipped her phone open, Ella took it from her.

'Give that back,' Christine cried out.

'Wait, let's get Lily settled first, and then we can talk about what we're going to do.'

'She's not called Lily. Her name's Daisy and you stole her from her mother. I know all about it, because the police were here and they told me what you did.'

'What they told you isn't true. Lily is my baby, and someone's trying to take her away from me.'

'Why would anyone do that?'

'It's complicated, but basically, she's crazy. She lost her own baby and now she's trying to get her hands on Lily, but I won't let anyone take her from me. You're going to help me

284

save Lily. Here, you hold her while I warm her milk.'

After that, for a while Christine was preoccupied with comforting the crying baby, but at last Lily was fed and changed and settled.

'Now give me back my phone,' Christine said.

'Listen, I'm not going to stop you calling the police if that's what you decide to do, but first you have to hear me out. A lot of people have been telling lies about me, and now even the police are involved, but it's not true what they're saying. None of it's true.'

Ella was so adamant that the baby sleeping peacefully in Christine's arms was called Lily that it was hard not to believe her. The account of a mad woman who had lost her own baby and had convinced the police that Ella had taken her was more difficult to understand. As Ella said, it was complicated. What was clear was that two women were claiming to be the mother of one baby. But nothing else about Ella's account made sense.

'The police can do tests to find out who the real mother is,' Christine said.

'No, they can't. Usually they can, but not in this case.'

'Why not?'

'Because – because – the woman who's trying to steal Lily from me is my long lost twin sister. We met after we left school, so you never knew about her. It's well known that twins often have babies at the same time, so our babies were the same age. When hers died, she went crazy and she's been telling everyone that Lily's hers. But because we're identical, that means the tests can't tell us apart. She's always been jealous of me, and since her baby died she's become unhinged. But she's very good at hiding her insanity, and now it's my word against hers. But my twin has – her husband is high up in the police and that's why they've taken her side.'

Ella explained that she had only taken Christine's money

285

so she could buy them both tickets to London.

'You didn't know I'd go with you,' Christine pointed out.

'I knew you'd come.'

Just then, the baby stirred in Christine's arms and she felt tiny fingers clutch at her hand.

'Lily really likes you,' Ella whispered. 'I think she loves you. So you can't let her down. You have to help us get away. If I try to leave the area on my own with her, the police are bound to find me, but they won't be looking for two women and a baby. Come with us, and we can get away and then Lily can live with us and we can say you're her godmother, or her aunt, or whatever you like.'

'I could be her mother,' Christine said tentatively, afraid Ella would be angry with her.

'Sure, of course, that's a great idea,' Ella replied with surprising enthusiasm.

'You're not just saying that so I help you get away?'

'Look how happy Lily is with you,' Ella replied. 'There's nothing I'd like better than to have you with us, always, helping to take care of her. But you need to decide now, because we have to go soon. Lily and I can't stay here. With or without you, we have to leave.'

Christine hesitated, but she was never going to be offered another chance like this. Maybe Ella was lying about letting her live with them, but she had to take that chance. She couldn't let Ella leave and take Lily away. Quickly she packed a few things into a bag, and they set off.

'You don't need that stick,' Ella said as she opened the front door. 'Just put your sunglasses on so no one knows who you are.'

'Of course I need my stick,' Christine protested. 'I can't go out without it.'

But Ella was adamant. 'We can't do anything that gives away who we are. Come on.'

It felt strange walking along the street without her stick to guide her, and several times she nearly tripped on uneven paving stones, even though she was holding on to Ella's arm.

'Be careful,' Ella warned her.

There was nothing Christine could do because she couldn't see the ground, and Ella was dragging her along at a fast walking pace so she couldn't even feel her way slowly. By the time they stopped walking a fine rain had begun to fall, and she didn't have a hood or a scarf. Her hair felt damp and she started to shiver.

'Is Lily getting wet?' she asked.

'Keep your voice down,' Ella hissed. 'She's fine. She's got a rain cover.'

'Where are we?'

'We're getting a coach to London. Once we're there, it'll be easy to disappear. I've still got some of the money left.'

'My money,' Christine thought, but she didn't say anything.

Once they were seated on the coach, Ella let Christine hold Lily, and she was able to relax and settle down to enjoy the journey. The coach was warm and she stopped shivering. Lily felt heavier in her arms than she remembered, and her weight was soothing.

'I think she's growing,' she said, and smiled. 'She must be healthy.'

'And happy. And we're going to make sure she stays that way.'

'I never thought I'd have a baby to look after.'

'I know, but remember to keep your voice down while we're out,' Ella muttered. 'There are people all around us. We don't want to draw attention to our situation.'

It was true. Christine could hear a muffled buzz of voices that she had been too preoccupied with Lily to notice. She nodded in Ella's direction and a few moments later the coach set off with a bump. She held Lily close, but the baby didn't seem to stir. If she put her head very close to Lily's face, she thought she could make out the faint purring of her breath mingling with the rumble of the engine. They hadn't gone far when they halted, and Christine heard a disturbance. Several people began asking what was going on, and above the commotion a loud voice rang out, ordering everyone to stay in their seats. At her side, she heard Ella swear. Without a word of explanation, Ella grabbed Lily who woke up and began to cry.

'You should have left her with me. She was fine,' Christine protested.

An unfamiliar voice called out their names. At first Ella didn't answer, but then she began yelling, 'Give her back! She's mine!'

Voices were shouting and Lily was crying, and Ella was screaming. Terrified by the commotion, Christine began to cry. She didn't know what was happening, but she was afraid Ella's evil twin had stolen Lily. Ella's shrieks faded and a woman's voice called Christine by name, and someone took her by the arm to help her out of her seat. Christine shrank back against the window.

'No, no, leave me alone. Where's Lily? Give her back! I'm not going anywhere without Lily.

There was a pause, and a muttering, and then the woman returned.

'Come on, then,' she said. 'We'll take you to Lily. But you have to come with me. Lily's not on the coach any more. Come with me, please.'

Still sobbing, Christine was guided off the coach and taken to a car and driven back to York. She was escorted to a cold room where, shaking and crying, she was led to a chair. Her social worker arrived and tried to calm her down, and a few moments later, she recognised the voice of the policewoman who had been to her house and told her that Ella had stolen a baby called Daisy.

'They took the baby,' she cried out. 'Where is she? Where's Lily? You have to get her back. Don't believe what that other woman says. They took Lily. Ella said I could help take care of her. She said I could hold her whenever I wanted. She's Ella's baby. She's ours!'

'It's all right, Christine,' her social worker said. 'Calm down. You're not in any trouble.'

'But they took the baby,' Christine wept. 'They took Lily.'

'Christine,' the policewoman said gently, 'the last time we spoke, at your house, you told me Ella stole money from you.'

'She did, she did,' Christine wept. 'But then she came back and said she needed me to help her with the baby. She only took the money so she could buy food for the baby.'

'You said she stole nearly three hundred pounds from you?'

'I thought she stole it, but then she came back. She needed the money to buy us tickets. We were taking Lily to London where we could all be safe. We were going to live together and I was going to help look after the baby. She said I could help take care of her.'

'That baby was not Ella's. She's called Daisy and now she's been reunited with her mother.'

'No, no,' Christine wept. 'It's not true. It's not true. Her name's Lily and Ella's her mother. Ella and me, we were looking after her. She loves me. Lily loves me.'

# 52

IF ANYTHING, ELLA WAS even more distraught than Christine.

'They took my baby,' she wailed. 'They took my baby.'

'But she's not your baby, is she?' Geraldine said. 'Because your Lily died from neglect when you failed to take proper care of her, didn't she?'

'No, no. It was him, it was him,' Ella replied. 'He did it, he did it.' A curious expression flickered across her face. 'He won't hurt either of us ever again.'

Geraldine leaned forward and lowered her voice, speaking to Ella as though the two of them were alone together. 'Who won't? Look at me, Ella. Who won't hurt you again?'

'Pete,' Ella replied, as though the question surprised her. 'Who do you think I meant? He was a vicious brute, and when I saw he was doing it to her too, I had to stop him, didn't I?'

'What was he –' Ian began, but Geraldine held up a hand to silence him.

'Yes, you did,' Geraldine agreed, smiling at Ella. 'You had to stop him. So what did you do?'

'He won't hurt anyone again,' Ella repeated.

'How can you be so sure?' Geraldine pressed her.

'Because he can't get out. He can't ever get out.'

It was not clear if Ella was laughing or crying. Before long she became hysterical and her lawyer insisted they take a break.

Geraldine turned to Ian. 'Something about this is very nasty, but I can't quite work out what.'

'A baby killed and another one abducted to take her place, isn't that nasty enough for you?'

Daisy had been taken to the paediatric ward of the local hospital where she was being carefully checked for injury or maltreatment. The report came in that she was in reasonably sound health and did not appear to be suffering any ill effects from her kidnapping. Jessica was with her.

Meanwhile, Geraldine had been reading Lily's medical record which mentioned several accidental injuries to her limbs and torso.

'Ella's crazy enough to have inflicted the injuries herself,' Eileen commented.

'But she took good care of Daisy,' Geraldine pointed out.

There was nothing to indicate Lily had not suffered a cot death, but there was enough to suggest that she might have been deliberately injured by Ella, or her boyfriend, Pete, who had apparently done a runner after the baby died.

'It's no wonder he scarpered,' Ian said angrily. 'If he is responsible for harming that baby, we need to find him and bring him to justice. A lifetime behind bars is too good for that scum.'

'They tried to find Ella's boyfriend, Pete, at the time of the baby's death,' Eileen said, 'but he was never traced. He's probably slipped out of the country by now. He could be anywhere. He vanished when Lily died, and there was no reason why anyone other than Ella would want to find him. A cot death is tragic, but it's not a crime. As for the baby's injuries, if they were deliberately inflicted, no one will ever know.'

'Her mother would have known,' Geraldine said quietly.

'You're looking thoughtful,' Eileen said. 'What's on your mind?' She frowned at Geraldine who shook her head.

'It's probably nothing,' she replied. 'But do you remember what Ella said to us when we were questioning her about Lily's death?'

291

'What specifically are you referring to?'

'All of it really,' Geraldine replied. 'Don't you remember what Ella said when we suggested she had neglected to care for Lily?'

'Remind me,' Eileen snapped. 'Don't play memory games.'

Without even glancing at her notes, Geraldine recited Ella's statement. 'She said: "It was him, it was him. He did it, he did it." And then she said: "He won't hurt either of us ever again." I asked her who she was talking about, just to be clear, and she replied: "Pete." She said he was a vicious brute and when she saw what he was doing to the baby, she had to stop him. And then she said: "He won't hurt anyone again because he can't get out. He can't ever get out." What if she found Pete before he could get away? What if he never got away?'

'That's all very well, but if you're right, then where is he?' Eileen asked.

Geraldine shook her head. 'I don't know, but there's a chance he never left, and that's why we couldn't find him. He could still be in her flat, hidden.'

Eileen stared at Geraldine for only a second before she was on the phone, expediting the issue of an emergency search warrant and barking at Geraldine to organise a search team. Questioning Ella further would have to wait. They were unlikely to get much sense from her anyway.

The search team went through Ella's flat room by room. It was filthy, and the kitchen stank of rotting food.

'No one could keep a baby here,' one of the team said. 'The health visitor would have it removed in a jiffy.'

'The place can't have been like this when her baby was still alive,' Geraldine agreed. 'She must have gone to pieces after Lily died.'

What was unusual was that every single room in the flat had bolts on the inside of the door. Wherever Ella went, she seemed to have wanted to lock herself in.

'It's as though she was afraid of being attacked inside the flat,' a constable said. 'How the hell she ever kept a baby here is just unbelievable. Did she lock it in with her wherever she went?'

'Talk about paranoid,' another officer added. 'She's an absolute maniac.'

'Do you think she was afraid of ghosts?' the first constable asked.

'Ghosts?' his companion echoed contemptuously. 'You think bolts can keep ghosts out?'

'Nothing can keep ghosts out, because they don't exist, you muppet.'

'Well, it may not have been ghosts, but she was keen to keep herself safe from something.'

'Or someone,' Geraldine said.

Every door in the flat had three bolts on the inside, top, middle and bottom. Only the door to the cellar was bolted on the outside. Geraldine watched as a constable pulled the bolts across.

'They're stiff,' he commented.

The door creaked open, and the officer drew back with a shout of disgust. The foul smell reached Geraldine who was standing a foot away, and she covered her mouth and nose at the stench with an involuntary grimace.

'I'm guessing there's a body down there,' the constable muttered, pulling a face.

But as he spoke, a grating voice cried out from the darkness at the foot of the stairs leading down into the cellar.

'Let me out! Let me out! Let me out, you fucking bitch. I'm going to kill you!'

The constable slammed the door shut and slid the middle bolt across. 'Fucking hell,' he whispered. 'There's someone in there!'

Geraldine approached the door and pulled it open, trying not to breathe in the horrible smell.

'Peter!' she called out. 'This is the police and you're under arrest for the murder of your daughter, Lily.'

In the light from a torch, Geraldine and a member of the search team made their way cautiously down the wooden stairs leading to the cellar. The walls were slimy with mould and damp; the smell became almost palpable as they reached the bottom. The constable shone the beam of light around to reveal a hideous crouching figure, covered in filth. His eyes, which were closed against the unaccustomed light, were crusted in filth and mucus and he was standing in a pool of vomit and excrement. A thick chain had been crudely wound around his arms and legs, pinning them to his sides, and preventing him from walking more than a couple of steps.

'Bloody hell,' the constable cried out. 'How long has he been here?'

'About three months,' Geraldine replied, struggling to control her nausea. She turned back to the stairs. 'I'll send someone down to help you get him out of here.'

Her colleague nodded. 'He was locked in here by the mother of a baby he killed, wasn't he?'

'That seems to be what happened.'

'I doubt if he'll be able to get himself up those stairs,' the constable said, speaking very fast, 'and it seems a shame to get our hands dirty moving him. Why don't we just leave him here?'

Geraldine hesitated, fighting the temptation to agree with the constable. With only the word of an insane woman to secure a conviction against him, Pete might evade a prison sentence. But Ella had taken the law into her own hands by punishing Pete herself, and that was a dangerous path to follow. Much as she abhorred the prospect that Pete might escape prison, Geraldine had devoted her life to the pursuit of justice. And that meant that even a villain like Pete had to face a fair trial, whatever the outcome. The other choice could only ultimately lead to chaos where the most powerful would inevitably triumph, regardless of right and wrong.

'We'll bring him out to face trial, and let's hope he spends the rest of his life behind bars where he belongs,' she said firmly.

'It's going to be tricky getting him out of there,' the constable said. 'Any attempt to move is going to be agonising for him, after he's been trussed up like that for so long.'

Geraldine and the constable exchanged a glance of complicity, although neither of them actually smiled.

'Make him crawl up the stairs,' she replied.

# 53

AFTER WAITING HALF A morning for the duty solicitor to arrive, Geraldine faced Ella in the interview room and started the tape running. With the preliminaries completed, she began with a direct accusation to see how Ella would react.

'You stole Jessica's baby.'

'No, I never,' Ella replied at once, her voice rising indignantly. 'If that's what she told you, then she's a liar. I never stole her baby.'

'If you didn't kidnap Jessica's baby, how do you account for your being discovered trying to escape from York with her?'

'I'm not saying I didn't have her, only that I never stole her.'

'I suppose you're going to tell us next that Jessica gave you the baby as a Christmas present?' Geraldine gave Ella's lawyer a patient smile which he did not return. 'Take as long as you like, Ella. Neither of us is going anywhere until you've told me the truth. Jessica never gave you her baby, did she?'

'Yes she did. That's what I'm telling you, if you'd only listen. That's exactly what happened. Jessica gave me her baby to look after, because she wanted to do whatever she could to protect Daisy from her father. Jason was a vicious man, just like Pete was. That's how come I understood her. I understood everything. Jessica showed me the bruises where he used to wallop her.' She rolled her eyes. 'I know what that feels like, I can tell you. When I warned her what might happen to Daisy if she kept her baby anywhere near that man, Jessica begged me to take Daisy away from their house. She said it was like sitting on a ticking bomb, waiting in fear for Jason to injure Daisy. She paid me to take the baby and look after her, and hide her from him. I never stole that baby. There was no need.'

'Jessica alleges you did.'

'That's because I refused to give her back.'

'It comes to the same thing,' Geraldine said. 'You kept her baby against her wishes. That's stealing.'

'I had to do it after Jessica told me what she'd done. She came to see me, all smiles, and said it was safe to take Daisy back home with her because she'd dealt with Jason. When I asked her how she could be so sure he wouldn't come back, she told me she'd killed him.'

'How did she do that?' Ian asked.

'She told me he was leaning over in the garage, and she crept up behind him and whacked him on the head with a hammer. He never got up again, so after a while she wrapped him in a blanket and lugged him into the car at night, and heaved him over a fence out by some allotments she'd driven past, somewhere she thought no one would see.'

'Jessica told you that?' Ian asked.

'That's exactly what she told me. So I had to refuse to give the baby back. I had to protect Daisy from her mother. If she'd killed once, who was to say she wouldn't do it again? I had to keep that baby safe. When she threatened me, I told her she could do her worst; only, if she took Daisy away from me, I'd tell the police what she'd confessed to me, about doing away with her husband. That shut her up.' She grinned. 'I never did tell, of course.'

'What happened then?'

'She complained to me that her money had run out and she couldn't afford to pay me any more. She thought that would make me give her back her baby, but I couldn't do that, could I? So I told her father what she'd done. I figured he'd be willing to pay a fair amount for my silence. He wouldn't want anyone else finding out what she'd done.'

'You blackmailed him?'

'No. I never did. It wasn't like that. I just wanted him to help me out now and again. Just a few quid here and there, for his granddaughter. He's a wealthy man. I was right. He wanted me to keep quiet about it only before he even gave me a penny someone topped him. Talk about bad luck!'

Geraldine and Ian exchanged a glance. With Ella's statement, the whole sorry story was beginning to unravel.

'So according to Ella's statement, which may or may not be reliable, Jessica killed her husband, allegedly to protect Daisy from his violent outbursts.' Eileen gazed around the assembled team. 'Ella says that Jason had hit Jessica on more than one occasion, and she was concerned for her daughter's safety. After handing the baby to Ella, Jessica murdered her husband and then asked for her baby back. Ella refused to give Daisy up, and went to David when Jessica refused to give her any more money. Shortly after that, David was killed.' Eileen paused. 'Did Jessica kill her father? She had a strong motive for silencing him once Ella had told him about Jason's murder.'

'I wonder why she didn't try to kill Ella, not her father?' Geraldine said. 'With Ella out of the way, the only accusation against Jessica would be hearsay, and in any case she could probably have convinced her father that she was innocent. Plus she would have been able to take back her baby.'

Eileen frowned. 'Let's see what Jessica has to say about her father's death.'

'She denies having killed her husband,' Ian said. 'But the forensic evidence points to her.'

Eileen sighed. 'If you can persuade her to confess, it would make our lives a lot easier.'

Jessica stared belligerently across the table at Geraldine

and Ian. 'When can I go home to Daisy?'

Anne Armstrong had employed a clean-shaven young solicitor in an expensive suit to represent and advise Jessica. He turned to his client.

'They have to release you in a couple of hours.'

'Unless we charge her,' Ian pointed out.

The solicitor returned Ian's glare impassively. Jessica seemed increasingly agitated, demanding to see her baby.

'Tell us again about Jason's disappearance,' Geraldine said gently.

'He went off to a stag do and never came back,' Jessica snapped. 'I've told you again and again. That's all I know. He didn't come home, and then ten days later the police knocked on my door and told me they'd found his body. He was dead.'

She broke off, as though she was overcome by emotion, but she dropped her face in her hands and Geraldine could not see her expression.

'Only Jason never went to a stag do.' Ian leaned forward and spoke very slowly and clearly. 'We've questioned all his friends and can find no evidence he ever went anywhere. We have a witness who claims you killed your husband because he physically abused you on a regular basis, and you were terrified he might injure your baby.'

Jessica hesitated and glanced at her lawyer who gave a slight shake of his head.

'No comment,' Jessica said.

'Is it true Jason used to hit you?' Geraldine asked.

'No comment.'

'We have medical evidence that suggests you suffered injuries over a prolonged period of time,' Geraldine pressed on. 'If you were provoked, were in terror of your life, and fearful for the life of your baby, a jury is bound to view your actions sympathetically –'

The lawyer interrupted. 'This is harassment and my client

is not going to respond. My client would like to go home now, with Daisy. She has not been charged with any crime.'

'Very well,' Ian said. 'We're charging her now. Is that what you want?'

He proceeded to read Jessica her rights and charge her with the murder of Jason Colman and David Armstrong. Her reaction was surprising.

'David Armstrong?' she repeated, her face flushing with some undefinable emotion. 'What are you talking about?'

'You know your father was murdered?'

'Murdered?' She sounded genuinely shocked. 'I knew he was dead. He died. It was – they told us he suffered a fatal haemorrhage.'

'He ingested a fatal dose of drugs, and when he collapsed, he was suffocated. He was murdered, Jessica,' Ian said.

'No, no, he can't have been,' Jessica replied.

She looked shocked.

'Where did you kill your husband?' Ian demanded, returning to the crime the suspect had not denied.

Jessica shook her head. 'He was my father,' she stammered. 'How can you think I was responsible? He was my father.'

But she did not deny having killed her husband.

'Did you kill Jason at home or had you gone out?'

'He deserved it,' was all she said.

'What I don't understand is why you didn't kill Ella instead of your father,' Geraldine said. 'With Ella out of the way, you would have been able to persuade your father not to tell anyone that you killed your husband. Your father would have done anything for you.'

Jessica shook her head. 'I couldn't kill Ella,' she replied. 'She told me she had her boyfriend locked in her cellar, and she said she was going to put me down there with him if I tried to take Daisy back.' She shuddered. 'I was afraid of what he would do to me down there. Ella frightened me.'

'Pete isn't going to do anything to anyone ever again,' Ian told her.

'Nor is Ella,' Geraldine added.

She did not explain that Ella was going to spend the rest of her life behind bars, probably in a secure mental institution. Nor did she add that a similar fate might await Jessica.

'So you killed your father?' Ian repeated.

Jessica burst into tears. 'No, no. Don't keep saying that. He was my father. How could I kill him? Do you think I'm a monster?'

Geraldine saw her own surprise reflected in Ian's face, but neither of them made any attempt to reply to Jessica's question.

# 54

'SHE DID SEEM SHOCKED to hear that her father was murdered,' Geraldine said.

'Or was she shocked that we discovered he was murdered?' Eileen replied. 'Jessica might have done it and thought she had got away with making it appear her father had died from natural causes.'

Ian nodded and looked at Geraldine. 'Did you see how agitated Jessica became when you talked about David's murder?'

'Yes,' Geraldine agreed. 'She appeared genuinely shocked on hearing her father was murdered, and we don't know she killed him. There are other possibilities.'

'If Ella told David that Jessica had murdered her husband, he might have threatened to tell other people. Jessica's liberty could have been at risk,' Eileen said.

'I'm still not convinced Jessica killed him,' Geraldine insisted.

'Who else could have been so concerned to keep it quiet they would have been prepared to kill David to protect Jessica from discovery?'

'Her mother?' Geraldine replied quietly. 'Isn't it at least possible that David confided to his wife what Ella had told him?'

'You really think Anne could have killed her husband?' Eileen asked.

'To protect her daughter?' Ian said. 'That would be a

horrible repetition of Jessica's crime, if she killed her husband to protect her own daughter.'

'This all sounds a bit fanciful,' Eileen said. 'Let's speak to both women again before we speculate any further.'

Geraldine and Ian went to see Anne Armstrong.

'What is this about?' she asked when she opened the door, scowling at them.

'Can we come in?'

'What do you want?'

There was no doubt she was nervous, but she stood aside to let them in. Sitting opposite them in her front room, she gazed anxiously at them, her fingers twisting in her lap. For a moment no one spoke, while tears slid down her pale cheeks.

'First my granddaughter disappeared, then I lost my husband,' she whispered, 'and now my daughter's being harassed. As if she could have killed anyone. It's an outrageous accusation. Outrageous. No one should have made that allegation against Jessica. The poor girl only just got her baby back, and now she's been taken into custody. It's monstrous.'

As she was speaking, a baby began to cry somewhere in the house and Anne jumped to her feet.

'Excuse me,' she said. 'I have to see to her.'

'Of course.' Geraldine glanced at Ian. 'I'll come with you.'

Anne turned back. 'Why? Do you think *I'm* going to run off with her?'

Geraldine followed Anne into the kitchen where the baby was lying in a travel cot, yelling. Anne scooped her up, making soothing noises as she fetched a small jar of baby food from a cupboard and settled the crying baby in a high chair. As soon as she placed a spoonful of the mush in the baby's mouth, the baby stopped crying and began slurping and gulping the food.

'She's beautiful,' Geraldine said, and Anne smiled.

'There's no way we're losing her again,' she said.

'Ella took good care of her for you,' Geraldine said. 'Fortunately, now Jason's gone you can put all that behind you.'

'Yes, Daisy's home where she belongs.'

'Jessica isn't,' Geraldine said.

A faint look of irritation crossed Anne's face, then she looked over at Geraldine with tears in her eyes. 'You have to help her. That man she married, he was a monster. He used to beat her. Whatever happened to him he had it coming. I swear, if she hadn't killed him, I would have done it myself.' Her eyes glittered as she spoke.

Geraldine waited while Anne finished feeding the baby before reiterating how beautiful Daisy was, and asking to hold her. Anne's eyes never left the baby as she handed her over and followed them into the front room where Geraldine nodded at Ian.

'We would like you to accompany us to the police station to answer a few more questions,' he said.

'You'll have to ask me here,' Anne replied. 'I need to put the baby to bed.'

'She's already asleep,' Geraldine said, without putting the baby down in the cot. 'I'll wait here with her until we have a vehicle to take her with us to the police station where she'll be well cared for until your release.'

'My release? What are you talking about? Jessica's already in custody for a crime she didn't commit, and now you want to take me as well? I don't believe this. I refuse to go with you. I'm calling my lawyer.'

'Good,' Ian said. 'He can meet us at the police station.'

Still protesting, Anne made her phone call before accompanying them to the police station. Daisy was transported in a separate vehicle with an appropriate car seat.

Anne's solicitor was waiting for them when they arrived.

A slickly dressed man in his thirties with a southern accent, he insisted on speaking to his client before they began to question her.

'That evil witch put you up to this,' Anne began when the interview commenced.

Geraldine and Ian had not yet posed a question but neither of them interrupted her. Anne was sufficiently agitated to make a blunder without any prompting from them. The lawyer narrowed his eyes and listened anxiously, ready to interrupt if it became apparent that his client was going to incriminate herself. On balance, Geraldine was fairly confident she would.

'That Ella, she set this whole thing up. She's crazy. We all know she lost her own baby, due to her neglect, and now she's trying to get her hands on Daisy. She's already stolen her from Jessica and attempted to run away with her. This is all down to her. She killed her partner because he mistreated her baby, and then she killed Jason and David, so she could keep Daisy. You can't trust a word she says. She's the one you should be going after her, not me or Jessica. Leave us alone. We've been through enough.'

Geraldine waited for Anne to finish before speaking. 'Anne, you can't keep this up. We know Jessica killed Jason –'

'It was Ella. It was Ella.'

'You know that's not true,' Geraldine said, hoping to persuade Anne to confess.

'Then it was me, it wasn't Jessica, it was me, and I'd do it again.'

'My client is clearly distressed by this line of questioning,' the lawyer cut in urgently. 'We need to take a break.'

'She's distressed because she knows her daughter is guilty,' Ian muttered. 'She's grasping at straws, blaming everyone she can think of to protect her daughter.'

'This is not the place to cast judgement –' the lawyer began. He glanced at Anne. 'I need to speak to my client.'

'You can't be serious about needing a break already. We've hardly begun,' Ian protested.

With the lawyer insisting on speaking to his client, Ian turned off the tape and he and Geraldine waited impatiently to resume their interrogation. Ian suggested they go along to the canteen during the break. As soon as they left the interview room, a constable brought them a message that they were to go to the briefing room where Eileen was about to address the team.

'That's all we need, a pep talk,' Geraldine muttered as they entered the room.

She struggled to focus on what Eileen was saying, especially as it quickly became apparent that there was nothing new to hear. Impatiently, she waited to return to the interview with Anne.

# 55

GERALDINE ENTERED THE INTERVIEW room ahead of Ian who gave her a quick nod as he took his seat, and a moment later Anne returned, accompanied by her lawyer.

'Tell us exactly how you killed Jason,' Ian began, when they had all taken their places and the tape was running again. 'Take us through it, step by step. You must have caught him off guard, because he could easily have overpowered you. So, tell us how you managed it.'

Anne shook her head. 'I – I can't – I can't remember –' she stammered.

'Do you seriously expect us to believe you can't remember how you killed your son-in-law?' Ian repeated in scathing tones. 'The truth is you have no idea how he was murdered, because you weren't there. You didn't kill him.'

Anne shook her head, and glanced sideways at her lawyer who gave her a warning frown.

'My client has no further comment to make,' he responded.

'Tell us what happened on the night David died,' Geraldine said gently.

Once again Anne shook her head, and Geraldine repeated her question.

'My client has made a statement about her movements on that night. She has nothing further to add to what she has already told you,' the lawyer answered for her.

Anne folded her arms and pressed her lips together, looking at her lawyer. He gave an almost imperceptible nod. Clearly he had instructed her to say nothing.

'My client has no further comment to make. She has already answered all of your questions.'

The lawyer stirred and gathered his papers, as though he was about to rise to his feet, indicating that the interview was over.

'She may have answered all of our questions so far,' Geraldine replied quietly, emphasising the last two words. 'But you are wrong to suppose she has answered all of our questions. You appear to think we have finished. We haven't.' She turned back to Anne. 'We have examined CCTV footage from your street, from your neighbour's and your own house and established that no one came to your house on the night of your husband's death, after he returned home on Tuesday evening, a few hours before he was killed.'

Anne nodded but she looked worried.

'Has the cause of his death been proven to be unlawful?' the lawyer demanded.

'Your husband was drugged before he was killed,' Geraldine went on, ignoring the interruption.

'David suffered from headaches so he took painkillers. He must have swallowed too many of them, and then he started drinking. I poured him a whisky, it's true, but I wasn't to know he had taken so many pills. His death was an accident. I'm sure he never intended to take an overdose.'

'You just accused Ella of murdering him,' Ian pointed out quietly.

'I was upset,' Anne muttered.

She flung a desperate glance at her lawyer who frowned at her, warning her to remain silent.

'That's a very serious accusation to make, even if you were upset,' Geraldine replied. 'I can't help wondering why you would accuse someone of murdering your husband, if you genuinely believe his death was accidental.'

Anne didn't answer.

'Post mortem injuries indicate that David was not yet dead when someone suffocated him,' Geraldine said. 'Whoever did that was determined to ensure he would never recover from his blackout.'

Anne had turned pale.

'I need to speak to my client,' the lawyer said.

'Did you have a towel in your hand when you went outside and found him unconscious on the drive?' Geraldine pressed on. 'It was dark. You knew your security lights were not working and no one could see you.'

Still Anne declined to answer.

'Someone pressed a towel over his mouth and nose, while he lay there dying, and murdered him.'

'I really need to speak to my client –' the lawyer intervened urgently.

This time it was Anne who ignored him, her words bursting out in a rush.

'All right, all right, I did it. It was me. But I never meant to do it. I saw him lying there, and I don't know what came over me. It was just a sudden impulse. I –'

She broke off and gazed around, looking stunned.

The lawyer began to protest, but Ian held up a hand and glared at him as, haltingly, Anne confessed. David had revealed to her that their daughter was responsible for her husband's death.

'You mean Jessica told David she murdered Jason?' Ian asked.

'No, no, Jessica never said that. No, it was her friend, that poisonous snake. She told David what Jessica had done. But it's a lie. It's all lies. It was Ella. She did it and then tried to blame Jessica, and David believed her. He believed her, you see.'

'And that's why you killed David?'

'I had to, don't you see? He was threatening to go to the police. I couldn't let him do that. Jessica's our daughter. I had to protect her. David kept threatening to go to the police.' She was crying now, stammering out the words between her sobs. 'Poor Jessica. She was terrified that vicious brute was going to turn on the baby. She did what any mother would have done, and killed that man to protect her baby.'

'So now you're telling us Jessica killed her husband?' Ian said.

'And that's what any mother would have done?' Geraldine repeated softly.

'Exactly. You understand, don't you?' Anne turned to Geraldine in a desperate appeal. 'Jessica never admitted that fiend was abusing her, but I could tell. A mother always can. One punch from that vicious brute's fist would have crushed little Daisy's skull. Jessica had to stop him. He got what he deserved. You have to understand now why we can't let Jessica go to prison for what she did. That can't happen, not to my daughter.'

'So you killed David to silence him about your daughter having murdered her husband,' Geraldine said slowly. 'Instead of leaving Jason, reporting him to the police, taking out an injunction against him, having him stand trial for what he had done to her, she decided to take the law into her own hands by murdering him.'

Anne was silent.

'You admit you were aware that your daughter had committed murder?' Ian said.

'No, no, it wasn't like that,' Anne replied. 'You make it sound so much worse than it actually was. You have to understand that Jessica was provoked beyond endurance. That's mitigating circumstances, isn't it? They can't call it murder, can they?'

Her lawyer confirmed that Jessica could plead diminished responsibility on the grounds of sustained physical abuse.

'Yes, that's exactly what it was,' Anne replied. 'Only David didn't seem to understand. All he could say was that we couldn't ignore the fact that Jessica had killed her husband. I begged him to keep quiet about it. Who was it going to harm? But he just looked grim and said he would have to think about it, before he decided what to do. "We're talking about murder" he kept saying, over and over. He said she needed professional help, and then he said he might go to the police, he hadn't made up his mind yet. I couldn't take that risk, not with Jessica's freedom. She has a baby to care for.'

'And so you killed him,' Geraldine said.

'Yes, yes, yes!' Anne cried out wildly, speaking in staccato bursts between sobs. 'That was me. I had no choice. He wouldn't listen to reason. She's my daughter. He was going to betray her. He wanted to tell the police – I couldn't let him –'

Anne dropped her head into her hands and wept without restraint. At her side, her lawyer stirred.

'I need some time alone with my client,' he said, his shoulders slumped in resignation.

'Take all the time you want,' Ian replied, switching off the tape. 'She's not going anywhere.'

# 56

THE CELEBRATORY DRINK IN the pub that evening was subdued. Two killers had been caught and were now behind bars, but as a result of those murders a baby had been taken into care. When she was older, Daisy might learn her family history, and live with the knowledge that both her mother and her maternal grandmother had murdered their husbands. She would never know who her father was. But for now, the team had gathered to celebrate the successful conclusion of the investigation.

'Well done, everyone,' Eileen said, raising her glass. 'That was a tough case.'

'And a particularly nasty one,' a constable added.

There was a murmur of agreement, while glasses were raised and clinked. Eileen was smiling, more with relief than pleasure, and most of the officers were talking at once.

'A mother and a daughter both killing their husbands has to be more than coincidence,' a constable said. 'There must be something in their genes.'

'Plus they both committed the murders for the exact same reason, to protect their own daughters,' another officer said.

While her colleagues discussed whether the case provided evidence that the ability to kill was hereditary, or if the similarity between the murders was coincidence, Geraldine remained silent, thinking about everything that had happened during the investigation.

'So you were right,' Ian said to her when they arrived home. 'What a family.'

'That poor baby,' Geraldine replied.

'Well, at least she won't be raised by a murderer. We now have two killers behind bars,' Ian said. 'Admittedly it's unlikely they were ever going to kill anyone else, but who knows? If either of them had seen someone else as a threat to them, they might have done it again. Once a killer...'

'What does that mean?'

'Just that people don't change.'

'Do you really believe that?'

Ian looked at her in surprise. 'Don't you?'

She shook her head. 'I don't know. To be honest, I've had enough of heavy conversations for one night. Can't we just pretend to be ordinary people with ordinary jobs who don't spend their time studying cadavers and crime scenes and interviewing the most horrifying people in town?'

Ian grinned. 'Sure. I'll be a construction worker. What do you want to be?'

Geraldine smiled. 'A hotel receptionist.'

'Dealing with all the guests' complaints?'

'No. OK then, a flower seller.'

'But your flowers wouldn't last long, so you'd be under pressure to sell them quickly.'

'Oh, I don't know, what job do you think would be the least stressful in the world?'

Ian frowned. 'Someone who sprays perfume on women's wrists so they can sample it? That has to be pretty safe, doesn't it?'

Geraldine laughed. 'But what if no one wanted to buy my perfume?'

'Then I'd come along and buy the whole shopful of perfume from you.'

'And what would you do with all that perfume?'

'Give it to you of course.'

They both laughed.

'Tell me,' Ian said, 'how did you used to unwind after an investigation, before I moved in with you?'

'Well, I'd pour myself a glass of wine, put my feet up, and watch something on the telly, or put on some music and read, anything relaxing to take my mind off the case.'

Ian smiled and put his arms around her. 'I can think of something to take your mind off the case,' he said, and he leaned down to kiss her gently on the lips.

# ACKNOWLEDGEMENTS

I would like to thank Dr Leonard Russell for his medical expertise.

My thanks go to Ion Mills, Claire Watts, Clare Quinlivan, and all the wonderful team at No Exit Press for their continued support over the years that Geraldine Steel has been conducting her investigations. It is a joy and a privilege to work with such professional and kindhearted people.

I would also like to thank my superb editor, Keshini Naidoo, for her brilliant insights, and my copy editor Jayne Lewis for her infallible attention to detail.

I look forward to working with the team again on Geraldine's future investigations!

# A LETTER FROM LEIGH

Dear Reader,

I hope you enjoyed reading this book in my Geraldine Steel series. Readers are the key to the writing process, so I'm thrilled that you've joined me on my writing journey.

You might not want to meet some of my characters on a dark night – I know I wouldn't! – but hopefully you want to read about Geraldine's other investigations. Her work is always her priority because she cares deeply about justice, but she also has her own life. Many readers care about what happens to her. I hope you join them, and become a fan of Geraldine Steel, and her colleague Ian Peterson.

If you follow me on Facebook or Twitter, you'll know that I love to hear from readers. I always respond to comments from fans, and hope you will follow me on **@LeighRussell** and **fb.me/leigh.russell.50** or drop me an email via my website **leighrussell.co.uk**.

That way you can be sure to get news of the latest offers on my books. You might also like to sign up for my newsletter on **leighrussell.co.uk/news** to make sure you're one of the first to know when a new book is coming out. We'll be running competitions, and I'll also notify you of any events where I'll be appearing.

Finally, if you enjoyed this story, I'd be really grateful if you would post a brief review on Amazon or Goodreads. A few sentences to say you enjoyed the book would be wonderful. And of course it would be brilliant if you would consider recommending my books to anyone who is a fan of crime fiction.

I hope to meet you at a literary festival or a book signing soon!

Thank you again for choosing to read my book.

With very best wishes,

*Leigh Russell*

**Sign up to our newsletter for great offers**

noexit.co.uk/newsletter

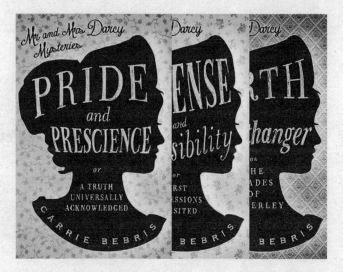

If you enjoyed this Rowland Sinclair mystery, you may enjoy Carrie Bebris' Mr and Mrs Darcy Mystery Series!

In the best Austen tradition with Regency backdrops, moody country houses, and delightful characterization – plus an added twist of murder and mayhem...

*Pride & Prescience*
*Suspense and Sensibility*
*North by Northanger*

Why not try Robin Paige's Victorian Mystery series?

Meet journalist Kate Ardleigh as she investigates her first case with amateur detective Sir Charles Sheridan in this popular series sure to delight fans of Sherlock Holmes and Agatha Christie.

'An intriguing mystery… skilfully unravelled' – Jean Hager, author of *Blooming Murder*